Wrath
of the
Savage

Center Point
Large Print

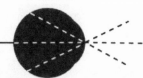

**This Large Print Book carries the
Seal of Approval of N.A.V.H.**

Wrath
of the
Savage

Charles G. West

CENTER POINT LARGE PRINT
THORNDIKE, MAINE

This Center Point Large Print edition
is published in the year 2014 by arrangement with
NAL Signet, a member of Penguin Group (USA) LLC,
a Penguin Random House Company.

The text of this Large Print edition is unabridged.
In other aspects, this book may vary
from the original edition.
Printed in the United States of America
on permanent paper.
Set in 16-point Times New Roman type.

ISBN: 978-1-62899-149-9

Library of Congress Cataloging-in-Publication Data

West, Charles.
Wrath of the savage / Charles G. West. — Center Point Large Print
edition.
pages ; cm.
Summary: "Unjustly court-martialed on a charge of cowardice, former
Lieutenant Brent Hollister and an old trapper named Coldiron rescue
two women held captive by Indians"—Provided by publisher.
ISBN 978-1-62899-149-9 (library binding : alk. paper)
1. Sihasapa Indians—Fiction. 2. United States. Army—Officers—
Fiction.
3. Kidnapping victims—Fiction. 4. Trappers—Fiction.
5. Large type books. I. Title.
PS3623.E84W73 2014
813'.6—dc23
                                                        2014012973

For Ronda

Chapter 1

Second Lieutenant Bret Hollister swallowed the last of his coffee and got to his feet. He took a few seconds to stretch his long, lean body before walking unhurriedly over to the water's edge, where he knelt down to rinse out his cup. When he stood up again, he glanced over to catch the question in Sergeant Johnny Duncan's expression. Knowing what the sergeant was silently asking, Hollister said, "Let's get 'em mounted, Sergeant. We need to find this fellow before nightfall."

"Yes, sir," Duncan answered, anticipating the order and turning to address the troopers who were taking their ease beside the stream. "All right, boys, you heard the lieutenant. Mount up."

He stood there, holding his horse's reins, and watched while the eight-man detail reluctantly climbed back into the saddle. When the last of the green recruits were mounted, Duncan climbed aboard and looked to the lieutenant to give the order to march. *A sore-assed bunch of recruits,* he thought, although not without a modicum of sympathy for their discomfort. Not one of the eight men had ever ridden a horse before being assigned to the Second Cavalry just three months before. Duncan knew that the reason they had been assigned to this detail today was primarily because of their greenness. He also knew that the reason he had caught the assignment was that Captain Greer felt confident he could nursemaid the raw troopers, and maybe the lieutenant in charge of the patrol as well.

Bret Hollister might make a good officer one day, Duncan speculated, depending upon whether or not he stayed alive long enough to wear off some of the polish associated with all new lieutenants coming out of West Point. He had only been with the regiment a year and a half, right out of the academy, and as far as Duncan knew, hadn't distinguished himself one way or the other. This rescue detail would be the first time the sergeant would report directly to Hollister, so in all fairness he supposed he should give the young officer a chance to prove himself.

Hollister had been posted to Fort Ellis in time to participate in the three-prong campaign to run Sitting Bull and Crazy Horse to ground. That campaign resulted in the annihilation of General George Custer's Seventh Cavalry at the Little Big Horn. By the time the four hundred troopers from Fort Ellis made the two-hundred-mile march to the Little Big Horn, they were too late to reinforce General Custer. So the only combat experience Lieutenant Bret Hollister had was in the burying of slaughtered troopers of the Seventh and relief of the survivors under Major Marcus Reno. It was hardly enough to test the steel in the young officer.

Duncan's thoughts were interrupted briefly by the order to march, but his mind soon drifted back to his dissatisfaction at being assigned to nursemaid a green patrol, commanded by a green officer. It was especially irritating when the rest of the regiment was preparing to move out to intercept a band of Nez Perce intent upon escaping the reservation. He didn't like being left behind by his company and regiment, the men he had soldiered with for more than two years.

"Damn it," he muttered, "orders are orders."

"Did you say something, Sergeant?" Bret asked, reining his horse back a bit.

"Ah, no, sir," Duncan replied. "I was just talkin' to myself."

Bret smiled. "Better be careful. Talking to yourself might be a sign of battle fatigue."

"Yes, sir," Duncan said. *Don't know what the hell you'd know about battle fatigue,* he thought. Then he reprimanded himself for his attitude. *Best forget about my bad luck and think about why this patrol was ordered out.*

The admonishment made him feel a little guilty, for the patrol was an important one. Reports of two separate raids on homesteaders along the Yellowstone River by renegade Sioux and Cheyenne had come in to the post just hours before the regiment was prepared to march to intercept the Nez Perce. From the report of the young man who had ridden to Fort Ellis with the news of the attack, both families were massacred. Duncan figured the Indians had too great a head start for there to be any reasonable chance of overtaking them. He supposed the real purpose of the patrol was to show some response from the army, even with only an undersized patrol of eight privates, one sergeant, and one officer.

Because of the nature of the mission, and the need to travel light, the men had been ordered to leave all personal items and clothing behind at Fort Ellis. Each man was issued four days' rations and told to take only one blanket, one rubber ground cloth, one hundred rounds of ammunition, no cooking utensils except one tin cup, and four days' horse feed. Those marching orders told the sergeant that they were expected to return to base as soon as they confirmed that the hostiles were no longer in the area.

Duncan had persuaded Captain Greer to let them seek out Nate Coldiron to help track the Indians responsible for the raids, just in case the trail was hotter than the young man reported. One day of their rations would already be gone in the time it would take to find Coldiron, but it couldn't hurt to have the old trapper along. He was a hell of a hunter, and Duncan thought the patrol might be out longer than four days in spite of their orders. If that was the case, he was confident that they wouldn't go without food.

Coldiron, a cantankerous old trapper and former

army scout, had a cabin on the east side of the Gallatin River at a point where a wide stream emptied into it. Duncan had been to the cabin once before when Coldiron had agreed to lead a scouting mission a year earlier. Duncan knew he could find it again, so he led the small patrol west from Bozeman to intercept the Gallatin River, the point from which they were now departing. As best he could determine, the stream that flowed by Coldiron's cabin was about twelve miles south, so the patrol set out to follow the river.

The farther south they traveled, the rougher the country became as they approached the rugged mountains that hovered over the narrow river. Along the way, they passed many streams that fed down into the river, all looking enough alike to make it difficult to identify one particular one, especially after a year's time. "Are you sure you'll recognize the stream we're looking for?" Bret felt compelled to ask Duncan. "It's not easy to tell one of these from all the others."

"Oh, I'll know it when I see it," Duncan assured him. "We ain't gone far enough to strike it yet."

It was toward the later part of the afternoon when they finally reached what Duncan referred to as Coldiron Creek. "This is it," he proclaimed, and pointed toward the top of the mountain. "It goes straight up that mountain. Coldiron's cabin is about half a mile up."

Bret could see why Duncan had been so confident in his ability to identify the proper stream. It emptied into the Gallatin between two big rocks. He followed the winding stream up the slope with his eyes until it disappeared into the thick foliage of the tall trees. Above the tree line the steep mountain peaks stood defiantly discouraging the casual climber. "It looks pretty rough. Maybe we'd better dismount and lead the horses up there."

"It looks rough," Duncan replied, "but there's a game trail followin' the stream up the hill, and we can ride it if we take it slow. It's just hard to see it from here. I'll lead the way."

He didn't wait for the lieutenant's order, but started up through a thick stand of fir trees that bordered the river. Bret fell in behind him with eight unenthusiastic troopers following him, complaining about the occasional branches that slapped at their faces.

"Quit your bellyachin' and keep up," Duncan called back over his shoulder, admonishing his men.

As Duncan had said, they soon struck a game trail that circled around from the north side of the mountain and started up the slope beside the stream. Bret couldn't help thinking how far removed he was from the cavalry combat training he'd been drilled in at the academy. There had been very little time spent on the basics of Indian fighting. He was convinced that it was certainly a worthwhile patrol. But what were the odds of tracking a war party of Indian raiders that had a two-day head start? Not very high in his estimation. Then he reminded himself not to question orders. He didn't want to start complaining like the privates following him. His thoughts were interrupted then by the sound of a rifle cocking, and a booming voice. "Somethin' I can help you soldier boys with?" The question was followed almost immediately by an exclamation. "Well, damn me—Sergeant Johnny Duncan! I thought you was dead."

"Not by a long shot," Duncan replied. "Where the hell are you?"

"I'm right here," Nathaniel Coldiron replied, stepping out from between two boulders on the other side of the stream.

Bret Hollister would never forget his first sight of the old scout. From behind the boulder, a man more closely resembling a grizzly bear pushed through a thicket of berry bushes and crossed the stream, oblivious of the water. Clad entirely in animal skins, he wore no hat. His long gray hair, tied in a single braid, hung down his back almost to his belt. A full beard, more gray than black, covered the bottom half of his broad face—so thick that, until he opened his mouth to speak, there appeared to be no hole there at all.

"What you doin' up here, Duncan?" he asked

as he eased the hammer down on his rifle—a Henry that looked unusually small in his over-sized paw.

"Lookin' for you," Duncan answered.

"What fer?" Coldiron asked, all the while casting a critical eye on the officer and enlisted men behind the sergeant.

"Got a little job for you," Duncan said. "That is, if you ain't got too old to do some trackin'."

Coldiron snorted scornfully. "If you thought I was, I don't reckon you'da drug your tired old ass up here lookin' fer me." He nodded toward Bret then. "Who you brung with you?"

Standing patiently by while the two old acquaintances greeted each other, Bret spoke up before Duncan could answer. "I'm Lieutenant Hollister. We came looking for you in hopes you might be able to track an Indian war party that massacred two white families over on the Yellowstone near Benson's Landing."

Coldiron nodded thoughtfully, openly distrustful of most army officers and all officers as young and green as this one appeared to be. "I heared about that raid," he said after a pause. "Two families got burned out. That was two nights ago. And you're lookin' to track 'em?"

"We're looking to try," Bret replied. "Those are my orders."

"Orders is orders. Ain't that right, Duncan?" He glanced at the sergeant and laughed as if he had made a joke. "That's a mighty cold trail you're lookin' to follow."

Bret began to lose his patience with the seemingly sarcastic brute. "That's the only trail there is. If you don't think you can help us, then I expect we'd best not waste any more of your time."

Coldiron chuckled and winked at Duncan. "Don't get your fur up, sonny. I didn't say I wouldn't help. I'll go over there with you and take a look around—see what's what."

"Fine," Bret replied. "That's all we're asking, but let's get one thing straight from the start. My name is Bret Hollister. I'll answer to Lieutenant, Hollister, or Bret, but don't ever call me sonny again. Is that understood?"

Coldiron jerked his head back, surprised by the young officer's spunk. It was only for a moment, however, before he chuckled heartily. "All right, *Lieutenant,* that's understood."

Also amused by the lieutenant's defiant attitude, Duncan said, "I reckon we'd best get started as soon as possible—cold as that trail is, and it's a pretty long ride if we have to go back the way we came." He looked up, trying to find the sun through the treetops. "It ain't gonna be long before dark in these mountains."

"I expect you're right about that," Coldiron said. "Ain't no use to start out till mornin', anyway. We ain't goin' back the way you came up the Gallatin.

We'll cut across through the mountains, and if we try to make it in the dark, we're liable to break a leg or somethin'. Besides, I got things to take care of before I can go. I gotta check my traps for certain." He turned to start up the slope. "You boys follow me and I'll carve off some deer haunch to cook for supper, unless you druther have that salt pork and hardtack the army gave you." His remark stirred a quiet murmur of anticipation among the eight troopers as they followed up through the steep path to Coldiron's cabin.

Afraid the horses might stumble as the path steepened even more, Bret had the men dismount and lead them the last fifty yards to the small clearing where the cabin sat, backed up against the slope. Coldiron had obviously built his small abode using logs from the trees he had cleared. Bret wondered if he had had help in the construction, but from the look of the man, he seemed capable of doing the job by himself. A short distance beyond the cabin was a sizable meadow where the huge man's two horses were grazing. Sergeant Duncan and the men took the horses there to graze overnight while Bret volunteered to help their host build a fire. "Them Injuns take anybody alive?" Coldiron asked when Bret brought an armload of wood from a pile near the cabin.

"Not according to the report by the thirteen-year-old boy who rode to Fort Ellis," Bret answered. "They killed everybody and set fire to the homes."

"Like I said," Coldiron replied, "I heard about the raid. I didn't hear about nobody bein' took alive, either."

"That's what I was told," Bret repeated.

"That kinda surprises me," Coldiron said. "Sometimes they'll carry off a young woman."

"The Sioux and Cheyenne have been known to take women hostages plenty of times before," Johnny Duncan commented as he walked up, having overheard the last remarks. "I don't see why these Sioux would be any different."

"Blackfoot," Coldiron said. "They was Blackfoot. They ain't Sioux or Cheyenne. They most likely were movin' too fast to bother with captives."

"Huh," Duncan grunted. "How do you know they were Blackfoot? We were told they were Sioux. Them and some Cheyenne renegades have been attackin' some farms along the Yellowstone for the last two months."

"The Injuns that hit Benson's Landing was Blackfoot," Coldiron stated matter-of-factly. "I seen 'em when they came down the river last week. I figured they was lookin' to steal horses or raid homesteaders, but there ain't no homesteaders on the Gallatin, so I reckon they moved on. They was a long way from home, if they were from that bunch up near the Judith. I thought that mighta been them comin' back when you soldier boys came ridin' up my trail."

"Maybe so," Duncan allowed. "Don't make much difference, though. Injuns is Injuns. Where's that haunch of deer meat you was braggin' about?"

Coldiron chuckled again. "Still on the deer," he said and pointed to a tree by the stream on the far side of the cabin, where a carcass was hanging from a limb. "I was just fixin' to butcher it when I heard you boys comin' up my trail soundin' like a freight train. I hadn't kilt it more'n fifteen minutes before that."

His comment surprised Bret. "We didn't hear a shot," he said. "If we were that close, I woulda thought we'd have heard the shot."

"Most likely because you boys was makin' so much noise comin' up through them bushes," Coldiron said, then waited for a few moments before explaining. "Coulda been 'cause I shot it with my bow, though." He looked at Duncan and laughed heartily. "If one of your boys can give me a hand, I'll go saw us off a haunch. Wouldn't be a bad idea if we smoked a supply of meat to take with us. We don't know how long it'll take to catch up to that raidin' party."

Duncan nodded toward Private Tom Weaver, motioning for him to follow Coldiron.

Although they had been grumbling most of the day, complaining about bottoms sore from pounding against saddles they had not come to comfortable relations with as yet, Bret's eight-man detail was able to enjoy the fresh venison feast. There was plenty, for Coldiron was not going to leave any behind, once they started in the morning. Long after they had eaten their fill, he continued to smoke strips of the meat over the fire, planning to take a good supply with them. He intended to feed the buzzards with what was left. While the enlisted men spread their blankets on one side of the fire, Bret and Duncan sat on the other, talking over the mission with their guide.

Bret was content to give the rough-hewn bear-like scout the benefit of the doubt as to whether or not he was a top-notch tracker. His first impression was of a bitter man who held a special contempt for officers, judging by his dismissive attitude toward him. Bret considered himself to be a fair man, but he was not one to be bullied by anyone, regardless of their expertise or experience. So he decided to ignore Coldiron's inadequately disguised arrogance for the time being, at least until he proved himself valuable or not.

The night passed peacefully enough, with every man's belly filled with venison and coffee. Duncan routed his troopers out of their blankets the next morning before the first rays of the sun found their way through the canopy of fir needles overhead. They saddled up while Coldiron closed his cabin and made sure there were no warm ashes left from the fire.

"Fill your canteens," Duncan ordered as he stooped to fill his. "We'll boil some coffee and eat breakfast when we stop to rest the horses." When satisfied that each man had filled his canteen and was standing by his mount, he looked at Bret and reported, "Detail's ready to mount, sir."

"Very well, Sergeant," Bret replied, and turned to see what progress his scout was making. Coldiron came from the cabin, leading a sturdy buckskin horse with a dark sorrel packhorse following behind.

"I reckon we're ready to go," he stated cheerfully.

"Ain't you got no lock or nothin' to put on your door?" Duncan asked.

"What for?" Coldiron replied. "I got ever'thin' I need with me. If I left a lock on the door, I just might come back with my door busted off the straps. Ain't nobody stumbled across my cabin that I know of. At least, if they did, they left it pretty much the way they found it. I left my sign propped up against the door, anyway."

"Your sign?" Duncan asked, straining to stare back at the cabin.

"Yeah. I can't read or make no letters, but I had Everett Bingham over at the fort make me a sign to leave when I'm gone."

Duncan laughed. "You think a sign'll keep anybody out?"

"Don't know," Coldiron came back, "but there ain't been no damage so far."

Unable to resist, Duncan walked back to the cabin door to see for himself. Sure enough, there was a sign propped against the door.

**THIS CABIN PROPERTY OF
NATHANIEL COLDIRON
BE WARNED
DON'T BE HERE WHEN I GET BACK**

Chapter 2

A trip of about forty miles as the hawk flies took the small patrol of eleven men almost two days owing to the rugged terrain and the frequent rests for the horses. Led by their imposing guide, they followed one small game trail after another, crossing mountains sparsely covered with spruce and fir, through rugged ravines and along ridges devoid of trees. Finally they descended into the Yellowstone Valley, striking the river precisely two hundred yards south of the trading post near Benson's Landing.

If there had been any question in Bret's mind regarding Coldiron's knowledge of the mountains between the two rivers, it had been properly put to rest. Speaking for himself, he knew with certainty that he would be unable to accurately retrace the way they had just come in the event he wanted to return to Coldiron's cabin. It was easy to attribute that skill to the fact that the mountains between the two rivers were, in essence, Coldiron's backyard. Bret would reserve his opinion of the man's ability to track once they found a trail to follow.

"If it's the two families that I heard about that got raided, they're about two miles south of here," Coldiron told them.

"You haven't been over here since you heard about the attack?" Bret asked.

"Didn't have no reason to," Coldiron replied indifferently. "It was too late to do them poor folks any good. Might as well wait to rest the horses till we get down there." He turned his horse upriver and led off toward the trading post. "I reckon you're gonna wanna see what the folks at Benson's have to say about the raid."

"That might be a good idea," Bret said.

On any given day, there were usually two or more trappers hanging around Benson's Landing, and this was the case when Lieutenant Hollister's small patrol rode up to the trading post.

"Here comes the army," Lloyd Turner called out facetiously from the porch, "and Nate Coldiron's leadin' 'em." Turner got up from the empty keg he had been using for a seat and walked out to the hitching rail to meet them. "I thought you was dead," Lloyd said in greeting Coldiron, a customary salutation between men who roamed the mountains alone.

"I ain't scheduled to go until right after you lose your scalp, Lloyd," Coldiron responded as he and Bret dismounted.

"Coldiron," acknowledged another man who had walked outside when he heard Lloyd's announcement.

"Leadfoot," Coldiron returned in recognition.

Lloyd took a long look at the lieutenant and the soldiers behind him. "I reckon you boys came over to see about the Injun raids up the river. They didn't send many of you, did they?" He addressed Bret then. "You boys wanna step down and rest a little?"

"No, thank you just the same," Bret replied at once. "We're pretty far behind on this patrol as it is. So I'd just like to see if there's anything else you might have to add to what we already know. Then I expect we'd best get about our business."

"Yes, sir," Lloyd replied. "I know you wanna do what you can to save those women."

His remark caused Bret to stammer in complete surprise, "Women? What women?"

"Them two the Injuns took with 'em," Leadfoot interjected when he saw the shocked expressions on the lieutenant's and sergeant's faces.

"We weren't told there were captives taken," Bret replied.

"I ain't a bit surprised," Coldiron allowed.

Needing to know for certain, Bret asked, "Are you sure about that? Two women?"

"The feller who can tell you for sure is layin' up in one of Lloyd's bunks with an arrow hole in his side," Leadfoot answered, then stepped out of the way when Bret almost ran over him in his haste to question the man.

"I saw 'em when they rode off with 'em," Tom Sayers told them. "Me and my little brother was helpin' Cliff Buckley plow up his corn crop. That night, me and Billy slept out behind the barn. We woke up in the middle of the night when we heard the Injuns attack. They had already hit the house and ever'one in it. We made a run for the woods, but they saw us, and that's when I got hit in the side. I told Billy to run for it, try to get to Fort Ellis. I figured they were gonna come finish me off, but I reckon they forgot about me layin' there in the cornfield. When it started gettin' on toward daylight, they took off, and they had Myra Buckley and Lucy Gentry with 'em. I figured they'd hit the Gentry house first."

It was a sobering testimony to be suddenly confronted with, and was enough to cast a new importance on their patrol. In Bret's mind, there was no longer a question of responsibility. He turned to Coldiron, and said, "Let's get up to that house and see if we can find enough tracks to see which way they headed from here."

It was as Coldiron had speculated. They came to the first of the two dwellings after a ride of a couple of miles, at least what was left of it. It had been burned almost to the ground, the still-smoking timbers attesting to the high risk of homesteading the Yellowstone Valley. Beyond it, another pile of burned timbers marked the spot where the barn once stood. At the edge of a cornfield, there were three graves, evidence that any attempt to aid the stricken family came too late. In the barnyard, the remains of a milk cow and several pigs lay half-eaten by scavengers, accounting for the odor of rotting flesh that drifted to Bret's nose as he gazed at the ghastly scene. "That's one of 'em," Coldiron said, breaking into his thoughts. "The other'n's around the bend on the other side of the river."

Bret sighed helplessly and dismounted. Turning to Duncan, he said, "Lead the horses upwind a little and we'll rest them here before we move on to the other house." Then he turned to watch Coldiron, who was already out of the saddle and looking around. "There are a helluva lot of tracks all over this place," he commented to the crusty scout. "It's gonna be pretty hard to sort out where the Indians went when they left here."

"There's enough to tell," Coldiron replied,

studying the ground carefully. "I ain't interested in the ones wearin' shoes. Those were left by the folks who came to bury 'em." Something caught his eye in the charred timbers of the house, so he stepped over the end of the fallen ridgepole and picked up the feathered end of a broken arrow. He studied the markings on the shaft and the way the feathers were fashioned. "Yep, like I said, Blackfoot, and I'll bet you they didn't have nothin' but bows and arrows—maybe an old musket or two—but I bet most of 'em was shootin' arrows."

"Maybe so," Bret conceded. He had no way of knowing if Coldiron was right or not.

"We gonna be here long enough to make a little coffee?" Private Bill Copeland yelled back to Sergeant Duncan, who was walking up to join Bret and Coldiron.

Duncan looked at Coldiron, who nodded. "Yeah, go ahead," Duncan yelled back to Copeland. Then thinking he should have checked with Bret before responding, he asked, "That all right with you, Lieutenant?" Bret nodded. The horses were due a rest before they started out again, anyway.

Coldiron paused for a few moments to cast a long glance in the direction of the patrol. "Damned if that ain't a sorry-lookin' bunch of soldiers you brought with you this time, Johnny," he commented. "Look at 'em—asses so sore they look like a bunch of cripples." He winked at

Duncan then and asked, "How 'bout you, Lieutenant? Your ass a little bit tender?"

"How about you keeping your mind on what the army's paying you to do, and I'll worry about my ass," Bret retorted. He started to walk toward the barn then, but paused to respond to the big man's attempt to provoke him. "To answer your question, no, my ass isn't sore. I expect I can sit a saddle as long as you can, maybe a little longer." Then he continued to the barn, leaving Coldiron at a loss for an immediate comeback, and Duncan with a wide grin on his face.

"Damned if he ain't a feisty one," Coldiron conceded. "I'll have to give him that."

"He is," Duncan agreed. "There may be somethin' inside that fancy blouse besides a typical West Point greenhorn."

Bret spent only a few minutes at the barn before walking to the river to look along the bank for signs of a crossing. He was kneeling down, studying a mixed trail of both moccasin and hoof prints, when Coldiron approached. Bret got to his feet and offered his interpretation of the sign.

"Looks to me like Sayers is right. They hit the other house first," Bret said. "They came across here, leading their horses at night."

"That so?" Coldiron asked, waiting to see for himself before commenting further. After a moment's study, however, he couldn't disagree. There were surely both footprints and hoofprints

27

leading up out of the water across an open sandy stretch of bluffs. "I reckon you're right," he said. "What tells you it was at night?" Tom Sayers had just told them the Indians struck at night. Coldiron wanted to see if the lieutenant was pretending to be a tracker.

"This spot they picked to cross," Bret told him. "If it had been in the daytime, they would have crossed back there where those trees come down to the bank. They figured at night they could take the easier crossing on this sandbar, thinking it was too dark to see them."

"Well, I ain't got nothin' to add to that," Coldiron said. "That's the same way I read it." Then thinking of something he could add, he said, "You can tell by the length of their stride, and the way the toes ain't dug into the sand, that they were sneakin' up on 'em and not chargin' outta the river."

"Right," Bret agreed. "So I think there's no need to waste extra time scouting the other farm. We just need to scout around the perimeter to see which way they headed when they left here."

"Most likely we can save some more time if we start lookin' for their tracks north of here," Coldiron said. "The Injuns that done this piece of business are Blackfoot, and I'm thinkin' they headed for home. Now, if I'm leadin' that war party, I'm not gonna wanna take on that bunch of trappers that hang around Benson's Landin'.

They've all got rifles, and I ain't got nothin' but bows and arrows—and maybe a shotgun or two I mighta got from the raid. So what I'm sayin' is, somewhere between here and Benson's, we're gonna find where they crossed back over the river and headed up in the hills."

"That makes sense to me," Johnny Duncan said as he walked up to join them. "But first, we need to make sure they headed north."

There were many tracks, going and coming, along the wagon road that followed the Yellowstone River, most of them recent. But Coldiron soon isolated the unshod tracks of the Indian ponies, and they were heading north, as he had predicted.

"Now all we gotta do is find where they crossed the river, but I'll guarantee you it'll be before we get to Benson's," he said.

"All right," Bret said. "We'll let the men drink their coffee. The horses should be rested by then." He turned to Coldiron. "You can go on ahead and scout the riverbanks if you want to, unless you want to have some coffee first."

"I don't need no coffee," the scout responded. "My horse is ready to go. I'll go on up ahead and wait for you boys." He took his horse's reins and started walking along the wagon track, his packhorse trailing along behind.

Over beside the river, a small fire was burning, and the eight troopers lay sprawled around it,

29

tending the metal cups that held the scalding black coffee.

"Look at 'em," Private Brice McCoy slurred, "over there lookin' all around that damn house for tracks. Hell, them Injuns are long gone."

"Maybe, maybe not," Private Tom Weaver remarked. "And maybe they're up ahead somewhere fixin' up an ambush, hopin' we chase after 'em." The eight men knew very little about each other, all being new recruits, and having known each other for less than a couple of months. But that was all the time needed to learn that Weaver was a chronic complainer, and the only one he could count as a friend was Brice McCoy, who complained almost as much. A tall, wiry man with dark eyes that peered out from under heavy black eyebrows, Weaver never volunteered any facts about his life prior to enlisting in the army. "I ain't anxious to get my ass shot full of arrows while Lieutenant Fancy Pants tries to go after some glory for himself," he drawled. "Ain't that right, McCoy?"

"Damn right," McCoy responded.

"I think you men mighta judged Lieutenant Hollister wrong," Private Pruett said. "He seems like a decent sort. I doubt if he wanted to go on this patrol any more than the rest of us."

"Shit, Pruett," Weaver snapped. "He went to West Point. That's what all them assholes are in the army for—medals and promotions to generals.

Hell, why do you think he went to West Point? I just don't want him steppin' on my dead ass to get his glory."

"All I know is I sure as hell didn't know what I was doin' when I volunteered for the cavalry," Private Joe Lazarra complained. "My ass is so sore I'm gonna have to sleep on my belly. If I had it to do over, I'd sure as hell rather be a walkin' soldier."

"Hell, I didn't get any choice," Bill Copeland chimed in. "They just sent me straight to the recruit depot at Jefferson Barracks in Missouri, and told me I was in the cavalry. I was hopin' to get sent to Washington, D.C., maybe to guard the president or somethin'." His remarks brought a derisive laugh from the others.

"Hold your tongue," McCoy warned. "Here comes Duncan."

"All right, ladies," Duncan mocked. "Let's get mounted—tea party's over."

"My horse ain't hardly rested enough, Sarge," Weaver complained.

"Is that a fact?" Duncan replied. "Well, in that case, I reckon you can tote him till he gets rested up enough."

"Nice try, Weaver," Pruett said sarcastically.

"Kiss my ass," Weaver shot back as he reluctantly climbed into the saddle.

The patrol rode for less than a mile before coming upon Coldiron sitting on a fallen tree trunk beside the river. He got to his feet when they pulled up to a stop.

"Here's where they crossed, Lieutenant, just like I figured." He pointed, then, across the river. "I expect they headed for that ravine yonder, figurin' on puttin' that ridge between 'em and the tradin' post."

It was not necessary to dismount. Bret could see the prints of a dozen or so unshod ponies leading across a thin strip of sand and into the water.

On the opposite side, the tracks seemed to be starting toward the ravine Coldiron had pointed out, so they headed for it at a lope, pulling up again at the mouth of the ravine long enough to confirm his hunch. Bret would ordinarily have sent two men out, one to each side, to act as lookouts, but owing to the narrow confines of the ravine, it was unnecessary. So they continued to follow Coldiron in a column of twos as they climbed toward the ridge above them. Once again confirming Coldiron's speculation, the Blackfoot war party did not continue up into the mountains, but descended on the other side of the ridge and cut back to the north.

"So far, they're doin' just like I figured," Coldiron said. "I didn't expect 'em to head on up into the Absarokas. They're headin' home. They'll be crossin' back across the river somewhere up ahead, most likely before the river takes a hard turn and heads east. Trouble is, it's comin' dark pretty soon, and I won't be able to see where they crossed."

"I was wonderin' about that myself," Duncan said. They had been following the Yellowstone on its northeast course since crossing over, but somewhere ahead of them, maybe twenty miles or thereabout, the river's course turned almost due east. And like Coldiron, he doubted the Blackfoot would follow it.

"Well, the horses are getting tired, anyway," Bret decided. "We might as well go ahead and make camp and get after them again in the morning." He let Coldiron and Duncan pick the spot they favored near a stand of willow trees at the water's edge.

When the horses were unsaddled and watered, and a good campfire was going, Duncan directed two of the men to string a rope between two trees to act as a hitching post for the horses. On Bret's orders, he then called out a sentry detail, starting with Private Lazzara and changing every two hours throughout the night. This was met with some disappointment by the eight troopers, but only one was vocal in complaint.

"Guard duty?" Weaver whined. "What the hell for? There ain't no Injuns within fifty miles of here."

"There's a helluva lotta things you don't know, Weaver," Duncan told him. "That's just one of 'em. But if you've gotta know the reason you're

33

gonna pull guard duty, it's because the lieutenant ordered it, and I, by God, said so."

Overhearing the last part of Weaver's complaining, Bret stepped a little closer and commented, "There's gonna be a horse guard tonight, and every night after this, because I don't intend to walk back to Fort Ellis. Is that reason enough for you?"

"Yes, sir," Weaver answered meekly.

"Good," Bret said. "Now, don't ever let me hear you question orders again. Is that understood?"

"Yes, sir," he mumbled, a childish pout upon his face. After Bret had walked away to sit down near Coldiron and Duncan, Weaver muttered under his breath, "Son of a bitch."

"Quit your bellyachin', Weaver," Pruett told him.

"Yeah," Lazzara said. "And Duncan said you're supposed to relieve me in two hours. Make damn sure you do it, or the sergeant ain't gonna be the only one wantin' a piece of you."

"Don't you worry, I'll be there," Weaver grumbled. "I sure as hell don't want any wild Injuns stealin' Lieutenant Fancy Pants's horse." He continued to gripe, however, as the men had their supper of coffee, hardtack, and smoked deer meat. "Ever' one of you knows this patrol ain't nothin' but a waste of our time. Those damn Injuns, Blackfoot or whatever they are, are long gone from these parts. And if we had an officer

34

with a lick of sense, he'd turn us around and get on back to Fort Ellis."

"What the hell did you think you was gonna be doin' when you joined the army?" Pruett asked then. "Maybe you thought you'd be guardin' the president with ol' Copeland over there." This brought a chuckle from the rest of the men.

"Go to hell, Pruett," Weaver spat.

"Seven o'clock, Lazzara," Sergeant Duncan called out from the other side of the little circle around the fire. "Keep your eyes open up there. Weaver will relieve you at nine."

"All right, Sergeant," Lazzara replied, picked up his carbine and blanket, and walked up a little rise beyond the willows where the horses were tied, that being the spot Duncan had selected to post his guards, where they would be able to watch the horses as well as the sleeping camp.

"I expect the rest of you boys oughta turn in pretty quick now," Duncan said. "Get a little sleep. We'll be in the saddle again early in the mornin'." The camp settled in for the night. Although it was still summertime, the Montana nights were normally quite chilly, so the troopers spread their blankets close by the fire. Bret noticed that Coldiron made his bed apart from the others, and seemed to be snoring as soon as he stretched his huge body out horizontally.

Feeling that sleep was not yet upon him, Bret moved away from the fire to sit down and finish the rest of his coffee. He found a spot in the low bluffs and propped his back against a short ledge. Once the camp got quiet, he could hear an occasional snort or nicker from the horses, and the gurgle of the river as it flowed gently by a fallen cottonwood extending out into the current. It was peaceful, but not sufficient to make him feel content with his life at this point. Commanding a patrol of greenhorns, guided by a man who seemed to have only contempt for them all, on a mission that held little chance of success, he was becoming more and more short of patience with the whole situation. He would never admit it, but Weaver was probably closer to the truth of the matter.

After a moment of disgust, he chastised himself for his attitude. He admitted that it was brought about simply because he had been left behind when the regiment marched to engage the Nez Perce.

Change your attitude, mister! he scolded himself. What about the two women hostages? Did they not deserve his every effort to find them? He tried to empty his mind of these troublesome thoughts and just concentrate on the murmuring of the river, and Coldiron's snoring. Convinced that he could not go to sleep, he nevertheless fell into a peaceful slumber.

Like a strike from a lightning bolt, he was suddenly jerked out of a sound sleep by the sounds of gunshots and he found himself at the edge of a whirlwind of fury. Unable to right his reeling senses at first, he soon realized what was taking place. The circle of sleeping soldiers was swarming with howling demons, slaughtering the surprised troopers with hatchets, knives, and random gunshots. It presented a hell like none Bret had ever seen before.

Realizing that he had not yet been discovered by the savage war party, he reacted in the only way he could. Grabbing his Spencer carbine and the Blakeslee cartridge box he carried, he started firing into the frenzy of Blackfoot warriors, knocking two of them down before they determined where he was. They turned immediately to attack him, but Bret heard the solid snap of Coldiron's Henry rifle at that moment, causing the charging warriors to back off and seek cover from both rifles.

Bret advanced toward the retreating Indians, firing as rapidly as he could, pausing only seconds to load seven new cartridges into the butt of the carbine. With the advantage of having the Blakeslee, he was able to load a fresh tube of ammunition before the savages could rebound to counterattack. The Blackfoot warriors had no choice other than to retreat under the continuous fire from Bret and Coldiron.

"Don't let 'em get to the horses!" Coldiron yelled as he came up from the bank of the river.

Bret sprinted past the bloody circle of slain

troopers to position himself between the warriors and the horses tied in the trees. On his way, he paused to pull Duncan back from the firelight. The sergeant was wounded in the gut, the arrow still protruding as he struggled to get to his feet.

"Can you hold on?" Bret asked hurriedly, although it looked doubtful as he dragged the stumbling man back away from the fire.

"I've been better," Duncan gasped painfully, his pistol in hand. "They got my carbine and two or three others."

"Stay here and keep low," Bret told him. "I've gotta get to the horses."

"Go," Duncan said. "I'll be all right. I can still shoot."

He paused for only a fraction of a second to look at the bodies of his men, unable to tell if any of them were alive.

"How many?" he asked quickly.

"Don't know," Duncan gasped painfully. "Four for sure, three might be wounded. I can't say how Weaver fared. He was on guard duty."

"I gotta go help Coldiron hold them off," Bret said when he had pulled Duncan to a spot where he felt sure he was out of the line of fire, and heard the sound of a new exchange of gunfire. It told him that the Indians were fighting back with the cavalry carbines they had taken when they overran the camp. He started running again, hoping the hostiles had not had the time or the presence of mind to take the ammunition, too. "I'll be back to help you."

"Over here!" Coldiron yelled when Bret came running through the willows toward the horses.

The big scout was hunkered down behind a low hummock, topped by a clump of willow switches. He fired a series of three quick rounds to give Bret a chance to cross an open gap in the trees.

"They're settin' back of that rise yonder," he said when Bret dived behind the hummock beside him. "A couple of 'em tried to get to the horses, but I got both of 'em."

He instinctively ducked when a few rounds from the captured Spencers dug into the sand above their heads.

"They're damn sure gettin' the hang of them carbines, but we've got 'em out on a limb right now. They can't get to the horses without crossin' open ground, and so far it's cost 'em every time they've tried it."

"You reckon they have any idea how many rounds those carbines hold?" Bret asked.

"I doubt it . . . maybe. There might be some of 'em that's seen one before."

"I may be wrong," Bret said, "but I'm betting they don't know what a Blakeslee cartridge box is. I don't think they've got any ammunition beyond what's in the magazines of the weapons they took. And if that's the case, they're gonna shoot that up soon. So if we can just hold them off till they run out, then we can take the offensive."

"I hope you're right," Coldiron said. "And if you are, them sons of bitches ain't gonna wanna be caught here after daylight."

"That's what I'm thinking," Bret replied.

So the two under siege sat tight and watched the rise for any sign of the hostiles trying to sneak across the open ground to the horses. There was only one more, and he met with the same fate as the other two, the only difference being the fact that he died from slugs of two different calibers.

Soon after, there was a period of almost no gunfire from the rise, with only a random shot to let the two white men know they were still there. It was during this lull in the battle that Bret had the opportunity to try to piece together the circumstances that allowed the camp to be routed so quickly. There had been no alarm, no warning from the sentry.

"How in hell could those hostiles just walk right into the camp and start hacking up my men, without anybody seeing them?" Bret wondered. "Did anybody hear the guard give a warning? I didn't. I was asleep."

"Hell, we was all asleep," Coldiron said. "When I woke up, they was already swarming all over them poor boys like bees on a hive. Seemed like a hundred of 'em when I first woke up, but I don't think it was more'n a dozen. Just seemed like more."

It was easy to come to the conclusion that the sentry must have been asleep with everyone else; either that or they managed to sneak up on him and kill him.

"Damn," Bret swore, feeling the responsibility of perhaps losing his entire patrol. "Can you hold on here for a little while? I've got to get back to Sergeant Duncan. He took an arrow in the gut, but he said he was all right till I got back to help him. I'll see who else is alive and try to bring them all back here. I think this is about as good a place as any to stand them off. At least we can try to protect the horses here."

When Coldiron assured him that he could hold that position against twice that many Indians, Bret crawled to the lower edge of the sand hummock and prepared to launch his lean body across the open gap between the trees. There was only one shot fired at him, from what sounded to be an old single-shot musket. It confirmed his speculation that the Blackfeet were running short of cartridges.

When he got to the spot where he had left Duncan, he found one of the men with him, Private McCoy. He had suffered knife wounds, but none so severe as to be life-threatening. He had had the presence of mind to pick up the remaining weapons from the dead before he ran for it.

"Is this it?" Bret asked as soon as he dropped down beside them. "Nobody else?"

"Just me," McCoy answered, "and I wouldn't have made it if you and Coldiron hadn't started shootin' when you did."

"That son of a bitch, Weaver," Duncan groaned. "He went to sleep. I know he did. I reckon he paid the price for it. They probably cut his throat."

"I hope to hell they did," McCoy growled. "The bastard's responsible for gettin' damn near all of us killed."

"Maybe so," Bret said. "We'll find out when we drive this bunch of Indians off. Right now let's get over to that hummock with Coldiron. There's better cover there, and we'll see if we can get that arrow out of you then," he said to Duncan.

"Well, I was wonderin' if anybody noticed the damn thing stickin' outta me," Duncan remarked between painful breaths.

"Take hold of his feet," Bret told McCoy, and the two of them carried the wounded sergeant through the willows to the open gap, where they paused to let Coldiron know they were coming in.

"Coldiron!" he yelled. "We're coming across. We're gonna need some cover fire when I tell you."

It wouldn't do to surprise the big scout without a warning. He might shoot at them, thinking he was under attack.

Bret looked at McCoy then. "Ready?" Then he

yelled out, "Now!" Coldiron peppered the rise with gunfire while they hurried across the open gap. When they arrived safely behind the hummock, they laid Duncan down as gently as possible.

Once Duncan was settled, Bret turned his attention to the arrow protruding from his stomach. Getting weaker by the minute, the sergeant was obviously dying. The arrow was embedded deeply inside him, but the head did not go all the way through, which would have made it much easier to break it off and pull the shaft out. Not sure what he could do without causing the sergeant a great deal of pain, Bret deliberated over it for a few moments, trying to decide if it could only be removed by cutting into the wound and enlarging the entry hole. But he couldn't leave the arrow where it was.

"Lemme see," Coldiron said, after Bret seemed to be hesitating. The big man crawled over beside Duncan, who now showed no ability to protest. Coldiron grasped the arrow shaft gently, testing its firmness. Duncan emitted a sharp grunt at the touch. "It's in there pretty good, all right," Coldiron decided. Then he turned to Bret and commented, "See them markin's there, they're Blackfoot, like I said."

"I don't give a damn who they are—" That was as much as Duncan could mutter before Coldiron tightened down on the shaft. With one massive paw on Duncan to hold him down, he suddenly yanked the arrow out, head and all, like uprooting a weed from the ground. It was so painful and unexpected that the sergeant was unable to make a sound for a moment before yowling weakly like a wounded coyote.

"Sweet Jesus!" he was finally able to gasp as a fresh flow of blood gushed from the newly enlarged wound.

"Yep," the imperturbable scout remarked casually as he held the arrow up to examine it. "It's Blackfoot, all right." He glanced back at McCoy. "You got anything to stuff over that wound? He's bleedin' out right smart."

McCoy reluctantly produced a piece of the cloth he was using to bandage his knife wound. It was obvious to him that Duncan was going to die, no matter whether they tried to bandage his wound or not. The sergeant was bleeding from his mouth as well as the hole left by the arrow. It didn't make sense to McCoy to waste his extra shirt on a dead man.

They waited out the few hours left before daylight, watching the rise intently, as well as the river at their backs. There was no further gunfire from the Indians, and when the first light of day began to find its way into the valley, the weary survivors roused themselves to be more alert.

As the sun climbed higher in the early morning sky, it was now easier to see the site of their camp and the bodies of their comrades slumped in eternal sleep around the ashes of the fire. What came as a surprise to them was the discovery that the bodies of the two warriors that Bret had killed were missing. Under the cover of darkness, the Blackfoot had crept into the camp to retrieve their dead. The light of day also revealed the absence of the bodies Coldiron had accounted for.

"They was already outta cartridges," he said to Bret. "They slipped out in the dark while we was settin' right here watchin' for 'em." He got to his feet then, certain he was right, and unafraid of being shot at. "Well, that's that," he announced.

Bret looked back at Duncan, who seemed to at last be resting peacefully. When he told him what the morning light had revealed, Duncan didn't respond. He had passed quietly during the long morning hours.

"Damn," Bret uttered softly. He had not had the opportunity to get to know the sergeant very well, but what he had seen up to this point had been enough to judge him a good man and a proper soldier. "He's dead," he reported when he looked up to meet Coldiron's inquisitive glance.

"I figured," was Coldiron's response.

Bret couldn't help wondering if the sergeant's death was hurried along by Coldiron's method of extracting the arrow. They went then to their campsite to check on their dead, six bodies lying grotesquely in various states of surprise as they

45

had been set upon in their sleep. The sight sickened Bret. He had seen mutilated bodies of soldiers when he had buried the dead at Little Big Horn, but these six were under his command, and were dead because of his failure to protect them. None of the other survivors of the attack might see it that way, but that was the way he saw it, and it weighed heavily upon him. Coldiron moved up beside him to comment, "They didn't waste any time, did they? They didn't even take time to scalp 'em."

Bret was staring at a couple of haversacks lying near Copeland's body. The contents that had spilled out on the ground were primarily his issue of Blakeslee cartridge cases. "If they had known what those were," he said, "we mighta had a battle for our horses." Thinking of his one missing man then, he told McCoy to go up to the little rise beyond the willows to look for Weaver's body. "We'll bring him back here and bury him with the others."

"That's a helluva lot of diggin' to do," McCoy protested. "And it don't make no damn sense to hang around here waitin' for those Injuns to come back."

Bret was in no mood to suffer the private's insolence. "I gave you an order, Private, and I don't want to hear any more of your mouth. Now get your ass up there and look for Weaver." McCoy hesitated a moment, burning inside before turning to leave. "I didn't hear you respond, Private," Bret said.

"Yes, sir," McCoy blurted. *You son of a bitch,* he said under his breath.

About fifteen minutes passed before McCoy returned. "He ain't there," he reported. "I looked all around that spot. Nary a sign of him."

Bret looked at Coldiron. "You think they captured him?"

"I doubt it," Coldiron replied. "If they thought there was a guard watchin' the camp, they woulda most likely killed him. I figure they just wanted to pick up their dead and get the hell away from here before daylight caught 'em without no cartridges for the guns they just got."

"Hell," McCoy put in, "even a damn Injun ain't got no use for Weaver."

Bret and Coldiron had already started digging graves, but they dropped the two hand shovels the patrol had brought with them and went to the rise then to see for themselves. There were traces in the sand where Weaver probably sat, and Lazzara before him, but there was no sign of a struggle having taken place, and no blood anywhere on the ground. Bret didn't like the picture forming in his mind. Coldiron voiced it for him. "Looks a helluva lot like he turned rabbit on us and took off." He pointed toward a trail left in the sand among the willows. "Looks like he was crawlin', leavin' tracks like that."

"That son of a . . . ," Bret started, then checked himself. "We'll take a wide circle around here to look for him. First, though, I wanna take a look behind that long rise where the hostiles were holed up. Maybe that'll tell us something."

A few days ago, he wouldn't have cared if Weaver had deserted. He would have figured the army would be better off without him. But if Weaver had deserted, leaving his fellow troopers to perish because of his negligence, then Bret was determined to run him down and let him answer for his crime.

An inspection of the low rise where the Blackfoot warriors had taken cover revealed nothing beyond evidence that they had been there. Bret was really only concerned about the possibility that Weaver's body might have been there. Coldiron, however, was puzzled about something else.

"I can't figure why they came back here to hit us," he mused aloud. "How the hell did they know we were trailin' 'em?" A notion suddenly struck him and he walked to the other end of the rise to confirm it. "It was that Blackfoot band, all right, but it was a different bunch that jumped us," he told them. "This warn't the same ones we was following. Their tracks came in from the south. It was just dumb luck that they came up on us. They didn't even know we were here." He looked at Bret as if caught napping.

Bret understood the reason for the big scout's guilty expression, for he had the same feeling. "I take the blame," he said. "We should have gone on to check on that second house around the bend of the river. If we had, we would have seen that the war party had divided after hitting the first house." He had been too anxious to follow the obvious trail leading away from the house to be thorough in his investigation.

McCoy, standing behind Bret, posed the question already troubling Bret's mind. "We gonna take what's left of us on back to Fort Ellis now?"

It seemed the sensible thing to do, but Bret was reluctant to make that decision. It was not an easy thing to abandon the two women who had been captured, but he had an obligation to report the massacre of his patrol. He turned it over and over in his mind before looking at Coldiron.

"This war party," he asked, "can you track them?"

Coldiron shrugged. "Yeah, I can track 'em."

"I'm thinking they'll lead us to the other war party that took the women, since it appears that the twelve or so you said were in the original party were just half of the whole war party. Is that the way you see it?" Coldiron said that it was the way he figured it. "All right, then," Bret went on, having made his decision. "McCoy, I'm sending you back to the fort to report what's happened here. Coldiron and I will continue on the trail of

49

the hostiles." He looked quickly at the formidable scout to check his reaction. "That's if you're agreeable with it."

Coldiron was somewhat surprised by the lieutenant's proposal. He would have bet that the three of them would be on their way back to Fort Ellis. He hesitated while he studied the earnest face of the young man. He had to admit that it might have been a mistake on his part for judging Hollister as a typical toy soldier fresh from the academy. He thought of the cool head and apparently fearless way he had handled himself in the heat of the attack—not to mention the accuracy he displayed with his weapon. He decided that Bret would account well for himself in any tight situation. His response on that night had confirmed it.

The fact that he and the lieutenant would be outnumbered bothered him a little, but since the two of them were armed with repeating rifles, while the Indians were without ammunition for the Spencers they had acquired, he was sure they could protect themselves. And it was likely that the warriors they were on their way to join would not be better armed, either. The third factor in his consideration was his skill as a tracker. He didn't intend to be discovered by the war party until he and Bret were ready to make their move. After quickly considering all of that, he answered the question.

"Yep. Suits me just fine. If we ain't in time for them poor ladies, maybe we can at least make them Blackfeet pay up for it."

McCoy started to protest. "Are you sure that's a smart thing to do, Lieutenant—just the two of you against a pretty good-sized war party, and me ridin' all the way back to the fort alone?"

"No, it's probably not the smart thing to do, but it's the right thing to do. Coldiron and I will be all right, as long as we keep our senses about us, and our eyes and ears open. You shouldn't have to worry about any danger to yourself. This close to the fort, that war party is obviously headed north as fast as they can go, and you should reach Fort Ellis by noon. Can't be more than about fifteen miles from here. Am I right, Coldiron?"

"That's about right," Coldiron replied. "You've come about full circle from my place on the Gallatin."

"Come to think of it," Bret continued, "for that distance, you could take the horses back with you. Might be best to load the dead on their horses and take them back to Fort Ellis to bury."

"Sir," McCoy protested, not at all happy with the idea, "I don't think one man can handle—" That was as far as he got before Bret stopped him.

"You have your orders, soldier," Bret snapped, confident that he himself could lead the horses back, and if he could, then McCoy should be able to manage it. "I'll take Sergeant Duncan's horse with me. If we're successful in rescuing those women, we'll need another horse. That'll give you one less to mind. Now let's get those bodies loaded. We're losing time here."

"Yes, sir," McCoy replied obediently while fuming inside.

Coldiron smirked at the complaining soldier and said, "That beats havin' to dig graves for all of 'em."

McCoy didn't respond vocally, but he told himself he'd gladly dig a grave for him and the lieutenant.

Private Tom Weaver climbed to the top of a deep ravine and anxiously looked back over the way he had come. It was two hours past dawn now and he had been walking since about ten thirty the night just passed. His eyes squinted, straining against the rising sun in an effort to see any sign of anyone following him. After a few long moments of peering back toward the valley, he sat down, relieved to be able to rest before starting out again. If anyone had seen him slink out of the camp, they would surely have caught up with him by this time. Taking another look back to the east just to be certain, he removed his right boot to examine his foot. Cavalry boots were not the best for walking and he feared he was getting a blister on the knuckle behind his big toe.

"Damn," he swore softly when he found the skin

broken. He took his handkerchief from his pocket and wrapped it around the injured foot, then pulled his sock over it. "Best I can do," he said. Thinking back to where he had just come, he added, "Helluva lot better'n gettin' scalped like the rest of the boys." The thought brought a smirk to his face, certain he had escaped a massacre. "My hair wouldn't look good on some wild Injun's lance.

"I reckon ol' Lieutenant Fancy Pants would like to say it was my fault those damn savages snuck up on us," he continued to himself. "I hope that bastard is dead." He applauded himself for having the good sense to escape when he had the chance. "Same thing any of the other boys woulda done in my shoes."

He pulled his boot on as carefully as he could, grimacing when the extra cloth under his sock made the boot tight. He got to his feet again and trudged back down the side of the ravine. He had no idea how far it was from the bend in the Yellowstone to Fort Ellis, but what little he did know about the location of the fort told him that it couldn't be far. He had left the river a couple of hours back; maybe he would make the fort by that afternoon.

As he walked, he thought about the chaotic moment when he was suddenly snatched from a solid sleep to discover screaming savages sweeping over his comrades, hacking and slicing like wild animals. He had his carbine, fully loaded, but it had occurred to him at the moment that he had not been discovered, hunkered down as he was on a little mound of sand in the willows. There was no thought of firing it and exposing his hiding place.

To run without being seen was the only thing he had any intention of doing, and the sooner the better, because it seemed obvious to him that the whole patrol was going to be slaughtered. His main regret was that he could not get to his horse without the prospect of being seen. So he grabbed his carbine and his haversack and crawled down through the willows until he reached the low bluffs beside the river.

Then he ran as fast as he could, even though he could hear the sound of gunshots that sounded like cavalry carbines. He was sure they were captured weapons in the Indians' hands. When he realized no one was running after him, he crossed the river and kept going in a direction he hoped would take him toward safety.

After another hour, he came upon a well-traveled trail, and he was sure he had struck the main road to Bozeman. Satisfied with his successful escape, he thought of his fellow soldiers and the fact that he didn't get along with many of them. The last image he had of them was of Lazzara with his face split open by a Blackfoot hatchet.

"I reckon you got more to worry about now than

whether or not I'm gonna relieve you on guard duty," he crowed aloud.

Maybe the rest of them would remember that he was the one who predicted Lieutenant Hollister would end up getting them all killed. His gloating was interrupted then when he heard the sound of horses beyond the bend of the road behind him.

A sharp feeling of fear gripped his spine, for he thought it might be the Blackfoot war party coming after him. Looking around him for someplace to hide in a hurry, he dived behind a clump of serviceberry bushes and readied his rifle to protect himself.

In only a few moments' time, a rider appeared around the bend trailing a string of what appeared to be packhorses behind him. After another couple of minutes, the rider came close enough for Weaver to recognize him as Brice McCoy. Then he realized that the horses weren't carrying packs. They were loaded with the bodies of the ill-fated patrol.

"Well, I'll be damned," he muttered, and got up from the ground.

Upon seeing someone suddenly rise from behind the bushes, McCoy jerked back hard on the reins and prepared to retreat.

"McCoy!" He heard his name called out, and discovered it was Weaver who had popped up out of a bush.

"Well, I'll be go to hell," McCoy blurted when he saw who it was, and urged his horse forward.

"How the hell did you get here?" he asked when he pulled up beside Weaver.

"I, by God, walked here," Weaver replied, "and I'm damn glad to see a ride." He walked back beside the trailing horses, looking at the dead. "I don't see Hollister's body, or that big-ass scout, either. What happened to them?" He turned back to look at McCoy. "And how come you're the only one left?"

"My number just ain't up yet," McCoy answered. He dismounted and told Weaver what had happened, and how he happened to be leading the dead back by himself.

"So ol' Hollister didn't get scalped with the rest of 'em," Weaver said. "That's right disappointin' news. You know, if I coulda helped you boys, I sure woulda, but there wasn't nothin' I could do. Looked to me like you was all dead, and I couldn't fight all them Injuns by myself. I was damn lucky to get out when I did."

McCoy fixed a skeptical gaze on him and smirked. "Oh, I know you woulda come a-runnin' if you thought any of us was still alive, but fact of the matter is, you was asleep when they jumped us. Ain't that right?"

"No, hell no," Weaver was quick to retort. "They musta sneaked up from the other side of them trees, where I couldn't see 'em. I'll admit that I was a little drowsy, maybe, but I never went to sleep."

McCoy snorted derisively. "Ain't no need to lie to me, Weaver. I don't care, as long as I came outta that mess alive. Hell, I'da done the same as you, if I hadda been in your shoes."

Weaver grinned meekly. "You know how it is," he said. "Look out for your own ass first."

"That's the way I see it," McCoy agreed. "So right now we can go back and play the heroes. If we're lucky, maybe the Injuns will take care of Hollister for us. I hope to hell he does catch up with 'em, 'cause that'll be the end of that son of a bitch, and that big-ass scout, too. If they ask me where he is, I'll just tell 'em I don't know."

The idea appealed to Weaver. He hadn't thought about playing the role of hero. *Leave it to McCoy . . . ,* he thought. "Hell, they might even give us a couple of medals," he said, grinning at the thought. "Wouldn't that be somethin'?" He paused then to look over the column of horses, a body across the saddle of each one. "How come you ain't got an extra horse? That's my horse." He pointed to a red roan with Copeland's body on it.

"Hollister took an extra horse with him and Coldiron," McCoy said.

"Well, I ain't ridin' back to Fort Ellis behind no damn dead man," Weaver snorted. He walked back until he came to a horse carrying Sergeant Duncan's body. "I'll ride this'n," he said, and dumped the sergeant's body off on the road. "It was a pleasure servin' under you, Sergeant," he mocked as he dragged Duncan's corpse off into the bushes. He stepped up into the saddle then, and the two heroes set out to lead their dead comrades back to the fort.

Chapter 3

Having sent McCoy off that morning with the bodies of his fellow soldiers trailing behind him, Bret returned with Coldiron to pick up the trail of the retreating warriors. It wasn't difficult to follow, and it led straight north. "They're ridin' to catch up with the rest of that war party," Coldiron said. "Looks like they was more interested in catchin' up than they were in hidin' their trail."

"I doubt they think we'll follow them, since they know how few we are," Bret replied.

"They stayed on this side of the river," Coldiron pointed out. "But if they're goin' where I think they're headin', they're gonna be crossin' over to the other side when the river turns back to the east. So we'll just keep our eyes open to see where they crossed."

They continued to follow the trail left by the dozen or so horses as the Blackfoot warriors followed the Yellowstone, carrying their dead with them. As Coldiron had predicted, they made a crossing of the river where it took a large turn to the east on its way to join the Missouri. Coming out of the river on the north side, the tracks held to a steady course across rolling, sparsely treed plains.

"If they keep on in this direction, they're headed for the Crazy Mountains," Coldiron said. He pointed toward the rugged peaks, clearly seen, even though they were half a day's ride away. "Hard to say what they've got in mind," he went on. "Maybe they're supposed to meet up with the bunch we've been trailin' somewhere up in the mountains. Maybe they'll stay clear of the mountains and go on up to the Musselshell. I reckon we'll find out."

After a stop to eat something and let the horses rest, they were back in the saddle to resume their mission. Eventually the trail led them to a small pond, fed by a strong stream coming from the mountains. The Indians had followed the stream from that point on, and the closer they came to the foothills, the more it became obvious that they intended to follow it up into the mountains.

At Coldiron's suggestion, they stopped when within about five miles from the odd cluster of high mountains sitting like an island of rocky peaks in the middle of the plains. The reason, Coldiron pointed out, was the ease that the two of them could be spotted on the rolling prairie by a lookout high up a mountain. So they held up in a stand of trees bordering the stream and waited for darkness to cover their approach to the mountains. Unwilling to risk even a small fire, they spent the time catching up on some of the sleep they had missed the night before, each napping while the other kept watch.

While Bret and Coldiron waited for the cover of darkness to advance farther into the Crazy Mountains, an interview was being conducted some thirty-five or forty miles southwest of them, as the crow flies. It was a serious fact-finding interview, the second since the two heroic soldiers had returned, leading their dead comrades on their horses. Colonel John Grice, acting commanding officer, since several companies of cavalry and infantry had departed the fort to intercept a band of Nez Perce fleeing their reservation, opened the questioning. "Now, Private Weaver, tell us again what happened to your patrol on the Yellowstone."

"Yes, sir," Weaver said respectfully, after a glance at Private McCoy. "Well, like we told the Officer of the Day when we came in this after-noon, we picked up the trail of them Blackfoot that massacred those poor folks, and we was followin' them up the river. Come nightfall, we made camp. About nine thirty or ten that night, the Injuns jumped us. We didn't have a chance before they was all over us."

Grice interrupted. "Did not Lieutenant Hollister post any guards?"

"No, sir," Weaver lied. "Sergeant Duncan asked

him if we shouldn't post some guards, but the lieutenant, he said we didn't need none—said them Injuns was long gone. I don't think he cared much whether we caught up with 'em or not." He paused while Grice cast a glance at the other two officers seated at the table with him.

"Go on, Private," Grice said.

"Well, sir, like I said, we never had a chance. They was on top of us so quick, we didn't have time to defend ourselves. Me and Private McCoy was just lucky we could get to our weapons and fight 'em off. They didn't have many rifles, so the two of us was able to kill enough of 'em to make 'em think twice about what they was doin'."

"Just the two of you," Grice commented. "What about Lieutenant Hollister and the scout, Coldiron? Where were they during the fighting?"

"Sir," Weaver replied, with another glance at McCoy, "we was wonderin' about that ourselves. We had our hands full, tryin' to fight them Injuns off. But as near as we can figure it, the lieutenant and Coldiron musta just cut and run, 'cause they sure weren't anywhere in sight when mornin' came, and me and McCoy was the only two left standin'."

"You haven't said anything about what happened to Sergeant Duncan. His body is missing. Did he go with Lieutenant Hollister and the scout?"

Weaver had to think quickly then. "The sad fact is, them Injuns mutilated poor ol' Sergeant

Duncan so that there wasn't enough left of him to bring back over a saddle. Me and McCoy figured the respectful thing to do was to just go ahead and bury what they left of him."

"Do you have anything to add to that?" Grice asked McCoy.

"No, sir. It's pretty much like Weaver said."

"But you were able to save all the horses?" one of the other officers asked.

"Yes, sir," McCoy answered. "Me and Weaver got between the Injuns and the horses where we had 'em tied in the trees. We saved 'em all, except Coldiron's and the lieutenant's, but they were already gone. The Injuns tried to steal 'em two or three times, but we finally convinced 'em that it would cost 'em every time they did. So they finally gave up and lit out."

"But there was one more horse missing," Grice pointed out. "So the hostiles must have killed one. Is that right?"

McCoy had to pause to think, remembering then that the lieutenant had taken Sergeant Duncan's horse with him. "Yes, sir," he replied. "That's right, they got off a lucky shot and killed one of the horses—Sergeant Duncan's, I think."

"When morning came, and the Blackfeet were gone, did you think about searching for Lieutenant Hollister and the scout?" Grice asked.

"Oh, yes, sir," Weaver replied. "We took a wide circle around that whole place, but there weren't no sign of either one of 'em. They was long gone."

"So then, you recovered all the bodies of the patrol and loaded them on their horses?" Grice asked.

"Yes, sir," Weaver replied. "We figured it was our duty as soldiers to bring all the boys back here to bury. If it had been the other way around, I know any of them would have done the same for me and McCoy."

Grice looked to the other officers at the table to see if anyone had more questions. When it appeared they did not, he addressed the two privates seated before them. "Well, I guess that's all we need for now. I want to commend both of you for your bravery and your outstanding performance of duty. I think you deserve a little time for rest and recovery after what you have just been through, so I'm advising your company commander to relieve you from all duty rosters for a couple of days."

"Thank you, sir," McCoy said. "That's mighty nice of you. I might add that we ain't got no hard feelin's against Lieutenant Hollister for runnin'. Every man's different when it comes to a hot fight, when it don't look like there's any way out of it but to fight or run. I reckon nobody knows what they'll do until they get throwed into it." They both got to their feet, saluted smartly, then turned and left the room.

Grice waited until the door closed behind the two survivors of the massacre before commenting to the other officers, "That's a damn disappointing report on young Hollister, and a sad one. I had higher hopes for him."

"Yes, sir," one of the panel said. "I thought he had the makings for a good officer. But I guess you can never predict how a man will respond to danger."

Outside the post commander's office, the two conspirators exchanged grins. "That went pretty well, didn't it?" Weaver remarked. "Two bona fide heroes, that's what we are, and ol' Lieutenant Fancy Pants ain't lookin' so good right now."

"I reckon so," McCoy said. "But what are we gonna say if Hollister shows up with those women?"

"Use your common sense," Weaver told him. "There ain't a chance in hell of them walkin' into the middle of a Blackfoot village and gettin' them two women. I'm bettin' that's the last anybody will see of those two bastards, and good riddance at that. You know Blackfeet ain't got no use for white men, especially soldiers, so I'm thinkin' they're dead men."

With the coming of darkness, Bret and Coldiron climbed into the saddle again and continued following the stream until reaching the foothills. They were forced to halt for the night then, since it became too dark to see the tracks. They made their camp close to the stream, which was now flowing deeper and stronger as it made its way from the mountain above, carving a rocky path down to a canyon beyond them, which seemed as dark as sin. Ready for some coffee, Coldiron gathered some branches and built a fire in a gully that ran from the spruce trees to the stream.

"It's been a while since I've been in these mountains," he said while he fussed over his kindling of small twigs and dried grass. "There ain't a lot of game that I was ever interested in huntin' in these mountains. Course there's a lot of small game and goats up high, but deer only occasionally. At least that's been my luck. I wonder where them Injuns is goin'. Best I can recollect, there ain't no way out of this canyon but the way you ride in." He looked at Bret and grinned. "That don't sound like we're in a very good spot, does it?"

"I was thinking that," Bret replied.

Coldiron chuckled. "I was just japin' you. There's a couple of ways out about a mile and a half in. When we start out in the mornin', we'll be climbin' right off. There's a waterfall about halfway up and a little lake above it. I've seen sign of Injuns camped there by that lake before, and I wouldn't be surprised if this bunch we've been followin' ain't been plannin' to meet up with their brothers there."

"Well, I guess we'll find out in the morning," Bret said as he moved some small rocks aside and spread his blanket, seemingly unconcerned, "if they don't decide to come back out tonight."

Coldiron chuckled again. "I'll tell you the truth, Lieutenant. I ain't run into many officers who would take off into this part of the country with nobody but a guide, especially an officer green outta West Point. Most officers I've worked for have got to have a detail of at least fifteen soldiers around 'em before they'd set foot outside the fort."

"Oh, I suppose there're quite a few," Bret replied casually. "You just haven't run into them yet." Now that the fire was showing signs of life, he got up and filled his cup with water and set it at the edge of the fire to boil. Then he sat down to watch it until it was ready to dump in the coffee, wishing he had a coffeepot so he wouldn't be eating half the grounds. "Why don't you stop calling me Lieutenant? My name's Bret."

"All right, Bret," Coldiron said with a parting of his whiskers to make room for a wide grin. "I won't call you Lieutenant . . . or Sonny." And he chuckled at his remark. "My friends and my late wife always called me Nate. I reckon I include you in that group."

Coldiron decided at that moment that Bret Hollister was worthy of being his friend, even if he was an officer.

• • •

The night passed peacefully enough for the two new friends. They started out the next morning, following the tracks they had followed the day before, but on this day they proceeded much more slowly and cautiously. It soon became obvious that it was unnecessary to look for tracks, because it became impossible to go up the rugged mountainside unless they followed the narrow trail. Boxed in on both sides by the enormous cliffs that formed the canyon, they saw very few places to hide from any lookout that might be stationed high above them. Both men constantly scanned the cliffs for any sign of a Blackfoot scout as they continued on. The trail had left the floor of the canyon now and started a steep climb up toward rocky ridges that looked too rough for a horse to travel.

Another half mile brought the trail out of the confines of the canyon and onto a ridge from which they could see smaller mountains to the east of them, ringed with tall spruce and pine around the lower portions. Bret commented that one of these would be an easier place to camp than the treacherous trail they continued to follow beside the stream that was now a rushing torrent as it steepened. Coldiron explained that the campsite by the lake over the falls was considered a holy place by several Indian tribes, so the Blackfeet probably hoped to make big medicine there.

"I reckon this is about as close as we better go with these horses," Coldiron advised when they reached the top of the tree line and a ledge that ran off to the right. "We can take 'em around on that ledge there and tie 'em in the trees, and go the rest of the way on foot."

After the horses were secured, they loaded up with ammunition and returned to the trail. "We'll be in a helluva fix if one of those bucks stumbles on those horses," Bret couldn't help commenting.

"You got that right, partner," Coldiron was quick to agree, "but we sure as hell couldn't sneak up on that camp with the horses."

Bret was soon to find out what he meant. They had not climbed for more than a quarter of an hour when the sounds of the Blackfeet camp came to them from above. The sounds of talking and war chants, although muted by the crashing of the water coursing down the rocky streambed, could be heard.

"To get us a good look into that camp," Coldiron said, "we need to go off to the side here and work our way up above the camp." So they moved off the trail about fifty yards and started climbing again, being careful now where they placed their hands and feet to prevent causing a shower of rocks to go rumbling down the mountainside.

"This oughta be high enough," Coldiron decided, so they worked carefully back to a point over-looking the edge of the lake.

When he got his first good look at the lake, Bret could easily understand why the Indians attached a sense of magic to it. It looked as if a giant hand had scooped out a huge portion of the mountain to form a basin for a high alpine lake. The natural beauty of the setting made Bret forget for a moment the reason he was gazing down on the peaceful lake, which spilled over the side to form the waterfall they had passed below. He was brought quickly back when his gaze swept across to the horses grazing in a small meadow near one side of the lake, and the warriors taking their leisure on the animal hides they used for bedding. He pulled his field glass from his haversack and extended it to search the camp. Taking his time to examine each individual on the far side of the small lake, he scanned back and forth several times.

"I don't see but about half a dozen Indians," he said. "Where are the rest of them?"

"Damned if I know," Coldiron replied. "But you're right. There oughta be about a dozen more of 'em if they joined up with the other bunch."

Bret scanned the edge of the lake again, slowly, but there was no sign of the two white women. "I don't see them," he said and handed the glass to Coldiron.

Coldiron put the glass to his eye and scanned the camp back and forth several times, then handed the glass back to Bret. "I don't see 'em, either. They ain't here."

Bret searched again to be sure, but could not find the women. He focused the glass on every boulder of size enough to hide someone. He had to conclude that, if they were in the camp, he could surely see them.

"Well, it seems pretty plain to me that the other bunch of warriors have got the captives with them, and they're still somewhere ahead of us, heading to who knows where."

"It 'pears like this bunch ain't worried about anybody chasin' after 'em, 'cause they don't seem in any hurry to leave."

"I can see why," Bret said. "They could hold off a regiment trying to come up that steep little trail." It was time to decide what to do next. He had to think about their odds of success, if he decided to punish the remaining six warriors for their part in the massacre of the two white families. Positioned as they were, high above the Indian camp, he and Coldiron could probably pick off two or maybe three of the six before they could scatter for cover. At that point, it might turn into a standoff that would likely last until dark. Then it would be a contest of stealth as each side would be stalking the other, with the hostiles standing between them and their horses below the lake. In the meantime, the war party that had taken the two women would be getting farther and farther away. He reminded himself that his primary mission was an attempt to save the women, so he told Coldiron that he had decided to leave the hostiles as they were and get on the trail of the other group.

Coldiron listened to Bret's reasoning with more than a little interest. "I'm damn glad you see it that way," he said. " 'Cause we'd be damn lucky to shoot all six of 'em."

In agreement then, they began to retrace their steps, working their way carefully back down the rocky slope above the lake. "I expect they're headin' for home," Coldiron said. "Most likely a village somewhere above the Big Belt Mountains, on the Musselshell, maybe. Might even be above the Missouri, on the Judith, or anywhere up that way. That's Blackfoot territory."

"What you're saying is you can't guess where they're heading," Bret said.

"What I'm sayin' is the only way we'll find those two ladies is if I can pick up their trail and follow 'em," Coldiron told him.

"Think you can do that?" Bret asked.

"I reckon," Coldiron answered, "if I can pick up their trail offa this mountain. Remember, I told you there were a couple of ways offa here without goin' back down that canyon. I just have to find which way they took." He stopped to listen when there seemed to be a pause in the voices above them. When they started up again right away, he went on. "Thought for a minute they mighta just found out they had company." Back to the subject then, he said, "If I can pick up some sign on whichever game trail they followed down, then there oughta be tracks enough when they get to the bottom."

"Let's give that a try," Bret said, and continued on his way back to the ledge where they had left the horses.

When they got there, Coldiron went back to where the horses had been tied in the trees. After looking around a few minutes, he spotted what he was looking for. He reached down and picked up a few clumps of horse manure one of the horses had dropped, and threw them over the side of the ledge. "No need to leave 'em a sign that we were here," he said, answering Bret's unspoken question. "That woulda told 'em how long ago we were here, too."

"Right," Bret replied, knowing it was something he never would have thought to do.

They descended along the rocky trail by the busy stream until reaching a place where an old game trail crossed it and led into the trees on the other side. "Right there's one of the ways outta here that I told you about," Coldiron said, pointing it out. "There ain't much use to scout around that trail. It'll take you down offa this mountain, but you'll just be deeper in between a couple others. I'm bettin' on the other'n a little ways down. It goes off to the east and comes out in the foothills. If I'm right, those Injuns will be headin' away from these mountains and goin' around the Big Belts on the eastern side."

When they came to the trail Coldiron spoke of, it turned out that he was right on his hunch, as he so often was. There were plenty of signs that the war party had taken the trail down, leaving hoofprints and broken branches as evidence. "Looks to me like the last thing they're worried about is somebody followin' 'em," he said. "Makes my job a sight easier."

At the base of the mountain, the trail emerged from the evergreens to cross a narrow valley between the mountain and a line of hills pointing toward the north. Once out of the hills, they pulled up while Coldiron dismounted and studied the tracks, to make sure they were the right ones, and not some older tracks. When he was satisfied and climbed back into the saddle, Bret thought he should check with the big scout to make sure he was comfortable with their chances. "I reckon I should have asked you back there on the mountain how you feel about pushing on into real Blackfoot country. You might not think it's worth the risk."

Coldiron shrugged. "I ain't gonna lie to ya. Our chances of catchin' up with that bunch ain't too good. There's a heap of Blood and Blackfoot bands up in that country, so it might take a long time to find the village they're headed for. How long are you expected to be gone from the fort?"

"We were issued rations and ammunition for four days," Bret replied. "I know I have to report back to Captain Greer, but if you're in agreement, I'd like to stay on this trail for a couple more days. Maybe we'll have some luck. If not, we'll have to report back, and I'll try to convince my superiors that it's worthwhile to mount a patrol to go in search of those women."

Coldiron shrugged again, seemingly indifferent. "Hell, whatever you decide, I ain't got nothin' better to do right now."

While following the trail was their primary objective, of equal concern was to put some distance between themselves and the unsuspecting hostiles still on the mountain behind them. They had to think that their presence at the camp had not been discovered. It would have been incredible luck if one of the six warriors had had occasion to scout the ledge where the horses had been tied. So they followed the trail the rest of the afternoon until, finally, they decided to find a place to camp for the night and continue early in the morning. When they came to a sizable creek, they followed it down a wide ravine and made camp where it took a sharp bend around a huge rock.

Coldiron got his frying pan from his packs to cook some of the venison he carried. "I still got a little of that smoked deer meat," he remarked. "Maybe we'll get a chance at some fresh meat before we have to fall back on that damn salt pork the army gave you to eat."

Neither man was really hungry, so a little venison and some strong black coffee were enough to satisfy them. Bret also had the urge to clean up a little, and maybe even shave the whiskers that had sprung up over the past couple of days. "How come you don't just let it grow?" Coldiron asked. "I decided a long time ago that it was a helluva lot easier to just leave it the way God planted it."

"I can see that," Bret remarked, joking. "But I reckon I got in the habit of shaving at the academy."

"Yeah, but you don't even wear a mustache," Coldiron insisted. "Don't your face feel kinda naked?"

Bret laughed at the big man's apparent serious interest. "I've grown one from time to time, but I got tired of it pretty quick, and off it came." The ordinarily gruff army scout surprised him occasionally with questions unrelated to the job at hand.

Chapter 4

Early the next morning they were in the saddle and ready to travel, after Coldiron had ridden up on a high ridge to take a long look over the ground they had traveled the day before. Satisfied that there was no sign of anybody in sight, he felt more confident that the Indians might never have known they had white visitors the day before. *Now maybe we can make up some ground on that bunch ahead of us,* he thought. He returned to the campsite to find Bret scattering the ashes of the fire and covering them with dirt in hopes of disguising their presence there. He had the right idea, Coldiron thought, so he didn't bother to tell him that a good tracker could see the ruse right away. And most likely every warrior in that bunch behind them was a good tracker.

Much of the final mile or so of their travel the night before had been guided by Coldiron's sense of dead reckoning when it had become too dark to see the tracks they hoped to follow. From the base of the Crazy Mountains, it appeared to him that the trail left by the hostiles was heading toward Coffin Butte, so he had continued on that way for a while after he could no longer pick out hoof-prints. Now before going farther, he wanted to find their tracks, so Bret scouted downstream while he rode upstream to see if they could find where the Blackfeet had crossed the creek. His intuition the night before was proven accurate when Bret sang out that he had found it. With a definite trail to follow, they set out to catch up with the Indians.

The tracking was not overly difficult since the Blackfeet apparently felt no concern that anyone was following them. Consequently they took the easiest route toward the Little Belt Mountains, and by noon, when the two pursuers skirted Coffin Butte and struck the Musselshell River they came upon the Indian campsite of the previous night. "They sure as hell ain't in much of a hurry," Coldiron commented as he looked around the riverbank. "We weren't more'n about twenty miles apart when we stopped last night."

"Maybe we'll catch up with them tonight, if we don't waste much time," Bret said.

"I expect we'd best rest these horses here for a spell, so we might as well have a little something to eat."

They built a small fire and prepared to partake of the usual fare of smoked venison and strong coffee, supplemented on this occasion by some hardtack that Bret had brought along. "I never thought I'd miss beans so much," Bret commented as he bit off a chunk of the stale hardtack, after he had wiped some of the mold from one side of it.

His comment caused a chuckle from Coldiron. The oversized scout found his young friend an interesting study. "Whaddaya think your superiors back at Fort Ellis are thinkin' 'bout you not showin' up with that other soldier?"

"Well, they know what we're trying to do. McCoy should tell them why we went on after the hostiles. I think it's what they would have wanted me to do. It's the right thing to do, anyway. When they sent us out to Benson's Landing, they didn't have any idea there were women captives. More than likely, they would have suggested that a patrol of fifteen or twenty troopers would have made more sense, but, hell, that young man didn't know the two women were captured."

"I reckon you'll find out when we get back," Coldiron said. "If we bring the women back safe and sound, I don't think they'll care one way or the other how long it took." He paused for a few moments while he studied the lieutenant. "I reckon you always wanted to be a soldier, I mean, you goin' to West Point and all?"

"I guess," Bret replied, although a little hesitant. "My father was a career soldier, and I reckon it was always a foregone conclusion that I'd be one, too."

"A what?" Coldiron responded, unfamiliar with the term.

"It was a safe bet that I'd go in the army," Bret rephrased for the benefit of the simple man.

"Your daddy," Coldiron asked, "is he a general or something?"

"A colonel," Bret replied.

"I thought your daddy had to be a general before you could get into West Point."

Bret laughed. "No, there's a lot of men at the academy whose fathers weren't even in the army. My father was a colonel. He might have made general, given a little more time, but he was killed at Vicksburg."

"That'll slow a man down, all right," Coldiron replied earnestly. Then thinking that he might have sounded a bit too crass, he commented, "Well, now, that's a shame. Maybe you'll make it to general and make your mama proud."

"Maybe so," Bret allowed, although he wasn't sold on the idea. "But it's already too late to make my mother proud. She died not long after my father was killed."

"I swear," Coldiron said. "That's bad luck. You got any brothers or sisters?"

"Nope," Bret replied. "I may have some relatives somewhere, but I don't know where that might be, or who they are."

"You're kinda like me, then," Coldiron said. "Ain't got no kin, nobody to answer to—except the army. I ain't sure about my folks, neither. I weren't much more'n five years old when my daddy sold me to a trapper, name of Henry Luce." Coldiron laughed at the recollection. "He was a hard son of a bitch to work for, but he taught me all there was to know about trappin'. I stayed with him for almost five years before we split up. I mighta stayed with him longer, but he got to thinkin' I'd make a good substitute for a whore. He only tried it one time, but that was one too many as far as I was concerned. I left him with a gash in his side about half a foot long courtesy of my skinnin' knife." He chuckled at the thought of it.

"That's pretty harsh," Bret said. "Did you go back to your home then?"

"Nah, hell no. There wasn't nothin' back there for me, and I could take care of myself by then, so I struck out on my own. So far, I ain't regretted it."

When it was time to mount up again, each man felt that he knew the other a little better, and Bret appreciated the fact that since the age of around ten, Coldiron had been a self-sufficient individual, living in the wild, a true son of the mountains and forests. The gruff, sarcastic facade seemed to have disappeared, replaced by an almost jolly countenance. In Bret, Coldiron saw a young man of strength and courage, too much to waste away his years in the army. It was a shame, he thought, but that was up to Bret to decide.

Crossing the river where the Blackfeet war party had crossed, they were surprised to find that, instead of continuing north, the trail split, with half of the party turning to follow the Musselshell to the west, while the other half rode in the opposite direction. "I reckon I guessed wrong this time," Coldiron confessed. "I thought sure as hell they were headin' up toward the Judith." He paused to watch Bret's reaction for a few moments. When it was obvious that the young lieutenant was weighing the dilemma in his mind, he asked, "Whaddaya wanna do?"

Bret didn't answer at once, for he was still wrestling mentally with his orders and his natural compassion for the unfortunate women captives. In the end, he reminded himself that he was an officer with explicit orders to follow, which he had already disobeyed by extending the search for two more days.

"We're no closer to the hostiles than we were two days ago. And now, since they've split into two parties, we don't know which party took the women with them. I have no choice but to report back to my post headquarters." He shook his head, frustrated. "But I swear I'll do everything I can to get them to authorize a search party."

"Whatever you say," Coldiron said. He could see that the decision was not one Bret found easy to make. But he also knew that there was no way of determining which trail they should follow. He hated to admit it, but he knew the odds weren't good that either one of the women would still be alive by the time he and Bret caught up with them, if they ever did.

Reluctantly they abandoned the search, with Coldiron leading them to the west in an effort to avoid a chance meeting with the party of Blackfeet behind them. His intention was to skirt the Crazy Mountains on their western side and travel south in the valley between them and the Big Belt Mountains. The gruff scout had lived in the wild long enough to accept the sometimes harsh consequences the untamed frontier dealt to Indian and white man alike. But the young lieutenant rode with a sickening feeling of helplessness in the pit of his stomach to think that he had failed the two women.

They approached the outer buildings of Fort Ellis early in the afternoon after a hard ride of two and a half days. "I'm gonna leave you here," Coldiron said, "and get on back to my cabin—see if anybody's been botherin' it."

"Aren't you gonna stop to get your pay before you go home?" Bret asked.

"Nah. You know as well as I do that they won't pay me till the end of the month when they pay ever'body else. I'll be back over here sometime to pick it up."

"All right," Bret replied. "I'll see that you're paid, and I just wanna tell you that you're a damn good scout. I appreciate your work."

"Why, thank you, Bret. Maybe we'll ride together again sometime—maybe if you persuade Grice to send out that patrol."

"I hope so," Bret said. "Take care of yourself."

"I always do," Coldiron responded, and turned his horse away.

Bret watched the big bear of a man as he rode toward the other side of the collection of buildings that made up Fort Ellis. He *was* a good scout and he sincerely hoped he would be with him when he returned to the Musselshell to search for some sign of the two women. With a renewed feeling of urgency then, he turned his horses toward the post headquarters.

Lieutenant Roger Oakes was the Officer of the Day on duty. He looked up with an expression of shocked surprise when Bret walked in the door. Sergeant Harold Baker, seated at a small desk by the door, seemed equally stunned upon seeing Bret. "Hello, Roger," Bret greeted Oakes. Like himself, Roger had not been posted at Fort Ellis for very long.

"Bret," Oakes returned briefly, still wearing an expression as if he had seen a ghost.

Surprised somewhat by his fellow officer's strange greeting, Bret told him that he was just returning from the field and wanted to report to Colonel Grice. Oakes seemed to be speechless for a few moments before finding his voice.

"Well, yes, I'm sure Colonel Grice wants to hear your report. Why don't you sit right down here, and I'll send Sergeant Baker to get the colonel?" He looked over at the gaping sergeant and said, "The colonel's at his residence eating dinner. Go get him and tell him that Lieutenant Hollister's back." Baker responded at once and was out the door, leaving the two officers to sit gazing at each other.

After a few moments, Bret sought to break the awkward silence, still baffled by Roger's bizarre behavior. He would have expected a less stiff reception after being out on patrol for a week.

"I brought Sergeant Duncan's horse back with me. We can have one of the men take it to the stables." Oakes merely nodded in response. "Anything of interest going on around the post?" Bret went on. "I've been away for a few days."

"Oh, not much," Oakes said. It was obvious to Bret that the lieutenant was not prone to make even casual conversation. So he gave up and waited in silence for the colonel to arrive.

It was not a long wait. In less than twenty minutes, Colonel Grice stormed into the office with two armed privates right behind him. Bret and Oakes jumped to their feet to stand at attention. Grice, a short man with drooping shoulders and a potbelly, glared up into Bret's face. "Well, by God, you've got your nerve showing up here at this post," he fumed. "I was hoping to hell you were dead."

"Sir?" Bret responded, stunned by the unexpected outburst.

"I have no patience for cowardice in any man, and especially in an officer," Grice ranted on.

"Cowardice?" Bret questioned, baffled by the colonel's attack. "What are you talking about, sir?"

"Cowardice!" Grice repeated in emphasis. "The cowardice of running to save your hide when your patrol was attacked by hostiles." He literally roared the accusation. "That, mister, is unforgivable of an officer under my command."

"Whoa!" Bret responded. "Wait a minute. Where did you get an idea like that? Didn't Private McCoy return with the horses and the bodies of my patrol?"

"Yes, he did. He and Private Weaver brought the bodies of their comrades back to be buried, after you ran away from the massacre of everyone but the two of them."

"I sent McCoy back to report on the attack," Bret insisted, hardly able to comprehend what could have given the colonel the idea that he had deserted in the face of combat. "Did you say Weaver? Weaver was missing."

"He wasn't missing when he and McCoy loaded the bodies on their horses and brought them back here," Grice charged. "And neither man had any idea what had happened to you."

"No, sir," Bret replied. "That's not the right of it. I sent McCoy back to tell you. The scout, Coldiron, and I went on to try to catch up with the hostiles in hopes of rescuing two women who were kidnapped."

"Is that your story?" Grice demanded. "You went after two captives?"

"It's not my story. It's what happened."

"Then where are the women? I suppose you were never able to catch the renegade Indians who stole them. For that matter, if Coldiron went with you, where the hell is he? Why isn't he here to corroborate your story?"

"He went home to his place on the Gallatin," Bret said, aware then that he had been so thoroughly demonized and realizing the guilty parties were McCoy and Weaver. "Sir, surely you're not going to take the word of two malcontent privates like McCoy and Weaver over that of an officer."

"An ex-officer," Grice responded, cooler now. "You were tried in absentia for your treason and found guilty of desertion under fire."

"I was what?" Bret gasped in protest. "On the word of a cowardly soldier who fell asleep on guard duty? I came back, didn't I?"

"Yes, you did," Grice replied unemotionally, "and that's the other mistake you made."

"So you've tried and sentenced me without ever hearing my side of the story? I don't even get my day in court to defend myself?"

Grice hesitated, then said, "I'm not an unreasonable man. I'll give you your trial. Ordinarily, since you were an officer, I'd leave you free on your own cognizance until your trial. But you've got a history of running, so you'll await your trial in the guardhouse." He nodded to Lieutenant Oakes. "March him to the guardhouse."

"This is all a mistake!" Bret protested as he was taken into custody by the two soldiers who had come with Grice.

"You'll get your day in court," Grice said, done with him for the time being.

Grice let him sit in the guardhouse for two days before informing him that his trial would be held this morning. It had been two days of anguish and disbelief that the army he had sworn to honor and serve could so drastically turn its back on him. Racking his brain, he could not recall when he had been so harsh on McCoy or Weaver to warrant such a hateful vengeance. Their only motive had to be to cover up their own cowardice. There was no doubt in Bret's mind that Weaver had fallen asleep at his post. Then when he could have joined in the fight to repel the warriors, he chose to run instead. Had he been awake and alert, he could have saved the lives of his fellow soldiers. That was certainly motive enough for lying.

His thoughts were interrupted then when he heard the guards coming to open the cell door. "Time to go, Lieutenant," one of them announced. They stood outside the cell and waited while he walked out to be marched over to the post headquarters.

"Good luck, Lieutenant," one of the other prisoners called after him, sarcastically, causing a titter of chuckles from the other three prisoners. Bret ignored them, much as he had ignored them during the two days he shared the common lockup with the enlisted men, all privates. He had not been allowed the courtesy normally shown an officer, even under arrest, and he had to assume that was because he had already been stripped of his rank in the absentia trial. He only hoped that in this reenactment common sense and the word of an officer would prevail, and this nightmare would be over.

He would never forget the walk across the parade ground when every soldier on work details he passed stopped to gawk at him as if he were a traitor. When he was escorted into the post commander's office, he was confronted with a panel of three officers, headed by Colonel Grice. Lieutenant Oakes was on one side of him, while Bret's company commander, Captain Greer, was on the other. They sat at a table that had been placed beside the colonel's desk, and he was directed to a chair facing them. On the other side of the desk were two empty chairs. Before sitting down, he snapped to attention and saluted. None of the three returned his salute.

"All right," Grice began. "Let's get this thing under way. Just so there is no misunderstanding, this hearing has been called merely as a courtesy to the defendant. A proper verdict on Lieutenant Hollister's conduct on the night of July nineteenth has already been decided. But since we now have the opportunity to hear the defendant's testimony, we will grant him that privilege." Looking at the guards then, he said, "Bring in the witnesses."

Bret almost came out of his chair when Privates Brice McCoy and Thomas Weaver entered the room and sat down in the two chairs. The sight of the two malcontents made his blood boil, especially when Weaver favored him with a sneer.

Addressing Bret again, Colonel Grice laid down the rules. "Be advised that, since this is an inquiry, your testimony will be confined to the answering of questions from any of the three of us. Is that understood?"

"Well, sir," Bret replied, not sure he was going to be allowed to give his complete side of the story. "I had hoped I'd get a chance to tell exactly what happened on the night we were attacked."

"You'll get that chance as long as you answer the questions," Grice said. "We'll start with the eyewitness report—Private Weaver."

"I object," Bret immediately exclaimed. "Private Weaver wasn't even among the survivors when the fighting was over." He was immediately reprimanded by the colonel.

Weaver made a convincing attempt to appear sincere as he related a fallacious account of the events on the night in question, during which he and McCoy performed heroically in their effort to repel the hostile attack. "And where was Lieutenant Hollister while this was going on?" Captain Greer asked.

"I don't know, sir. He wasn't nowhere around. Him and that scout, Coldiron, kinda got off by theirselves when it was time to go to sleep." He glanced at McCoy for confirmation. "We all wondered why they didn't bed down with the rest of us. Anyway, come daylight, they was both gone."

"That's a damn lie, and you know it!" Bret exclaimed.

"This is the last time I'm going to warn you," Grice said, and pointed a stern finger at Bret.

There was little doubt in Bret's mind that the verdict was already decided and the inquiry was merely a formality to soothe Grice's conscience as the hearing continued. He was questioned by all of the three judges, but the questions were specific, and he was not allowed to expound on his answers. In the end, it came down to taking the two witnesses' word over that of the officer. It was a farce, and he found it hard to believe that it was allowed to happen. It would not have made any difference, he decided, had Coldiron been there as a witness for the defendant. The panel came to the inquiry with the verdict already established. And when it came time for the verdict, Grice asked the prisoner to stand up while he read it.

"Bret Cameron Hollister, it is the verdict of this hearing that you shall be reduced to the rank of private. If you do not wish to serve in that capacity, you may resign your commission and be discharged dishonorably from the United States Army. Do you have anything to say to this panel?"

Surely I will wake up from this nightmare, he thought, but he knew it was real, as real as the stoic look on Grice's face—as real as the smirks on the faces of McCoy and Weaver. Fuming inside, he finally replied to the question. "Yes, I've got something to say. I made a big mistake by coming back here to report. In doing so, I'm afraid I might have jeopardized the lives of two innocent white women. I wish that I had continued the search for them. As for the choice you distinguished officers have offered, I'll not serve at the rank of private. In fact, I prefer not to serve at all in an organization with officers of such limited intelligence as yourselves. I willingly surrender my sword, if you haven't taken it already from my quarters."

Grice and Captain Greer recoiled haughtily from his comments, while Lieutenant Oakes shook his head sadly, thinking about the years the prisoner had spent preparing for a career in the military. Grice got up from the table and walked around to stand before Bret. With a knife he had brought with him in anticipation of the act, he reached up and meticulously cut the insignia of rank from Bret's shoulders.

"This hearing is concluded," he announced officially. Then to Bret, he remarked, "We're letting you off easy. I could have sent you to prison for a few years. Your quarters have already been stripped of everything of army issue. You may keep the uniform you're wearing and any personal items, but that is all. I suggest you remove anything you have left from the BOQ before mess call."

He felt completely drained, and the desire to cry out at the magnitude of the injustice he had been dealt was almost overwhelming, but he knew it would do him no good at all. He chose not to give them the satisfaction of witnessing his anguish, so he contained his anger and struggled to maintain his calm. Without another word, he turned and walked out of the room, at the very least a free man—at the most, a man with no possessions beyond the disgraced uniform he wore and the few personal items left in his quarters. He was not without means, however, for he had a tidy sum in savings in the First Bank of Bozeman—inheritance from his late father's estate. He had thought to use it for something worthwhile at some point, possibly a land investment of some description, but nothing so far had caught his interest. He was struck with the irony that a portion of it would be used now to completely outfit himself.

After leaving the post headquarters, he walked directly to the Bachelor Officers' Quarters. The door to his room was open and his scant belongings were in a bag on his bed, which had been stripped and the mattress rolled up. *They couldn't get rid of me soon enough,* he thought as he unrolled the mattress and dumped the contents of the bag on it. His personal items were all there, plus two pairs of socks, two changes of underwear, his bankbook, writing papers, and a pen. That was his estate, in addition to a roll of money hidden in one of the pairs of socks. *Enough to get a room and some supper in the hotel at Bozeman,* he thought. He went to the tiny closet in the corner of the room and discovered that all of his uniforms had been removed.

"I'm lucky they didn't turn me out on the road in my underwear," he muttered. He was as eager to leave the post as Grice was to get rid of him, so he put his personal items back in the sack and headed for the door. It was about a three-and-a-half-mile walk to Bozeman, so he figured he'd better get started.

Fort Ellis was not a traditional frontier post in that it was not surrounded by a stockade. Instead it consisted of a collection of buildings to house the cavalry and infantry companies assigned there to protect the settlers moving into the Gallatin Valley. As he walked across the parade ground toward the outermost buildings, he thought about his short stay at this Montana post. He had not developed any close friendships with his fellow officers, but he had always been on a congenial basis with most of them. He could not understand why any of them would believe the charges brought against him.

Striking the road to Bozeman, he picked up his pace, telling himself to put it all behind him, and knowing that it would not be an easy thing to do. For he could not at this moment see any future for himself. Since he was a boy, he had been groomed for a career in the military, destined to follow his father's illustrious career. What would his late father think of him now? He immediately told himself that his father knew the truth of the matter. These troublesome thoughts were suddenly forgotten when he rounded a bend in the road to discover a couple of soldiers sitting in the shade of a large tree beside the wagon track. As he approached them, they got to their feet and he was startled to recognize McCoy and Weaver. He continued toward them, not really surprised to see them, knowing them for the kind of men they were.

"Well, now, lookee here, Brice," Weaver drawled sarcastically, "if it ain't our old friend, Private Fancy Pants."

"Well, damned if it ain't," McCoy remarked. "How you doin', Fancy Pants? Whaddaya doin' walkin' out here all by yourself? Ain't you got no horse?" His remarks brought a round of chuckles from them both.

"By God, the shoe's on the other foot now, ain't it, Fancy Pants?" Weaver prodded. "What was it he called us—mal-somethin's? Whatever it was, it didn't sound good. I expect he'd wanna beg our pardon right now."

"Malcontents," Bret stated calmly. "Malcontents was what I said you were, and I think now it's too good a word for scum like you two." He stopped to face them when they strolled casually off the side of the road to stand in his way. "Especially you, Weaver, you no-good piece of shit. The lives of those men are on your conscience. They died because you went to sleep, and then you ran like the coward you are."

"Why, you snotty son of a bitch," Weaver blurted, his tall wiry body tensing as he took a step closer. "You're fixin' to get your ass whupped good. Me and McCoy are gonna give you somethin' to remember us by."

With no weapon, and facing two-to-one odds, Bret had no choice other than to defend himself as best he could. The only thing he saw in his favor was the absence of firearms on either man. Their intent, evidently, was to administer a physical beating and leave him lying in the dust of the road. He did not plan to go easily. In fact, he welcomed the opportunity to strike out at the two smug privates who had made a mess of his life.

McCoy started to crowd in for the fun as Weaver took another step closer. Bret took a step back, waiting for the first one to strike. Thinking he was retreating, Weaver lunged for him, swinging wildly with his right hand, the intended haymaker landing harmlessly against Bret's sack of personal items. Having blocked Weaver's punch, Bret had time to tattoo McCoy's face with a rapid series of rights and lefts that left the surprised soldier stunned. He wobbled backward until tripping over Bret's foot and going down hard on his back. Although much quicker than his two assailants had anticipated, he could not avoid Weaver after McCoy went down. The wiry private leaped piggyback on him and clamped a forearm around his neck in an attempt to crush his windpipe. Staggering off the road with Weaver stuck to his back, Bret backed up to the big cottonwood that had provided shade for his antagonists. He then repeatedly banged Weaver against the trunk until he was forced to let go when one blow knocked the wind out of him. Bret turned in a flash and landed a punch on the point of Weaver's chin that snapped his head around and dropped him. Bret then returned his attention to McCoy, who was rousing himself up from the ground, less enthusiastic about the confrontation at this point. With blood running out of his nose and one eye already beginning to swell, he took a defensive stance, his hands held high like a boxer's. Bret moved straight toward him, but instead of striking out with his fists, he suddenly landed his boot squarely between McCoy's legs. With a loud grunt, McCoy dropped to his knees with no chance of getting up again anytime soon.

With one less to worry about, Bret could now give Weaver his full attention. Just beginning to regain his breath, Weaver got up as far as his knees before Bret, anxious to expel all his hateful vengeance upon the men who had ruined his career, wound up and delivered everything he could against the side of Weaver's face. Weaver dropped like a sack of flour. Bret, his thirst for revenge not yet slaked, turned again to McCoy, who raised his head to gaze pitifully at his executioner. Walking deliberately up to him, Bret slammed him with one more right hand, this one sufficient to end the assault, leaving McCoy flat on the ground.

Satisfied that there was no further threat from either, Bret had to stifle the urge to make their misery permanent by killing both of them with his bare hands. He gave it another moment's thought before deciding he didn't need to have the military after him for murder.

"Gentlemen, it was a pleasure," he said, turned to pick up his sack, then continued on his way to Bozeman. It had been the two enlisted men's misfortune to pick a fight with a man who had been one of the best heavyweight boxers to graduate from West Point.

Chapter 5

After paying for a hot bath and supper in the hotel dining room, Bret went up to his room and got a good night's sleep. He planned to have a busy day in town the next morning preparing for the rest of his life. Sleep didn't come easily, however, for he found it impossible to put the events of the last three days to rest in his mind. Colonel Grice's hostile attitude was something he could not understand. Grice had graduated from the academy in the same class with Bret's father. They had served in the same regiment in Major General John McClernand's XIII Corps. Grice had even courted Bret's mother before his father swept her off her feet at the graduation ball held at the academy. That thought caused him to pause and reflect for a few moments, but he immediately discarded the notion as ridiculous. A man of Grice's stature would hardly let something like a college fling influence his decision on something as important as an officer's destruction.

As soon as the bank opened the next morning, he withdrew a good bit of the money he had deposited there. Leaving a still sizable balance of his inheritance, he decided to keep it right where it was until he figured out what he was going to do with the rest of his life. Next he went to the stable on the other end of town to look over any horses there for sale. He found the owner, Ned Oliver, cleaning out a stall in the back of the stable. "Mornin'," Ned greeted him. Bret returned the greeting and told him he was interested in buying a couple of horses if he had any for sale. "I sure do," Ned replied and propped his pitchfork against the wall of the stall. "I've got some good ones. Let's walk out to the corral and we'll look 'em over." Bret followed him outside. Standing outside the corral, Ned pointed out the horses for sale, then let Bret pick out any he was interested in. "Don't the army furnish you with a horse?" Ned asked, curious about his customer, who was dressed in an officer's uniform, but without any insignia of rank.

"I'm not in the army anymore," Bret answered briefly. "I'll take a look at that paint in the corner."

"That's a right smart choice," Ned said. "Strong horse, that one, Injun pony, won't have to shoe him, broad through the chest for an Injun pony, too."

"Is he saddle broke?" Bret asked.

"Yes, sir, saddle broke and gelded," Ned assured him. "That horse ain't but about three years old."

"Let's put a saddle on him, and I'll try him out," Bret said.

Ned took the paint out and threw a well-used single-rigged saddle on him, studying the soldier intently as he did. It occurred to him that he might be a potential horse thief, arriving as he had with no visible possessions other than a cotton bag— and wearing a uniform stripped of all insignia. There was a distinct possibility that when he took the horse for a trial ride, he might just keep going. "How you figurin' on payin' for this horse?" Ned asked while still holding the reins.

"How much are you asking?" Bret replied as he examined the paint's mouth.

"Oh, I'd have to get fifty dollars for a horse as stout as this one."

"I'll be paying cash money," Bret told him as he continued to look the horse over. "He's closer to six than he is three years old, and I'll have to ride him before I make up my mind." He climbed into the saddle, not waiting for Ned's reply, and gave the paint a little kick with his heels. The horse reacted immediately and they were off at a jump. Ned stood, helplessly watching his property gallop out the end of the street to vanish around a curve in the road.

Bret liked the horse immediately. It was quick with good wind, and responded to commands given with a light touch. He rode the horse for a couple of miles, before stopping to give it a closer inspection. His mind made up then, he climbed aboard and returned to town, approaching the stable and an anxious stable owner at a comfortable lope. "Whaddaya think?" Ned asked when Bret looped the reins over a rail of the corral.

"I need a packhorse, too," Bret replied, "that one." He pointed to a sorrel standing in the middle of the corral watching them.

"You got a good eye, mister," Ned said. "You picked out my two best horses right off, and since you're buyin' two, I'll let you have both of 'em for a hundred dollars."

Bret wasn't sure if that was a good price or not. He hadn't been in the market for one for some time, but they seemed worth it to him. "All right," he said. "I'll give you one hundred, but you'll throw in the saddle and a pack rig for the other horse." He pulled out a roll of bills and started to count it out.

"I don't know about that," Ned said, scratching his chin whiskers thoughtfully. "That's a mighty fine saddle. . . ." He stopped when Bret folded the money back and replaced it in his pocket, then was quick to accept. "All right, I'll do it. Mister, you drive a hard bargain."

Bret's next stop was the small building next to the saloon that proclaimed itself to be a gun shop and hardware store. Since he could afford it, he was immediately attracted to the Winchester '73 displayed prominently in the shopkeeper's window, and he told himself that he was going to need a good rifle. He was soon on his way with the rifle in his possession, along with an ammunition belt and a good supply of .44 cartridges. He was certain he would need them for what he had planned to do, a decision made during the sleepless portion of the night just passed. With that thought in mind, he went from the gun shop to the general store to outfit himself with supplies and cooking utensils for a long trip. When all his purchases were completed, he left the little town of Bozeman and turned the paint in the direction of the Gallatin River. Since most of his day had been spent preparing himself for his existence after his brief career with the military, he traveled for only about fifteen miles before making camp for the night.

Starting out early the next morning, he rode up the eastern side of the Gallatin River until reaching the stream that rushed out of the mountains and emptied into the river between the two huge boulders—the stream Sergeant Duncan had called Coldiron Creek. He followed it up the mountain, half expecting the big scout to suddenly appear to challenge him. But there was no sign of the bearlike man. And when he made his way up the narrow passage to the cabin, there was still no sign of Coldiron. At first, he thought he might have made a useless trip in hopes of finding the scout, but he immediately changed his mind. Coldiron's sign was not propped against the door of the cabin, and when he looked around back, he saw one of his horses in the small corral adjoining the cabin. So he figured Coldiron was somewhere close about, and would be returning soon enough.

With that in mind, he unsaddled his horse and unloaded the packhorse. That done, he decided to make himself at home while he waited.

After building a fire in the ashes of many earlier fires, he took his brand-new coffeepot to the stream and filled it with the cold mountain water, then put it near the flames. When it got hot, he dumped his coffee in and watched it until it started to boil. When he deemed it ready to move back a little from the flames, he poured himself a cup of the steaming black liquid and sat down to enjoy it. He had begun to get a little drowsy in the warm glow of the campfire when he was suddenly jolted awake by a booming voice.

"Mister, you've got a helluva lot of gall, parkin' yourself in my cabin," Coldiron charged. "I don't recollect sendin' out no invitations."

"I figured it didn't matter since the sign wasn't up," Bret replied.

"Bret?" Coldiron questioned, recognizing the voice. "Is that you?"

"Reckon so," Bret replied. "I see you're as hospitable as ever."

"Well, I'll be . . . ," the big man stammered. "What the hell are you doin' here? They kick you outta the army?"

"As a matter of fact," Bret replied.

Thinking he had been japing his young friend, Coldiron realized then that Bret was serious in his reply. He then noticed the missing symbols of rank on his shoulders, and immediately felt embarrassed. "I swear, I didn't mean . . . ," he started. "I mean, what the hell did you do?"

"Pour yourself a cup of coffee, and I'll tell you the story," Bret said. He then proceeded to relate his reception at Fort Ellis, his time in the guardhouse, and his subsequent trial by three of his fellow officers. Coldiron was left shaking his head in amazement when Bret had finished.

"Well, hell," he said. "We can fix that up right quick. I'll just ride on back to Fort Ellis with you and tell them officers the straight of it."

A tired smile spread on Bret's face. "I appreciate it, but I'm afraid that won't work. They painted you with the same brush. Those two privates testified that you and I both ran off when we were attacked, and left them to fight the Indians alone."

"Ha!" Coldiron blurted. "That'll be the day." He quickly returned the focus to Bret. "It don't matter a helluva lot to me what they think I did. You're the one just gettin' started on your military career. They've ruined your life. Mine's pretty near over."

"It's over and done with," Bret insisted. "Maybe it's somebody's way of telling me the army's not the life for me."

"Well, those low-down, dirty skunks," Coldiron said, thinking again of McCoy and Weaver. "They ain't worth the powder it'd take to blow 'em to hell. Whaddaya aim to do about it?"

"There's not much I can do about it," Bret said. "They know how I feel about it, though." He held his hands out to show Coldiron his bruised and scraped knuckles. "I reckon that was about it."

"Well, I'll be damned," Coldiron swore. "If that don't beat all. They kicked you outta the army on the word of those two." He still had difficulty believing it. Then remembering, he asked, "Where'd you get the horses?"

"With some money I had saved up. I had to buy everything I needed. The army took everything."

Coldiron shook his head again. "When I came down the mountain, I thought I was gonna have to throw somebody outta my house. I saw that paint and the sorrel in my corral, and I knew they didn't belong to anybody I knew. So what are you aimin' to do now?"

"That's the reason I came looking for you," Bret said. "I don't have any idea what I'm going to do with the rest of my life. And since I don't, I'm heading back up on the Musselshell to see if I can find those women we started out after. I feel kinda responsible for quitting on them when we weren't that far behind." He looked at Coldiron and shrugged. "That's what I'm gonna do. I just came looking for you to see if you wanted to go back with me. Whatever the army paid you, I'd be willing to pay—at least till the money gives out." He paused to wait for an answer, but the big scout just seemed to be gnawing on his lower lip as he gave it some thought. "Of course, I wouldn't be the least bit surprised if you weren't interested," Bret went on. "I expect you've got your own life to live."

Coldiron still did not reply, his broad, bushy face knotted in deep concentration as he processed the proposition. Finally he spoke. "You're wantin' me to go ridin' off up in Blackfoot country again—just after we got back with our scalps still on? Without no detachment of cavalry soldiers— just the two of us? Without a chance in hell of ever findin' those ladies?" He shook his head as if flabbergasted by such a proposal, then replied, "Why, hell yeah, I'll go!"

It didn't take long for Coldiron to get ready to leave again. He was always in a state of leaving on a moment's notice. Bret suspected that the abandonment of Myra Buckley and Lucy Gentry had weighed a bit heavy on the big man's conscience, even though he gave the impression that he didn't have one. Evidence of that was apparent when he declined payment for his services.

"If you'll pay for the supplies and cartridges we'll need, that'll be payment enough. Hell, I wasn't gonna do nothin', anyway, but do a little huntin' before winter set in good."

"All right, then," Bret said. He'd had a feeling that he could count on Coldiron all along. "We'll start back north in the morning."

With that settled, they turned their attention to the coffeepot again. "Looks like you got yourself all fixed up to go huntin' Blackfeet," Coldiron remarked. "Lemme see that fancy new rifle you got there."

Bret pulled the Winchester from the saddle scabbard and handed the weapon to him. Coldiron looked it over closely.

"That's the model 'seventy-three, ain't it?"

Bret nodded. Coldiron brought it to his shoulder and aimed it several times, brought it down, then repeated the motion again.

"It's got good balance to it. I like that furniture under the barrel," he said, referring to the wood forearm. "The barrel on my Henry gets pretty hot to hold if you do a lotta shootin'." He handed the rifle back to Bret. "Can you hit anything with it?"

"To be honest with you, I don't know," Bret confessed. "I've only fired it a few times, and that was just to get an idea how it shoots. And a tree doesn't move around much while you're trying to hit it."

"You'll be all right with it once you get used to it," Coldiron predicted. "I've seen you in a tight spot with that army-issue Spencer you had."

He had seen enough evidence of Bret's natural instincts to recognize the young man's efficiency with a weapon when it counted. There was none of the tendency to lose precious moments to take deliberate aim before pulling the trigger. For most accomplished marksmen, the weapon became an extension of the shooter's mind, sending the bullet where his eyes were looking without thinking about whether or not the rifle was aimed properly. It would be the same with the Winchester as it had been with the Spencer.

"That looks like an Injun pony you got there, too. Which one are you ridin', the paint or the sorrel?"

"The paint," Bret replied. "He *was* an Indian pony, I reckon. He's not wearing shoes, and his feet are nice and hard, with no evidence he ever has worn shoes."

"That ain't a bad idea where we're headin'," Coldiron said. "How 'bout the sorrel?"

Bret shrugged. "Shod."

"So's my packhorse," Coldiron said with a chuckle. "That'll give anybody trackin' us somethin' to think about, I reckon."

They passed the evening quietly talking about what their odds were for a successful mission. Common sense told them that they were playing a long shot, but Bret couldn't think of anything of more importance in his life at the present time. As for Coldiron, if the truth be told, he was reaching a stage in his life when calls for his services came much less frequently, and he was happy to be needed. There were a great deal more silver threads in the long ponytail hanging down his back, but he was not yet close to the time to crawl off someplace and die. On the other hand, if he was closer to that time than he thought, this task they were about to set out on was as good a cause as any to cash in his chips. Besides, he had decided that he liked young Bret Hollister.

Starting out early the next morning, they were already on the move when the sun found its way through the spruce trees behind them on the mountain. Being an optimistic sort, Coldiron packed a couple of extra saddle blankets to be used to make beds for the women. He also packed his bow. Bret had purchased some basic supplies, but they figured to rely heavily on wild game for their food. Before they left the log hut on the mountainside, Bret had to remind his big partner that he had not propped up his sign to trespassers.

"Thanks for tellin' me," he said. "I plumb forgot about it." That was only partially true. He had let himself forget because of a gnawing feeling that he wasn't coming back to his cabin.

When they left the Gallatin River, they cut across the foothills north of the mountains and retraced their recent journey up the valley. After three full days of travel, they reached the Musselshell River once again, and scouted the banks to see if the tracks were still there. They soon recognized the spot where the Blackfeet had crossed the river, and split up on the other side. But they had no clue which direction they should go. The tracks, more than a week old now, still told no story beyond the fact that they had to choose which party to follow. They made their decision by flipping a silver coin. It landed heads up and consequently sent them to the west, following the Musselshell. Tracking was out of the question, since they soon found themselves on a well-used trail, and the tracks they sought were mixed in with those of many others, going in both directions.

"I reckon we'll just have to get lucky," Coldiron remarked.

Later in the afternoon, they came upon another trail that joined the river trail they were on. Then more trails were joined, telling the trackers that they must be getting close to a sizable village, and from the looks of the many trails, one that had been there for some time.

"I got a kinda itchy nose that's tellin' me we'd best find us a place to keep outta sight till the sun goes down."

With respect for the big man's instincts, Bret didn't argue, and they picked the first likely spot they came to, a horseshoe bend in the river with plenty of foliage on the banks and a grove of cottonwood trees in the closed end of the horseshoe. They watered the horses and led them back up out of the river to nibble on the sparse patches of grass between the serviceberry bushes and the trees. Satisfied that it'd be hard for anyone to come upon them, they settled down to wait out the daylight.

When the sun dropped below the mountains close by, they climbed into the saddle again, and proceeded to follow the common trail along the river. Darkness was not long in finding the river valley, but they continued on. According to Bret's gold pocket watch, it was eight thirty when they rounded a bend in the river and saw the rosy glow of campfires on the night sky.

"There she is," Coldiron announced.

"Looks like it might be a good-sized village," Bret remarked.

"Looks like," Coldiron agreed. "Plenty of Injuns to go around. We won't have to worry about runnin' out of 'em." Both men pulled their rifles and checked to make sure they were fully loaded before dropping them back in the saddle slings. A sudden shift in the evening breeze brought the sounds of singing and drums to them then.

"Sounds like they're havin' a dance," Coldiron said. "I thought they were up kinda late, from the sight of all them fires. That oughta help us out a little. They'll have that on their minds."

Holding the horses to a fast walk, they approached close enough to see the individual fires that had combined to form the glow in the sky. They paused then to try to pick the best spot to get a look into the camp.

"North of it, I'd say," Bret volunteered. "That

111

way, we'd have those hills behind us, in case we have to get outta there quick." Coldiron agreed, so they turned off the trail and rode around a large horse herd to reach the first of a line of foothills before the Little Belt Mountains.

Approaching from the north side of the camp, they rode as close as they thought sensible, then tied the horses in a narrow ravine about two hundred yards from the camp. Then they went the rest of the way on foot until they reached a clump of laurel bushes that were near enough to the outer tipis to get a good look into the center of the camp. What they saw confirmed their earlier guess. A huge fire in the center of the lodges was being fed more wood as a ring of warriors danced and chanted a war song. It was the first such sight that Bret had ever seen.

"Does that mean they're getting ready to go to war against somebody?" he asked.

"Maybe," Coldiron replied, keeping his bull-like voice as low as he could manage, "but not always. Might not be a war dance. They might be thankin' Man Above for somethin'."

"You see any sign of the women?" Bret asked as he took his field glass out. Coldiron said that he did not. Bret put the glass to his eye and focused it on the women and children sitting outside the ring watching the dancers. Scanning carefully over every group he could see, he started to hand the glass to Coldiron and said, "Damned if I see anything that looks like a white woman." As soon as he said it, he exclaimed, "Wait a minute!" Then he scanned back toward the outer circle of tipis. "There's one of them!" He handed the glass to Coldiron then and said, "Look at those lodges on the left, on the outer ring. There's a woman sitting beside one of them. It's hard to tell in this light, but it looks like she's wearing white women's clothes." It might be too much to hope for, finding the two women in the first village they came to.

Coldiron took the glass and brought it to focus on the woman. "You may be right, might be why she's settin' there by the tipi, instead of up there watchin' the dance. It'd help if she'd raise her head, so I could see her face."

"Somebody's walking toward her," Bret told him. "One of the men."

As if hearing Coldiron's request, the woman raised her head when she heard the warrior approaching. The light from the huge fire gave Coldiron a clear look at her face.

"She's white, all right," he confirmed. "She's just settin' there 'cause she's tied to a stake in the ground." He handed the glass back to Bret, who was anxious to see for himself.

He got just a quick look before she dropped her chin to her chest when the warrior reached her, but it was enough for Bret to agree that she was white. The warrior threw something on the ground before her, looked to be saying something to her, then returned to the dance. When he had gone, she reached down with both hands tied together and picked it up. When she attempted to brush the dirt from the object, Bret realized that it was a piece of meat. And as she eagerly bit into it, he couldn't help thinking, *Like you would feed a camp dog.*

"That's one of the women, all right," he said. "I'd have to guess that it's the older lady, Myra Buckley. Now we've got to find the other one."

"Well, damned if I can see her, so far," Coldiron said. "At least she don't seem to be staked outside a tipi like that one. She might be tied up inside one of 'em. Ain't no way to find out except askin' the one we see. Might be a good idea to wait and watch a little longer. Maybe the other'n will show up. It sure would be a whole lot easier if she was in one of the other tipis on the back row, like that one, 'cause I don't see no real trouble to sneakin' up there and snatchin' her."

He looked at Bret, who nodded his agreement. "Besides, the longer we wait, the more these bucks will get into the spirit of their dancin', and nobody's liable to pay attention to us."

"That makes sense to me," Bret said, so they continued to search out the village for some sign of the other woman.

They remained where they were for at least an hour, before deciding that wherever Lucy Gentry was being held, she was not going to be seen from where they sat. There was also the possibility that the woman they were watching was not one of the two they were looking for, but she was obviously there against her will. As they had anticipated, however, the entire village seemed to be captured by the dance, as the young warriors became more and more lost in the ritual.

"We might as well make our move," Bret decided. "The young one's not gonna show up."

They left the cover of the bushes then and made their way across a wide area of open meadow to a position only a few yards from the woman tied beside the tipi. There they paused to make sure there was no sound of alarm from anyone who might have seen them. When there was none, they decided on the best plan for abducting the unsuspecting woman. Since they couldn't count on the tipi being empty, they decided that Bret should snatch the woman while Coldiron entered the tipi in case the younger woman was inside. And if she wasn't, he was prepared to silence anyone else who was.

After finishing the piece of dried antelope, Myra Buckley wiped her hands on her skirt and dropped her head down again. Although still grieving the death of her husband at the hands of the savages who now held her captive, she was more angry than mournful at the moment. She didn't understand why she was taken and not killed with the rest of her family. What did they intend to do with her? She knew why Lucy was abducted. She was young and pretty, and the warrior who claimed her had definite plans for her. The thought of it sickened Myra.

As for herself, she felt slightly guilty for not dying with her husband and her sons, and if she ever had an opportunity to strike back in vengeance, she would not hesitate. Her thoughts were interrupted then by a slight sound behind her, which distracted her for no more than a moment. A second later, her head jerked back suddenly when a firm hand was clamped over her mouth and a strong arm surrounded her shoulders, holding her helpless.

"Steady," a low voice spoke softly. "I'm not gonna hurt you. I've come to rescue you. My name is Bret Hollister, and I've come to take you away from here. I'm gonna take my hand away now, so don't make a sound. All right?" She nodded, enthusiastically, hardly able to believe her ears.

He removed his hand from her mouth and went to work on her bonds with his knife. "Are you Myra Buckley?" She nodded again. "Where are they holding Lucy Gentry?"

"She's not here," Myra whispered.

"Not in the camp?" Bret asked.

"No, they took her away, some other group of Indians." She looked distressed to have to tell him. "Poor Lucy, she's scared out of her mind. I'm afraid they're gonna do her terrible harm."

She rubbed her wrists vigorously when her hands were free and watched nervously while he cut the rawhide cord around her neck, looking back at the campfire in fear they might be seen. Turning her attention back to him, she jumped, startled, when Coldiron came around to join them.

"It's all right," Bret assured her. "He's with me."

"Thank goodness for that," she gasped, awed by the size of the man.

"Ma'am," Coldiron acknowledged, then asked Bret, "You 'bout through there, partner? We'd best not push our luck too far. What about the other woman?"

"She's not in the village," Bret answered. "So let's get the hell outta here and get back to the horses." He took one more quick look back toward the fire to make sure no one was running to stop them, then started toward the horses at a trot. There was no need to encourage Myra to keep up. She kept pace with the two men. When they reached the ravine where they had left the horses, Bret told her that they had an extra horse, but no saddle for her. "Can you ride a horse?" he asked.

"Indeed I can," she replied. "Which one?"

"Here you go," Coldiron said as he led the sorrel from the ravine.

She didn't answer right away, distracted as she peered beyond him to the ravine behind him. "Where are the rest of the soldiers?" she asked, assuming he was in the army, and expecting to see an entire detachment of cavalry waiting for them.

"I'm afraid this is it," Bret said.

"Don't worry, ma'am," Coldiron said. "A whole bunch of soldiers woulda made too much noise."

She still found it hard to believe. "You mean the army just sent the two of you to overtake a whole band of Indians?"

"Well," Bret answered, "not exactly. There were more of us the first time we started out looking for you, but they were killed by a band of Blackfeet."

Coldiron stifled a chuckle. "That don't make you feel much better, does it?" He picked her up then and hefted her up to set her on the sorrel's back, as easily as if lifting a child. "Since there ain't no more of us, I expect it'd be a good idea to put a little distance between us and this village." When she was settled, he remarked, "Sorry we ain't got no saddle for you, but you can hang on to that packsaddle pretty good."

"Don't worry," she assured him. "I'm not gonna fall off."

The sound of the drums and the singsong chanting of the warriors faded away behind them, with no sounds of alarm as they rode deeper into the hills, continuing to ride until deeming it a safe distance to stop and decide what to do next. Guiding the horses up a low hill where they could see the moonlit prairie behind them, they pulled up and dismounted. "We'll catch our breath here for a minute," Bret told Myra as he helped her dismount, "and you can tell me what happened to the other lady, Lucy Gentry. You said some other group of Indians took her somewhere. Who were they? Do you know where they took her?"

"First thing," she replied, "I wanna thank you two for coming after us. God love you. I never thought we'd see the light of day after they grabbed Lucy and me. I reckon at my age I was better able to handle it than poor Lucy. I wish you coulda got here sooner. I kinda helped her hold on to her wits, and I'm fearful for her all by herself with those savages that took her from here. I don't really know who they were. They were just Indians like the ones who stole us. They were here in that village when we got here, and they were more like visitors. Well, one of them, one of the scariest-looking savages I've ever seen—didn't have but one ear—took a fierce craving for Lucy as soon as he saw her, and he wouldn't rest till he convinced the one who grabbed her to trade her to him for a whole bunch of horses."

"That don't sound too good for her," Coldiron said.

"It worries me no end," Myra said. "I've grown kinda fond of that little girl since we came from Missouri in the same train, and built our homes right across the river from each other. She's like one of my own children. Since I just had two sons, she was the daughter I never had. Just like me, those savages killed her husband."

"Do you have any idea where these other Indians were going?" Bret asked.

"I don't," Myra said. "I'm sorry, but I don't have any notion where they took her. I don't even know where I am. Even if they talked about it, I couldn't understand any of that Indian gibberish they talk."

"I reckon not," Bret said. "Did you see them when they left the village, which direction they went?"

"They rode off up the river, pretty much the same way we just rode out."

"From what the lady is tellin' us, it sounds like maybe some visitors from one of the other bands of Blackfeet was the ones she's talkin' about—the Piegans, or the Bloods," Coldiron mused. "The Blackfeet ain't friendly with too many other tribes, so it'd be a good bet that's who traded for her. It's been over three years since I've been up this way, but back then there were several bands of Bloods that liked to camp on the Smith River, near where Hound Creek runs into it. From where we are now, I'd say that's about a two-and-a-half or three-day ride. But maybe this bunch are headin' to a village up that way."

Bret considered what Coldiron was saying, but he was now faced with a decision that was not easy to make. What should his first responsibility be—to the lady just rescued, or to the one still in captivity? Should they settle for the one woman rescued and take Myra back to safety, or should they proceed on to search for Lucy Gentry? It would not be fair to expose Myra to the danger they might face if they ventured farther into Blackfeet territory, and yet he found it difficult to abandon Lucy.

Coldiron watched him carefully. He guessed that his young friend was grappling with yet another tough decision. "Whaddaya think we oughta do?"

"Whatever we do," Bret answered, "we'd better do it quick before those hostiles back there find out their captive is missing." He turned to Myra then, thinking he owed her an explanation for his decision. "I don't want to turn my back on Lucy Gentry without trying our best to find her, but I feel responsible to you to get you back to Fort Ellis and out of danger right away. I don't feel like I've got the right to take you two or three days deeper into Indian country—country that's not friendly to white people right now. But I promise you this, I will come back to try to find Mrs. Gentry as soon as I possibly can after I know that you are safe."

"That might be too late," Coldiron remarked.

"I know that," Bret replied. "We might be too late already. We don't know if we can find this new bunch."

Myra didn't hesitate to let him know in no

uncertain terms where she stood on the matter. "We've got to find Lucy," she said. "That's the most important thing right now. That poor darlin' is liable to go out of her mind if we don't find her." She looked at Bret, pleading. "It would be a sin not to try to save her. If you're really worried about me, you can stop right now. I don't have anything to go back to. Lucy's the closest thing to family I've got now, so let's go look for her."

Bret looked at Coldiron's serious face, then looked back at Myra's concerned frown. He shrugged and said, "Well, if we're gonna find that Blood village, I reckon we'd better get started." His decision was met with determined smiles on both the lady's and the huge scout's faces.

"Those bucks back there mighta found out that Myra's gone by now, but they'll most likely think she ain't got very far, so we oughta have a little head start. But I can't do much trackin' in the dark, 'specially when I don't know what tracks I'm supposed to be followin'." He left the obvious conclusion for Bret to express.

"There really isn't any trail to follow," Bret said. "So why don't we just head up the river like Myra said they did, and see if we can find a village?"

"Suits me," Coldiron said. "We need to go ahead and ride on up the river a ways tonight before we make camp, anyway, in case some of the boys back yonder decide to look for Myra up this way."

"Makes sense," Bret said, then looked at Myra. "You ready to ride?"

"I'm ready," she replied confidently. She had been completely honest when she told them she was not afraid to go farther into Blackfeet country. There was nothing to fear anymore, as far as she was concerned. Her husband of almost twenty years was gone, along with her sons. So why worry about what might happen to herself now?

Chapter 6

They continued on for another two hours, following the south fork of the Musselshell before feeling it safe to make camp. The spot they chose was on a small creek that fed down from the Little Belt Mountains. As an added precaution, they followed the creek back for a couple hundred yards and settled on a spot surrounded by trees. The men took care of the horses while Myra built a fire. They decided to use a little of their precious coffee to wash down the salty bacon that Bret had bought in Bozeman, causing him to remark, "We're already running short of some of our supplies. I wish we could find a trading post or some place to resupply."

"There used to be one at the fork where Hound Creek joins the Smith River," Coldiron said. "He might still be there, feller name of Jake Smart."

"That would put him right in the middle of Blackfoot territory, wouldn't it?" Bret asked, surprised that a white man would be allowed to stay there.

"Yep," Coldiron replied. "He's been there quite a spell—gets along with the Injuns, because he married a full-blooded Blackfoot woman, I reckon. Most of his trade is with the Blackfeet."

"I've still got a fair amount of the money we started out with," Bret said. "It should buy us some coffee and maybe some beans, so we could have something besides salt pork to eat."

"If you have enough for a few ingredients, I might be able to make some pan bread," Myra suggested.

"That would surely be to my taste," Coldiron muttered, and rubbed his belly.

"We'll see if Jake Smart is still in business," Bret said. "I would enjoy some bread myself."

"We're gonna have to take some time to go huntin', especially if Jake ain't there no more," Coldiron said. "We could use some fresh meat."

Besides hunger, Myra had one additional need, and she expressed a desire to take care of it. "I really need to give myself a good bath," she announced. "There hasn't been an opportunity since those savages carried me off from my home, and I feel like I'm covered with grime from head to toe." She pointed toward a sizable boulder that extended out into the creek. "I suppose the other

124

side of that rock is as good a place as any for the ladies' washroom."

"I can understand how you feel," Coldiron said. "I get the urge to wash up, myself, from time to time—when the bugs start to bite, or my socks get a little rank. But it'll be a while yet before then. Too much washin' will weaken a man. I think a little sweat and trail dust builds a protective coatin' around your hide, keeps you from catchin' pneumonia and stuff like that. So I'd better build the fire up a little, so you can warm up good when you're done."

"Thank you, sir, I would appreciate that," she said with a contrived lilt in her voice. "I'm so fortunate to have been rescued by such gentlemen."

"You're welcome, ma'am," Coldiron replied, completely unaware that she was joking, or why she and Bret were both grinning at him.

"Sorry I don't have any soap to offer," Bret said, "but I guess you can at least rinse off. There may be something in one of those packs to dry off with when you're done."

"I declare, if she ain't a proper lady," Coldiron said after Myra had disappeared behind the boulder.

Alone for the first time since being captured, except for the brief time when she had been tied to a stake while her captors participated in their war dance, Myra suddenly allowed herself to feel the weight of her misery. A heavy weariness settled about her shoulders as she stepped out of sight of the two men who had rescued her, and her mind's eye recalled the horror of witnessing the slaughter of her husband and her two sons. Cliff had been in the barn when the savages attacked. She had no idea of the evil descended upon her family until Boyd, her eldest, staggered inside the kitchen door and fell forward on the floor, three Blackfeet arrows in his back. When she had run to help him, she saw her youngest lying facedown in the front yard and a line of savages advancing toward the house. Her screams brought Cliff running from the barn, only to be felled by a Blackfoot hatchet as he came out the barn door. She must have collapsed then, because her only recollection of what happened after that was when she found herself with hands and feet bound, lying in the yard while her home was engulfed in flames.

Born with a fighting spirit and a natural determination to overcome adversity, she had refused to let her captors see her grief, no matter how they tried to provoke her. Then when Lucy Gentry was captured, Myra had to assume a posture of strength and comfort for the young woman's sake. Poor devastated and frightened Lucy, she was so close to losing her mind, she had to have someone with strength to rely upon. So Myra was forced to take on that responsibility and lock her own grief away inside her in an effort to instill a sense of silent defiance in her for Lucy's benefit. That facade of boldness was still displayed even after Bret and Coldiron freed her, but now, in the calm quiet of the night, when she was alone with her thoughts, she released the pretense and let her sorrow out.

She had kept it buried too long, so when she freed it, it became impossible to stop. She fell to her knees at the edge of the water, sobbing silent tears of fear and loneliness, grieving for her family, lost to her forever. She cried until there were no more tears left to fall and her body was racked with dry sobs until, finally, she called again upon the inner strength that had sustained Lucy.

Feeling weak and exhausted, she got to her feet and waded out to the middle of the creek where the water was waist deep. She had always had a fear of water over her head, but she submerged her whole body in the cold, swift current. As the water closed over her head, she remained there, holding her breath for as long as she could. The thought entered her mind that it would be best for her to remain under the water until it took her to be reunited with her husband and sons.

But at the moment when her breath was gone, she could not do it. Her fear of deep water was too strong. That, combined with a fighting spirit to overcome, was too much to allow her to drown, and she lunged up from the watery grave, coughing and sputtering with the water attempting to enter her lungs. She at once berated herself. Lucy needed her strong shoulder to rely upon. What would Cliff think of his usually determined wife?

"That's the last time you'll ever have a failing like that, Myra Buckley," she admonished. "You're a fighter—always have been." She wrung the water from her hair as she turned and waded out of the creek.

Shivering now, as she stood naked on the bank, she dried herself as best she could with the blanket from the bedroll that had been tied behind her on the packhorse. She had searched the packs as Bret suggested, but there had been no article of clothing there. She would try to dry the blanket by the fire before she turned in for the night. Thoughts of what luxury some clean clothes would be right then made her sigh in resignation as she got back into her cotton frock.

"Well, sure looks like you took a good one," Coldiron blustered when she returned and he saw her hair wet and dripping. "Come on up here close by the fire before you take sick in this night air." He threw one of the extra saddle blankets he had brought down closer to the fire for her to sit upon.

"It'd take a lot more than a little dip in the creek to make me sick," she replied smartly. "This ol' bird is tougher than you think."

"I reckon," Coldiron snorted with a laugh.

"Here, put this over your shoulders," Bret said, and pulled his shirt blouse off to drape over her.

Coldiron laughed again. "Now you're wearin' the lieutenant's coat, so I reckon you're the boss—although it ain't got no bars on it no more."

Having not approached the subject to that point, she thought it time to ask. "Why didn't the army send some more men with you? You are in the army, aren't you?"

"No, ma'am," Bret replied. "I just haven't gotten around to buying myself some clothes." He saw no purpose in giving specifics pertaining to his disgraceful separation from the military.

"So the two of you just took it on your own to try to find Lucy and me? Well, then I'll say it again. God bless you both."

"Best not bless us till we get you outta this country to somewhere safe," Coldiron remarked as he spread the other saddle blanket he had brought for her bed.

Up with the sun the next morning, the three searchers made ready to get under way once more. Bret and Coldiron loaded the packhorses, adjusting the makeshift saddle they had fashioned for Myra. When Myra asked if she should revive the fire, Bret told her that they would get a little farther up the river before stopping to rest the horses, and then they would fix some breakfast.

When all was ready, Coldiron led as they retraced their ride of the night before, following the creek until it emptied into the Musselshell, then turning northwest once again.

After a ride of about twenty miles, they stopped at a point where the Musselshell took a decided bend straight to the north, toward its origin in the high mountains. "I betcha I camped on this very spot," Coldiron claimed as he led them to a clump of trees near a bank covered with knee-high grass. "I was trappin' on up this river with Big Sam Swift, musta been a hundred years ago. I killed a deer around that bend yonder. I bet deer still cross the river at that spot."

"After we eat some breakfast, maybe we'll take a look," Bret said, then helped Myra gather limbs for a fire. When the fire was going well, he pulled a slab of bacon out of one of the packs and unwrapped the cloth around it.

Referring to his earlier remark, he said, "I'm sure we'd better check that deer crossing you talked about, because this pork is starting to look a little more green." He took his knife and sliced off an end piece and showed it to Myra. She scrunched up her nose in response.

"Well, hell," Coldiron remarked, "it ain't gonna kill us, long as we cook it up till it's really done."

"That pork's not that old," Bret complained. "I guess I should have taken a closer look at it. I hope the rest of it's not as bad as that slab."

"I reckon that means we're goin' huntin'," Coldiron said.

"I hate to lose any more time," Bret told him, "but we've gotta eat, so I guess we'd better see if we can find some kind of game before we go any farther. We haven't seen any signs that would tell us we're anywhere near a village, so we'd better do it before we get any closer to one."

"We might spot some deer this early in the day," Coldiron speculated. "We'd have a better chance if it was evenin', and they was comin' out to feed. But, hell, maybe we'll be lucky."

"I'll stay with the horses," Myra said.

"Will you be all right alone?" Bret asked. "We haven't seen any sign of Indians, so far."

"Oh yes," Myra replied. "I'll be all right. I'd feel a lot safer if I had a weapon of some kind, but I'll be fine."

"Maybe I can fix you up with one," Coldiron said, and went to his packhorse to untie the bow and quiver of arrows he had brought with him. "Can you hit anything with that?" Bret asked when he caught up with him.

"You've been eatin' deer meat that I killed with it ever since that first day on the Yellowstone," the huge man replied. "If we was to happen to get close enough, I'll guarantee you I can hit somethin' with it. And I was thinkin' it might not be such a good idea to use a rifle, anyway. I don't know if we're close to a village or not, but there

ain't no use to make noise if we don't have to."
Bret couldn't disagree with that. Myra looked a
bit skeptical, thinking she might as well be
unarmed as left with a bow and arrow. But
Coldiron assuaged her fears. "I'll leave you my
rifle." He handed the Henry to her. "It's got a full
magazine. All you have to do is crank the lever
and it's ready to shoot."

Relieved, she said, "I can do that."

It was not a long walk to the place in the river
that Coldiron remembered as a deer crossing. And
much to his delight, it appeared to still be in use
by deer, antelope, and all kinds of animals, for
there were tracks of all shapes and sizes leading
down to the water. "What did I tell you?" Coldiron
gloated, pointing to the tracks. There were no
animals in sight, but they had been there recently.

They walked around a dense thicket of berry
bushes and followed a trail the animals had beaten
through the tall grass on the bank—Coldiron with
an arrow notched on his bowstring just in case.
When almost to the water, they heard a sudden
rustle of leaves in the thicket they had just passed.
Turning at once, the startled men saw a small herd
of deer flushed from the bushes and scattering
through the trees.

"Damn!" Coldiron blurted, and swung around,
drawing his bowstring. Bret, who was walking
behind him, was quick thinking enough to drop to
the ground to give Coldiron room to shoot. He

only had time for one shot before the deer were gone, and his arrow was deflected harmlessly by the thick bushes. Bret scrambled to his feet and both men ran back up the bank in an effort not to lose sight of their prey, but it was too late. "Well, if that ain't somethin'," Coldiron complained, frustrated. He had no sooner said it than they heard a rifle shot in the direction of their camp.

"Myra!" Bret exclaimed. "We shouldn't have left her alone." Both men started running back through the trees, skirting thickets and jumping gullies in an effort to come to her aid.

Bret, being the younger, as well as the slimmer, outran the older and heavier Coldiron, but not by a great length. With rifle ready to fire, he approached the camp, looking frantically from side to side in an effort to spot the raiders. He saw Myra then, standing near the bank of the river, Coldiron's rifle in hand. She turned when she heard him pushing through the willows, and gaped at him in astonishment.

"What is it?" he gasped. "Are you all right?" She was about to answer when Coldiron charged into the clearing behind him, equally alarmed. She didn't answer Bret's questions. Instead she turned back toward the river and pointed. The two confused hunters moved up beside her and looked where she pointed to see a four-point buck lying dead at the edge of the water.

"It ran right through the camp," she explained.

"I was holding the gun until you came back. The fool thing almost ran over me, so I shot it."

Bret and Coldiron exchanged glances of astonishment, neither man knowing what to say until the big scout muttered sheepishly, "Well, ain't that somethin'?"

Bret laughed then. "I guess we know now who should do the hunting." He looked again at Coldiron. "I reckon you and I can at least do the butchering. But before we drag that carcass up from there, it might be a good idea to take a look around to make sure nobody heard that shot." The two men walked back to a low rise beyond the trees and scanned the horizon for any sign of visitors, but saw none. "Looks all right, but we'd best take another look every now and then. I'd hate to be surprised by a Blackfoot hunting party."

They dragged the deer up on the bank and hung it from a tree limb while Myra built the fire up. Then Coldiron gave them a lesson on how to skin and butcher a deer in a short amount of time. He had two interested students, for neither Bret nor Myra had ever actually done it before. By the time Bret had cut some green limbs to serve as spits, Coldiron had sliced off some cuts of meat for roasting. The process took on an almost festive air as the aroma of roasting venison filled the tiny clearing in the cottonwoods—so much so that Bret had to remind himself that it was time to walk back to the rise for another look around. There was no one in sight, so he hurried back to partake of the feast.

Crow Killer lay flat on a grassy hilltop two hundred yards from the grove of cottonwoods by the river, and studied the white man on the low rise close to the trees. *A soldier . . . what was he doing here?* Crow Killer wondered. *Where were the rest of the soldiers?* He looked back to signal his friend, Rides With Fire, who was holding the horses.

"Come," Crow Killer said. "Soldiers."

Rides With Fire dropped the ponies' reins and crawled to the top of the hill to see for himself. "Where are the others?" he asked, for like his friend, he could see only one soldier. They had been hunting back in the low hills when they heard the single shot and had followed the sound to this point. There had been no sighting of army troops entering their country for some time now. The word from the trader, Jake Smart, was that the army was occupied with the Sioux and Cheyenne, and just recently sent many soldiers to fight the Nez Perce. So the Blackfeet had no concern for the army's plans against them. Maybe Jake Smart did not know everything the soldiers were doing.

In answer to Rides With Fire's question, Crow Killer said, "I think they must be in the trees. Maybe that one is a guard."

"We must warn our village that the soldiers are here," Rides With Fire said, "so they can be prepared to fight."

"First, let's see if we can get a little closer to their camp to see how many they are," Crow Killer said. "If they are not too many, perhaps a war party can ride out to meet them before they get to our village."

"You are right," Rides With Fire said, then remarked, "Look, he has gone back in the trees." They looked the situation over and decided that as long as there was no guard on the rise before the trees, they should be able to circle around the lower end of the grove and get close enough to see into the camp. Agreed on the plan, they pushed back away from the hilltop and jumped onto their ponies.

Using the line of hills for cover, they rode a wide circle to approach the stand of cottonwoods and willows upstream from where they figured the camp to be. Once they reached the cover of the trees, they tied their horses and made their way closer on foot. Sliding silently through a stand of willows near the river's edge, they suddenly caught sight of the camp. They dropped at once to the ground and crept closer until they could clearly see into the small clearing. With a look of astonishment for his companion, Crow Killer whispered, "There are only three: a soldier, a man the size of a buffalo, and a woman."

"Maybe they are scouts, and the rest of the soldiers are somewhere behind," Rides With Fire suggested.

"We would have seen them when we came this way," Crow Killer replied. "Besides, they are obviously alone and they have a woman with them. Soldiers would not have brought a woman with them. The big one is butchering a deer. There are no soldiers."

"But what are they doing here?" Rides With Fire was still puzzled.

"I don't know. I think maybe they are lost. I think, too, that it is bad luck for them. They have guns and horses. I think this will be a better day to hunt than we thought." He looked at Rides With Fire and smiled, then sniffed the air. "After we kill them, we will feast on the fresh meat they have cooked."

Armed only with bows, the two hunters sought to move even closer to the camp before risking a shot. When reaching a position as close as they dared, they decided on their targets. Crow Killer took aim on the soldier, while Rides With Fire concentrated on the larger target still busy carving the carcass hanging from the limb. Seeing their victims' weapons close at hand, they knew it was necessary to make the first shots count. They took dead aim and released their arrows.

Bret suddenly leaned forward to catch a piece of hot venison that Myra playfully tossed to him, forcing him to lunge to keep it from landing on the ground when her throw was short. It was the only thing that prevented his being struck in the stomach by the arrow that glanced instead off his shoulder. Catching the flash of the arrow as it flew by him, Coldiron instinctively pulled the deer in front of him in time to catch the second arrow in the carcass.

"Get down!" he yelled, and all three hit the ground as two more arrows narrowly missed their targets. "In the willows!" Coldiron yelled again as both men rolled over to snatch up their weapons. In a matter of seconds, they proceeded to pump round after round into the clump of willow trees, halting the flight of arrows almost at once.

"Keep low!" Bret shouted to Myra as he and Coldiron scrambled to find protected cover to shoot from. Having almost emptied his rifle, he called over to Coldiron, who was using a tree trunk for protection. "I'm down to one shot. My extra cartridges are all back in my saddlebags. How about you?"

Coldiron, who was in the process of reloading his Henry rifle, answered, "I've still got some extra in my pockets." They remained where they were for a few moments with no more arrows coming from the willows. "We mighta hit somebody," Coldiron said. "Couldn'ta been many of 'em, for no more arrows than that."

Bret was of the same opinion. There couldn't

have been much protection from the volley he and Coldiron leveled at that thicket. Impatient, he called out, "I'm gonna go see." He jumped up and ran toward the cottonwoods before the willows.

"You damn fool!" Coldiron blurted, but it was too late. Bret was already among the trees.

Pressing his body tight up against a tree, Bret inched his way around the trunk until he could see the patch of willows from which the arrows had come. He stopped abruptly, his rifle ready. There was no one to be seen, so he cautiously pushed through the willows, looking around him, searching for anyone. He saw no one, but then he heard the sound of breaking limbs and knew at once that someone was retreating through the bushes.

He didn't hesitate, for he knew he couldn't afford to let anyone get away to alert the village to their presence. He plunged into the bushes behind the fleeing Crow Killer, running as fast as he could, afraid the Indian had too much of a head start. But he could see branches swaying on trees and bushes ahead of him, and he knew he was gaining. A few yards farther and he spotted the two horses tied in the trees, and the wounded Indian, limping desperately to reach them. He pushed himself to run faster, but Crow Killer reached his pony and crawled onto its back. Bret fired his last cartridge, hitting the Indian in the back, but the hostile would not fall. He turned the pony toward the open prairie and lashed it with his reins. The pony jumped to his command, but Bret was close enough to dive at the wounded warrior and pull him off the horse. They landed with a thud on the hard ground, rolling over and over before parting.

Desperate, Crow Killer pushed himself to his feet and charged Bret with his knife drawn. Still on the ground, Bret looked frantically around him for his rifle. Even though it was empty, he could use it to defend himself from the Indian's knife. He didn't have time to see where it had fallen, and Crow Killer was almost upon him, his long skinning knife poised to slash. There was no time to think, so when he felt a biscuit-sized stone near his knee, he took the only option he had. He grasped the stone and threw it at the charging savage as hard as he could, striking him in the chest.

The solid thump of the stone on his chest was enough to startle and confuse Crow Killer, causing him to pause. When he did, it gave Bret the opportunity to lunge up under him and knock him off his feet. With Crow Killer down, Bret wasted no time in attacking. He launched his body at the wounded warrior, grasping the wrist of the hand that held the knife while he clutched Crow Killer's throat, pressing against his windpipe as hard as he could. It seemed like minutes, although was actually only seconds, before the struggling warrior's hand finally relaxed, releasing the knife. Bret took the knife and, even though Crow Killer was no longer fighting, sliced his throat to make sure he was dead.

He stood there, looking down at the dead warrior, hardly able to believe that he had escaped unharmed, except for a slash on his shoulder from the arrow that glanced off it. Now that it was over, he wondered why the Indian had stopped charging when he threw the rock at him. It gave him time to catch him by surprise. He had to assume that the stone had struck him so solidly in the chest that he thought at first that he had been shot. *You were damn lucky, Hollister,* he thought. "Damn, you're a helluva man," he muttered in tribute to the bloody body. He turned then when he heard Coldiron crashing through the bushes behind him. "There were only two of them," he stated calmly when the huge man burst through to join him, "but I don't know where the other one is." He pointed to the two ponies standing a couple of dozen yards away. "There're the horses."

"Let's pack up and get the hell outta here," Coldiron said. "Ain't no tellin' how many other bucks heard that shot."

Not willing to leave the deer they just killed, Coldiron hurried to butcher the carcass while Bret went to get the Indians' horses. He found them still standing in the trees upstream where he had last seen them. Leading them back toward the camp, he came to the thicket where their assailants had taken cover when they shot at them. There, he also found the body of the other hostile, his hand still clutching his bow. He had evidently been killed immediately when he and Coldiron had returned fire. Bret pried the bow from the Indian's hand and stood up to test the pull of the bowstring. Interested, he pulled the hide quiver of arrows from the body as well, thinking it might be a good idea to learn to use the weapon, as Coldiron had done.

When he walked back into the camp, leading the two horses, he found that it had not taken the big scout long to cut the portions he was saving and wrap them in the deer's hide. "Ready!" he called out to Bret, while still loading them on his packhorse. He stopped what he was doing then to examine the Indian ponies.

"Appaloosa," he announced, nodding toward one of them. "Most likely stole it from the Nez Perce. How do they look to you?" he asked.

"I haven't looked them over that closely," Bret replied. "But they seem to be in pretty good shape." He smiled at Myra, who was also looking them over. "Both have Indian saddles on them—might make it easier on you than riding that packhorse." The remark definitely caught her interest.

The two ponies became a little nervous when the strangers gathered around them, prompting

Coldiron to advise, "Might better pull the shirt offa one of them dead Injuns and rub it over the faces of them horses. Maybe that'll calm 'em down till they get used to our smell." His suggestion seemed to work on the captured ponies, for they calmed down enough for a thorough inspection, and when it was done, he concluded that they were of good quality—a conclusion that Bret had already arrived at.

Their horses had not rested as long as they had planned, but they were watered, so the little party of white people left the banks of the Musselshell and struck out for the Smith River. "It can't be more'n ten or fifteen miles to the Smith," Coldiron said. "We can rest the horses again when we get there."

When they reached the Smith River, they made camp for the night and Myra helped Coldiron cut the venison into strips for drying over the fire. "It's a good thing it didn't take us much longer to get here," she said. "A little bit longer and this meat wouldn't be fit to eat, smoked or otherwise."

"Oh, we coulda still ate it," Coldiron said. "It'da just turned over a little while in your belly before it settled down."

Myra shook her head slowly and said, "It's a wonder you've lived as long as you have." She turned her attention back to the meat she was roasting for their supper, and he continued to fashion drying racks out of green willow limbs for the jerky.

During the next few days, they saw many trails leading along the banks of the river, but they did not happen upon any village, as they had hoped to do. On the second day, they came upon the site of a previous village, but the tracks left by the departing Indians were over a week old. Bret counted evidence of sixty lodges.

"Fair-sized village," he remarked, "not big, not small." Once again, he was struck by the feeling that their chances of finding Lucy Gentry were becoming more remote.

Coldiron, sensing his partner's concern, made the only suggestion he could think of that might have some potential.

"Look here, this trail is gettin' colder and colder. Why don't we push on up to Jake Smart's place? We might run up on a village between here and there, maybe the one that used to be here. But if we don't, Jake mighta heard somethin' about a white captive with one of the bands in this part of the country." He shrugged and added, "I reckon he's still there—if that wildcat he married ain't killed him."

That sounded to be as good a plan as any, as far as Bret was concerned. There was never a thought from any of the three about giving up the search, for with all three, there was nothing pulling them back. When Bret made no comment, Myra gave voice to the decision.

"Let's quit lollygagging and get started, then. Lucy's got a chance just as long as we keep looking for her."

The journey was not an easy one. The river made its way through the rugged country between the Big Belt Mountains and the Little Belt Mountains. With many twists and turns, it led them past miles of narrow canyons with steep walls, and pine-covered slopes. There were also gently sloping meadows here and there that might have been perfect sites for a village, but there were none.

Still, they followed the river as it flowed to the northwest until late one afternoon they topped a low butte and spotted a log cabin with a small barn and a corral behind.

"Well, the cabin's still here," Coldiron remarked.

As they drew closer, they could see a man sitting in front of the cabin in a rocking chair. There was a small porch on the cabin, but the chair was sitting on the bare ground in front of it. Like Coldiron, the man was dressed in animal skins, so it was difficult to tell if he was white or Indian until they rode down the slope to the river.

Having studied the three riders intently since they appeared at the top of the butte, Jake Smart turned his head to call to his wife inside the cabin.

"We got company—white, one of 'em's a

woman, and one of 'em might be a soldier. I ain't shore."

He remained seated in his rocker, but knocked the tobacco from his pipe on the side of the chair and dropped it in his pocket. Inside the house, his wife, Ruby Red Bonnet, reached behind a short counter, picked up a double-barrel shotgun, and positioned herself next to the door.

It was not an everyday occurrence for white folks to visit the little trading post, especially one wearing a uniform, so Jake was a little more than curious. He settled his eye upon the man dressed in buckskins, thinking he was reminded of someone he knew, especially considering the apparent bulk of the man. After a few more moments passed, and the strangers reached the edge of his front yard, a slow smile spread across Jake's face.

"Ruby!" he called again. "No need to worry. It's Nate Coldiron—don't know who he's got with him, though." He settled back in his rocker then, not bothering to get to his feet to greet his visitors.

"Jake Smart, you ol' son of a bitch!" Coldiron called out as they rode up to the cabin. "You got so old you can't ride nothin' but a rockin' chair?" He glanced then at the Indian woman, who appeared in the open doorway. "Ruby," he acknowledged. She made no response.

"I heard you was dead," Jake responded.

"Who told you that?" Coldiron replied.

"I just heared it somewhere. Figured it was most likely true, 'cause you was long overdue." He got up from the chair and nodded toward Bret before asking, "You still doin' some scoutin' for the army?"

"Some," Coldiron replied.

"Ain't much of a patrol you're ridin' with right now. I hope there's a heap more soldiers behind you. Ain't you a little worried about runnin' into a Blackfoot war party?"

"Some," Coldiron repeated. "There's just the three of us," he continued then. "We're lookin' for a young white woman some of your Injun friends run off with. She was took with this lady, here, but they split up back on the Musselshell, and some other bunch has got the other one. Myra here says the ones who took the girl were just visitin' the village. I figured they was more likely Bloods. I thought maybe you'd seen somethin', or heard somethin' that might put us on their trail."

"Is that a fact?" Jake responded. Then without responding to Coldiron's query, he turned his attention to Myra. "'Scuse my manners, ma'am. You folks step down and come in outta the sun. My woman'll fetch you a dipper of cool water from the spring. Or maybe you'd enjoy a cup of cider. I've got a barrel that just come off a boat last week." He offered his hand to help Myra dismount. "I declare," he commented, "they've got you ridin' on an Injun saddle."

"It does just fine," Myra told him. "A cup of water would really be appreciated."

While Bret and Coldiron stepped down, Jake looked back at the sullen woman watching silently from the door. "Ruby, fetch a dipper of water for the lady." Without a change of expression, Ruby turned and disappeared into the cabin. Turning his attention back to Coldiron, Jake said, "You boys need somethin' from the store? Like I said, a boat just come up the Missouri last week, so I've got most anythin' you might need."

"Maybe a few things before we go," Bret said. "Let's talk a little bit first."

Jake studied his face for a few moments. "Why don't we set here on the porch in the shade?" he suggested. "I've had to move my rockin' chair twice already to keep in the shade. Might as well set it on the porch now." He picked up the rocker and carried it to the porch. "You can set yourself down here, ma'am." There were no other chairs, so Bret and Coldiron sat down on the edge of the porch with Jake. "You fellers want some water, or cider, or coffee?"

"Is it hard cider?" Coldiron asked.

"No," Jake replied at once. "You know I can't keep nothin' like that around here. I don't even keep a bottle of likker for myself. Old Chief Black Bear would have what little hair I've got left if he found out I was sellin' any spirits to his warriors.

I don't know how long I'd last if anythin' was to happen to Ruby, anyway."

"Let's make it coffee, then," Bret decided, and Coldiron agreed.

Jake went inside to give Ruby instructions to make a new pot of coffee. When he came back, he handed a dipper of water to Myra. Then he sat down on the edge of the porch again and started to fill his pipe with tobacco. Coldiron controlled his patience until Jake's pipe was filled, lit, tamped down, and lit again. With the pipe pulling satisfactorily, Coldiron pressed for the information he had come to find.

"Damn it, Jake, you've been livin' with Injuns too damn long. You know anythin' about the bunch we're lookin' for, or not?"

"Maybe a little," he said, his voice lowered almost to a hush. He glanced back to make sure Ruby was back in the kitchen before he continued. "You know the only way I hear anythin' about things like that is from Ruby. The only reason they allow me to stay here is because it gives 'em someplace to trade, and they don't think I have any love for the army." That comment caused him to interrupt himself and ask, "What about you, young feller? Are you in the army, or what?"

"No," Bret replied. "I'm not in the army."

"Well, lemme give you some good advice. Get rid of that damn uniform. Soldiers ain't too welcome around here."

"I thought about that myself," Bret replied. "But I don't have any other clothes, and there's no place to buy them, anyway." He realized he should have done it back in Bozeman when he was outfitting himself with horses and weapons.

"I can fix you up with some deerskins," Jake suggested, "like me and Nate's wearin'. Ruby's a dandy seamstress. She makes clothes all the time, and if I tell her you ain't friendly with the army, she'd do it. Matter of fact, I'll tell her you got throwed out of the army 'cause you wouldn't fight against Injuns."

"All right, let's do that," Bret said. Jake didn't catch the smile of irony on his and Coldiron's faces.

"She's already got plenty of hides cured and softened up," Jake went on. "A shirt and trousers are worth about four dollars. How you thinkin' 'bout payin' for 'em? You got somethin' to trade?"

"How about cash money, U.S. dollars?"

"Cash money?" Jake echoed. "Yes, sir-ree, that'll do just fine. How 'bout a good pair of moccasins, too? Cost you five more." It was a rare occasion when he had an opportunity to do anything on a cash basis. Cash would come in especially handy the next time he bought supplies from the riverboats that traveled the Missouri. "I'll tell Ruby you took that uniform offa a dead soldier you killed. She'll do you a special good job then."

Even more impatient, although he agreed that it was a good idea for Bret to get rid of the uniform, Coldiron interrupted. "This is all fine and dandy, but now can we get back to what we came here for? What do you know about the other white woman?"

Jake took a cautious look toward the door again before lowering his voice and returning to the subject.

"I'll tell you the truth, Nate. Ruby said there was a Blackfoot war party that raided some farms down along the Yellowstone, and they came back with two women captives. And I reckon that's who had this lady that's ridin' with you now. Accordin' to what Ruby was told, their village had some warriors visitin' 'em. They were Piegans, not Bloods, and one of 'em took a real fancy to the young lady you're lookin' for. He came from a village above the Missouri on the Marias River is what Ruby said." He saw the deep frown of interest in all three of their faces, so he was quick to caution them. "Don't let on to Ruby that I told you anythin' about this. If she thinks I told you where to go to look for that woman, she'd go straight to Chief Black Bear, and he'd have a war party on your behinds right now." He paused to stroke his chin whiskers thoughtfully before adding, "And she'd most likely geld me while I was sleepin' some night." He flashed a sheepish grin at Coldiron, as the conversation was ended with the arrival of Ruby Red Bonnet carrying a coffeepot with her apron filled with cups.

In an effort to thaw the icy reception they had received from the stoic Indian woman, Myra set the dipper on the floor and got up to offer her help with the coffee. "Here, Mrs. Smart, let me give you a hand with those cups."

Ruby said nothing in response, but stood still while Myra took the cups from her apron, watching the white woman closely, as if expecting a trick. When Myra distributed the cups, including one Ruby had brought for her, Ruby spoke her first words to them. "I pour. Coffee hot." Then she took the pot back to place it on the corner of the stove.

Jake grinned sheepishly. "She don't talk much white man talk, but she cooks pretty good." Remembering then, he added, "And she's a helluva seamstress. Don't take her long, neither, once she gets started."

"I don't know if we can take the time to get some clothes made," Bret remarked, rethinking his commitment earlier.

"Two days, if she gets goin' on 'em right away," Jake said, anxious about losing the money. "And I'm gonna tell you what's the truth. Walkin' around with them army clothes on is the same thing as havin' a target on your back." He looked solemnly at Coldiron then. "You know I've always been straight with you, Nate. And I'm tellin' you, this ain't a good time for a white man to be seen on this side of the Missouri. And it's worse on the other side, up toward the Marias. It'd be a whole lot better for you folks if the Injuns think you're just a couple of trappers."

Coldiron nodded thoughtfully. "I expect he might be right," he said to Bret. "I don't wanna hold up any longer, same as you, but we might avoid some extra trouble if we wait till we can get you outta that uniform."

Bret looked at Myra before answering. She nodded, so he said, "All right, we'll wait." Turning to Jake then, he asked, "How soon can you get her started?"

"Ruby!" Jake called out immediately. When the sullen woman appeared at the door, he told her, "These folks heard about how good you make deerskin shirts and trousers, so they come all this way to see how fast you can make some clothes for this feller so he don't have to keep wearin' them army clothes." She didn't seem to be very enthusiastic about the prospect, so Jake went on. "He's gonna pay in government money, and we can buy a lot of things offa the boat with that." She nodded then and returned to the kitchen.

"Nothing fancy," Bret said. "I don't need any fringes or stuff like Coldiron's shirt has on it. That'd be quicker, wouldn't it?"

"It would at that," Jake replied. "Same price as one that is fancy, though."

Ruby returned then with a long length of rawhide cord. "Stand up," she said. Bret got to his feet, and she used the cord as a measuring tape, tying a knot in it for each measurement taken. In a matter of seconds, there was a knot after the length of his arm, another after the length of his leg, and so on until she had all the measurements she needed on one length of cord. "Two days," she said when finished, then left them to drink their coffee.

"Best not say anythin' to Ruby about lookin' for that other lady," Jake warned them again, his voice lowered almost to a whisper again. "She's full-blooded Blackfoot, and she thinks like they do on most about everythin'." His advice was unnecessary, for the woman's cool demeanor toward them was enough to make them feel they were in the enemy's camp.

"I reckon we'll see about settin' up our camp, then," Coldiron said.

"Best thing to do is camp down the creek a ways behind my place," Jake advised. "Ain't likely anybody'll bother you there. There ain't no good reason anybody'd even know you were there. There's a clearing with good grass right next to the creek for your horses. I notice you're leadin' a couple extra horses. And if I had to guess, I'd say two of those horses, the ones with the Injun saddles, mighta belonged to previous owners who most likely died of lead poisonin'. Whaddaya aim to do with 'em?"

"We was thinkin' about tradin' 'em to you," Coldiron said. He winked at Bret. "If you got anythin' worth tradin' for two fine ponies like them."

"Wait a minute," Myra spoke up then. "You ain't trading my horse." She had become quite comfortable riding the Appaloosa gelding.

"I reckon I was wrong," Coldiron allowed. "I forgot to check with the boss of this outfit."

"You didn't get 'em from around here any-where, did you?" Jake asked. When Coldiron told him how they came to have the horses, Jake said, "Good, just as long as none of Black Bear's warriors recognize 'em."

When Myra had interrupted to protest the prospect of trading her horse, Bret suddenly realized he had been blind to further needs the lady had. She had no clothes other than the dress she had been captured in, and it was getting pretty ragged from the hard wear it had been subjected to. He felt remiss in not being more observant. "Have you got any ladies' clothes in your store?" he asked Jake. His question corralled Myra's interest immediately.

"Why, no, I ain't," Jake replied, somewhat sur-prised that Bret should ask. "I ain't got much call for ladies' clothes. I got some bolts of cloth that some of the women from the village make clothes out of, but that's all. The only clothes I sell are some trousers and a few shirts, but they're men's."

"That'll do," Myra sang out, "a lot better than a dress."

"I'll show you what I've got," Jake said. "You'll have to gimme a few minutes to dig 'em out of my storeroom. Like I said, I ain't got much call for clothes, men's or women's. Matter of fact, I don't know why in the world I ever bought 'em in the first place." He gave her a wide grin. "Maybe I knowed you'd come along sometime."

They made camp on the grassy clearing Jake told them about, but kept the horses on a rope line close to them just in case Jake might have been overly reassuring regarding their safety.

"I don't care if we are right behind the tradin' post," Coldiron said. "Injuns is Injuns, and Blackfeet ain't never had much love for the white man." With that in mind, they made their beds on the sand beneath the creek bank, so they would have cover in case of a surprise attack. "I've knowed Jake for a good many years," Coldiron said, "but he's been livin' with the Blackfeet for a long time now, and he ain't about to do nothin' to bring ol' Chief whatever-he-said-his-name-was down on him. I reckon I'll sleep with both ears open tonight."

"That might be a good idea," Bret said.

Myra shifted around from one side to the other on her blanket, trying to gain a comfortable position to sleep. Her new shirt and pants felt stiff and unyielding, but they were a welcome addition to her scanty wardrobe.

"That is one scary woman he's married to," she commented when she finally settled down.

Coldiron laughed. "That's the truth, all right. Ol' Jake's been married to that woman for a long time."

"He must see something in her that doesn't show on the outside," Myra said.

"I think whatever he saw in her when he married her dried up long ago, and now he's too scared to kick her out, scared if he did, he'd end up with his throat cut." Coldiron stroked his chin whiskers, thinking back. "They had a young'n, but I never heard what happened to him. Jake don't ever talk about him. Knowin' that woman, she most likely had a panther. He mighta gone with his mama's people." He paused to consider that. "He'd be a man now."

Chapter 7

"What these people want?" Ruby asked when she placed a plate of food on the table before Jake and sat down to face him.

"I told you, hon," her husband replied, forgetting that he had advised Coldiron not to tell Ruby why they were here. "They musta hired Coldiron as a guide, and they're just passin' through this way, lookin' for that young white woman that some of your folks snatched down on the Yellowstone."

"What you tell them?" she asked, concerned, for she knew who had the woman and where she was.

"Ah, you know me, hon," Jake said. "I told 'em I didn't know nothin' about them two women that was took. Ain't none of my business. That ol' gal they got with 'em was one of the two, and they got her back. They oughta just figure that's good enough, and go on back down where they came from."

"I don't trust them people," Ruby groused. "I make clothes fast, so they go from here quick." Were it not for the money they would receive for her sewing, she would have refused to make clothes for the tall white man.

"They'll be gone in a day or two, and we most likely won't see 'em no more." He paused then when he heard a faint noise outside the door of the cabin. "You hear that?" She nodded, and they both got up from the table, for it was late for a customer to be calling. Jake went to the counter near the door where his shotgun was handy.

"You're too slow, old man," John Lame Dog scoffed. "You'd already be dead if I wanted to kill you." He pushed the door open then and walked into the store. Lean and dark, with a constant look of contempt, he smirked at the man behind the counter for a moment before turning to face the woman coming to greet him. "Mama," was his only acknowledgment.

"John." Ruby uttered the word softly. "You stay away so long. Come, you must be hungry."

He scowled at her greeting, annoyed by her use of the name his father had insisted upon. He preferred his Blackfoot name, Lame Dog, a name that had come to him when he went into the mountains to seek a vision. She led him to the table and sat him down where Jake had been seated.

"Eat," she insisted, and pushed the plate toward him, unconcerned that it was her husband's supper. He obliged, stuffing a piece of boiled pork in his mouth.

Accustomed to his place in his wife's ranking of importance, Jake went to the cupboard to get another plate for himself. He dipped some more of the pork onto the plate and sat down at the other end of the table. "What brings you back here?" he asked, knowing that the only reason would be that he was in need of something.

"I wanted to see my daddy," Lame Dog replied sarcastically, and grinned. He paused to bite off a large mouthful of meat. "I need cartridges," he said then. "I need other things, too." He glanced up from his plate to give his mother a grin.

"You know, it'd be a help if you was to bring some pelts or somethin' with you to help pay for all the stuff you come here to get," Jake couldn't resist commenting.

"Jake," Ruby scolded. "He's your son."

"Well, he don't hardly act like it," Jake complained. "Whaddaya need cartridges for, anyway? I don't reckon you're wantin' to go huntin' for buffalo, are you? I gave you two boxes of cartridges last time you was here. How'd you use them up so fast?"

"Killing white men like you," Lame Dog said with a sneer.

"I swear, you're makin' a mistake, runnin' with that wild bunch of Piegans. We hear about them raids on white settlers on the Marias and the Judith. You forget you're half white yourself."

Lame Dog paused to look up at him and snarled, "Yeah, and that's the thing I'd change if I could. I'd kill that half. The half of me that's Blackfoot is the only half I claim."

Making an effort to head off the violent argument that was sure to follow, Ruby placed her hand on her son's shoulder. "You are great Blackfoot warrior. Your mother is proud of you."

Lame Dog calmed down enough to change the subject. "Someone is camped down on the creek. I saw their fire when I rode in, but I couldn't see who they were."

"Just some travelers passin' through," Jake hurried to answer before Ruby could. "A man I've known for a long time. Ain't nobody important. Your mama's sewin' some hides for one of 'em."

"That so?" He looked at his mother for confirmation.

She nodded. "How long will you stay?" she
asked. He always stayed in Chief Black Bear's
village when visiting, refusing to stay in a white
man's home. She did not want him to decide to
stay the night with them this time for fear he
might have a confrontation with the white men
camping at the creek. She was familiar with Nate
Coldiron's reputation as an Indian fighter, and the
young man with him impressed her as being a
formidable warrior.

In answer to her question, Lame Dog replied,
"Only long enough to get the things I need. Then
I will go to the village."

"Well, I reckon I can get your stuff together
right quick, so you don't get to the village too late
to find you a lodge to sleep in," Jake said.

Thinking along the same lines as his wife, he
wanted to send Lame Dog on his way as quickly
as possible. Without finishing his supper, he got
up right away and went to his storeroom to get a
box of .44 cartridges. Afraid that Lame Dog would
come to look for himself, Jake hid the balance of
his supply of cartridges under a pile of deer hides.

"Well, you got my last box. I reckon I'll have to
get some more pretty soon," he said when he
returned to the kitchen.

"I need more'n that," Lame Dog complained.
"When are you gonna get some more?"

"Won't be for a month," Jake lied, "when a boat comes upriver with some."

He avoided Ruby's eyes, in case she happened to know how many cartridges he really had in the storeroom.

Clearly unhappy about the number of cartridges he would have to settle for, Lame Dog gulped the rest of his food down and got up from the table.

"Well, maybe I'll find some somewhere else. Let's see what else I need."

Jake followed him around the little store as the disgruntled half-breed grabbed anything that struck his fancy. Before he was through, he had filled a bulging sack of supplies.

His mother followed him out to talk to him while he tied the sack on his saddle. "Must you stay in Black Bear's village tonight?" she asked in the Blackfoot tongue.

"Why shouldn't I?" he asked. "My village is too far from here to start out before morning."

"The men camped at the creek have the other white woman with them. They are searching for the young one. I'm afraid, if they know you are here, they will try to follow you back to your village."

"Huh!" Lame Dog snorted. "How many are they?"

"Two," Ruby answered, "but one of them is the white scout Coldiron. The other one looks to be strong as well. It's best that you leave here before they see you."

"Huh!" Lame Dog snorted again. "Two men? And one of them is as old as the worthless white man you married. Maybe I'll ride down to the creek and kill those two. Then you won't have to worry about them following me."

"No!" she retorted. "Listen to your mother! It is best to leave them alone and return to the Piegan village. They don't know to look for the woman there." She was unaware that Jake had told Coldiron that Lucy Gentry might be in the village on the Marias. "Give me your promise that you will not go near the white men's camp."

He shrugged as if casting the notion aside. "All right, if it pleases you. I must go now." He climbed onto his horse and rode up the path to the river trail. She watched until he was swallowed up by the evening darkness.

Once he was out of her sight, Lame Dog turned to ride along the bank of the creek, back from the point where it flowed into the river. He intended to satisfy his curiosity about the people who were camping behind his father's trading post. His father had been pretty anxious to see him leave, and now, thanks to his mother, he knew why. He frowned when he realized that Jake had not warned him about the two men hunting for the woman. He cursed the day when his mother had married a white man.

Making his way down from the bluffs, he

walked his horse along the creek until reaching a point just before the clearing where they were camped. He pulled his '66-model Winchester from the sling and dismounted to go the rest of the way on foot. It was dark enough to easily conceal him as he walked through the trees along the bank, but he was forced to stop at the edge of the clearing, some seventy-five yards short of the campfire.

Beyond the fire, he spotted a group of horses, evidently tied close to the water, but he could not see well enough to count them. The clearing before him was brightly lit by a three-quarter moon just rising over the mountaintops behind him, making it risky to try to sneak up closer. So he continued to sit where he was and watch to make sure that there were no more people in the camp than his mother thought there were. Lame Dog wondered who the man with Coldiron was, for there appeared to be more than a few horses tied by the creek. The thought of acquiring those horses was more than enough incentive to make a try for them.

Coldiron's reputation was well known, so Lame Dog was not inclined to run across a moonlit clearing of seventy-five yards. He was not so foolish as to test the scout's alertness, or his aim. But he reasoned that if he could manage to slip into the camp and steal the horses, not only would he increase his wealth, but the white men would be on foot. Finally, his mind made up, he decided to go back to his horse and ride out of the trees to circle around and come up from the opposite side. That would put the horses between him and the campfire, and he might possibly be able to steal them before their owners knew what was happening.

After riding a wide arc around the camp, he found that he could get a little closer to the horses than it had appeared from the other side of the clearing. He had only about twenty-five yards of open grass to cover before he would be in the midst of the trees where the horses were tied. He slid out of the saddle and crept silently to the edge of the clearing. He was close enough to count the horses now. There were six. With his rifle in one hand, and his knife in the other, he crept into the clearing, having taken only a dozen or so steps when he felt the snap of a rifle slug stinging the air by his head. It was followed almost immediately by the sharp crack of a Henry rifle.

Lame Dog rolled over and over for several yards as fast as he could manage, a maneuver made difficult by the weapons he was holding, but accomplished in his desperation. He hoped to make himself an elusive target until he could scramble to his feet and dive into the cover of the trees. Several bullets flew around him to hurry his flight, but luck was with him and he gained the protection of a large tree trunk.

Once he had avoided being hit, he fired at the

creek bank from which he had glimpsed muzzle flashes—then cranked in another cartridge and fired again. His return fire set off an eruption of rifle fire that filled the air around him and forced him to hug the ground. Seeing at once that he was facing far too much firepower from his intended victims, he backed carefully away, trying to keep the large tree between himself and the rifles. It was obvious that he had no chance of stealing any horses on this night.

Cursing his luck, he jumped upon his horse's back and kicked it into a gallop, ignoring the branches that whipped his face and body as he crashed through the grove of trees.

"How'd you know?" Bret asked when there were no more return shots from the trees.

"I didn't," Coldiron confessed. "I just couldn't sleep. Maybe I was expectin' somethin' like this, and that's why I couldn't sleep. I was just layin' there, and I heard a couple of the horses nicker. It made me kinda curious, so I rolled over and took a look out at the clearin', and there he was, tryin' to get to the horses."

"I heard his horse running like hell through those trees," Bret said. "I only heard one, so I think he was alone."

"Well, I know I'm not going to sleep anymore," Myra announced. "I thought we were all right this close to the trading post."

"I wouldn't worry no more tonight," Coldiron told her, "at least not from that child. I expect he found out it might not be too good for his health to go after our horses."

"I wonder if he just happened to find us, or if somebody told him where we were," Bret speculated. "How much do you trust your friend Jake?"

"Oh, about as far as I could throw him when he's settin' on a horse," Coldiron replied. "Tell you the truth, though. I ain't as worried about Jake as I am about that woman he's livin' with. She's got all kinda kin in that village up the river, and I expect they'd all like to have some extra horses."

"We might have made a mistake, staying here for a couple of days," Myra suggested.

"We're probably just as safe here, where we can hole up in that tradin' post if we have to," Coldiron said. "We need to get Bret outta that damn uniform for one thing. Ain't no use in paradin' that target around in front of a bunch of scalp-happy Blackfoot bucks. It'd be a pretty big coup for one of 'em to kill a soldier. Somebody in that Injun camp knows we're here now, and that ain't good, but like I said, we can hold 'em off in Jake's place. I don't think they're gonna wanna burn him out, 'cause then where would they get their coffee and flour and calico, and all that other stuff he gets for 'em?"

"Now, what the hell?" Jake had exclaimed when he heard the shooting from the creek. The first thought that came to mind was, *He had to go stir up trouble. He couldn't just leave them alone.*

Even more alarmed than her husband, Ruby exclaimed, "Lame Dog!" fearing that he had been shot. She ran to the back door and followed Jake out in the yard to listen for more gunfire. All was quiet now, which caused Ruby to worry even more.

"They might have shot Lame Dog," she said fearfully. "You need to go down to creek to see."

"And get my ass shot full of lead?" Jake responded. "Right now ain't a good time to go walkin' up on that camp. That hardheaded son of yours oughta stayed away from there, like we told him. Now they're liable to shoot at the first thing they see."

"If you not go, I go," Ruby declared. "Make sure my son all right."

"No, damn it," Jake replied. "Ain't no sense in you gettin' yourself shot, too. I'll go down there."

He knew the woman would do what she said, and he wouldn't be any kind of man at all if he let his wife risk the danger of getting shot. He couldn't avoid the thought that went through his mind that his life might be more peaceful without her. But he wasn't sure how long the Indians would let him stay there if she was gone.

"No, you just stay right here, and I'll go find out if that was John that caused all the shootin'." It was a little more than a mile, so Jake put a bridle on his horse but didn't bother with the saddle. Using a rail of the corral as a stool, he crawled up onto the horse's back and rode off along the creek, leaving Ruby still in the yard, listening.

Approaching the camp through the trees, just as Lame Dog had done, Jake pulled up short of the clearing to announce his presence. "Hello!" he yelled. "Nate, it's me, Jake. You hear me?"

"Yeah," Coldiron called back. "We hear you. Come on in."

"Anybody hurt?" Jake asked when he rode up to the fire and slid off his horse.

"Don't reckon so," Coldiron replied. "We looked in the trees there, where this feller came from, but he's gone away from here. Don't know if we hit him or not. It's too dark to tell if there was any blood around, and he lit out like his tail was on fire. I think me and Bret made it a little too hot for him to make another try for the horses."

"Well, I'm glad nobody got hurt," Jake said. Then remembering his manners, he asked, "You all right, ma'am?" Myra said that she was. Turning back to Bret and Coldiron, he said, "I don't know how anybody knew you folks were camped here. Musta been one of those young bucks from Black Bear's village. Probably stumbled on you by accident." He was hoping it was too dark to see the traces of the lie on his face.

"Likely so, I reckon," Coldiron said. "Just cost us a little sleep and a few cartridges is all."

"Well, I expect I'd best go on back to the house and let the old lady know all you folks are all right," Jake said. "She was a little worried. I reckon I'll see you in the mornin'." He made an attempt to jump on his horse's back but failed by a couple of feet. Coldiron clasped his hands together to make a step for the short little man, and boosted him up on the horse. "Much obliged," Jake said, and turned the horse back toward his cabin.

"Why do I get the feeling that ol' Jake there might have an idea who our visitor was?" Bret wondered aloud.

"I don't know," Myra said, "but I wonder why I have a hard time believing that Indian woman he lives with was worried about our safety."

As Ruby Red Bonnet had estimated, it took her two days to complete Bret's new outfit of deerskin, including winter moccasins. All traces of his life in the army disappeared when he tried them on, and he was pleasantly surprised to find how well they fit him. Bret had expected a rather baggy creation of stiff leathery hide to have been finished in such a short time. He had been certain that it was not a job Ruby relished, for her icy disposition toward them never improved. But he should have suspected that the woman's pride in her sewing would not permit her to turn out a product of inferior quality. There was the possibility that he might tell someone who did the job. Although he was keen to try the moccasins, he planned to keep his boots in case the moccasins didn't work out.

"You look like you belong in these mountains now," Coldiron told him. "All you need is to get 'em broke in a little bit, and take some of the new shine off 'em."

There had been no more visits from any horse thieves during the night, but both men took turns watching the horses anyway. Bret had in mind the possibility of trading the two extra horses for winter coats, probably bear skin or buffalo, if their search for Lucy Gentry took them into the winter. According to Coldiron, their best bet to trade for any supplies they needed would be at Fort Benton, which was ten or twelve miles short of the confluence of the Marias with the Missouri.

"Is that a military post?" Bret asked. "You think a band of Piegans would have a village that close to an army post?"

"It used to be the Blackfoot Agency," Coldiron said. "But it ain't no more, not since they moved it to Choteau. The army weren't the first to use the fort. It started out as a fur tradin' fort before trappin' went to hell. Last I heard, the settlers built a right good-sized town around the old fort. I expect we can find about anything we need there."

When all the trading that was to be done with Jake Smart was finished, the three travelers said farewell to the little man and his stoic wife. Ruby walked out to stand beside her husband and watched them ride up the slope to the river trail.

"Why they don't ride toward the village?" Ruby asked, referring to the Blood village of Chief Black Bear. "They don't look for woman there?"

"Why, I don't know, hon," Jake replied. "Maybe they plan on circlin' around the village and watchin' it from the other side." He could not tell her that he had told Coldiron the woman was taken to a Piegan camp, the same village their son resided in. In an effort to get her mind on something else, he said, "That sure was a fine piece of work you did on that young feller's outfit."

"Huh," she snorted. "I hope if I see it again, it's got arrow hole in it."

Fearing that time was against them, and concerned that the young woman they searched for might already be dead, they followed the river north for half a day until it reached the Missouri. Then, after resting the horses, they followed the Missouri northeast for another fifteen miles by Bret's estimate before camping for the night.

There had been no sign of any Indian activity

after leaving the confluence of the Smith River with the Missouri. In fact, they saw a couple of isolated homesteads across the river on the north bank. The sight was a reassurance for Myra that the entire country was not a savage wilderness.

In the evening of the third day, they made camp within a few miles of Fort Benton, where the river turned in a series of curves to form an S. Coldiron told them that they were going to go a bit farther the next morning before crossing over to the north side of the river.

"If we cross here, we'll have to backtrack just to keep from havin' to cross it again." The fort and the settlement growing up around it were all on the north side.

The prospect of swimming the horses across was not one that Myra looked forward to. All during the day's ride, there had been no section of the river that appeared to offer an easy ford, at least in her opinion. She would never admit to her fear of deep water, or the fact that she could not swim. She thought about the night they had camped near the Musselshell, when she had gone behind a big boulder at the edge of the creek and tried to drown herself. The idea of water trying to enter her lungs had terrified her, causing her to abandon any thoughts of suicide in that fashion. And that was in water no deeper than her waist. What if she fell off her horse during the crossing? Realizing that if she continued thinking these things she was going to be a nervous wreck by morning, she ordered herself to forget about facing it until the time came.

"What are you workin' so hard on in your head?" Coldiron asked her. He had been watching her from the opposite side of the small campfire as they finished their supper. "I don't think we have to worry too much about the Injuns this close to Fort Benton. A lot of the Injuns come into the town to trade. The Blackfeet were the ones who got the American Fur Company to build Fort Benton on the north side of the Missouri, so they'd have a place to trade their furs."

"I'm not worrying about the Indians. My mind was just somewhere else," Myra said, refusing to admit her fear to Coldiron. "I'm tired, I guess. Maybe I was worrying a little bit about Lucy, and what's happening to her while we're sitting around this fire drinking coffee and eating venison."

The next morning, the three travelers followed a well-used trail along the river. Coldiron and Bret took some time to look over the banks, trying to decide on a good place to cross over to the other side. After passing up one possibility after another, because of steep banks, or swirling water, Bret made a suggestion.

"This trail we've been following looks to me like it's well traveled, not only hoofprints, but wagon tracks, too. More than likely these folks were on their way to Fort Benton, so I'd bet we just need to keep following the trail and see where they ford the river. That's most likely the best place to cross."

Grinning, Coldiron responded, "Well, now, that makes a helluva lotta sense, don't it?" He turned his sturdy buckskin gelding back toward the trail, without any discussion. They were within sight of some of the buildings of the town when the trail took a sharp turn down to the river.

"I reckon this is it," Coldiron said. They paused on the bluff to look over the crossing. An island situated more than halfway across split the ford into two phases. The first appeared to be the deepest and the widest.

"Might as well take a look," he said, "see if there's any trouble." He nudged the buckskin, and the big horse went forward without hesitation into the water. "Bottom seems pretty good," he called back when nearly halfway across the channel. "Ol' Buck's swimmin' now, though," he said when the water came up on his thighs. He started to come out of the saddle when the horse seemed to struggle, but realized that the buckskin had found footing again. Coldiron reined the horse to a stop when it came up on the island. Then he turned and beckoned for Bret and Myra to follow.

Bret tied Coldiron's packhorse on a lead rope behind, thinking it best if he led two horses while Myra led one. "You go next, Myra," he told her.

"I'll come behind you in case I have to fish you out of the river." Although he was teasing, he thought it a worthwhile precaution.

"You're not gonna have to fish me out," she blustered confidently. "I might have to come back and fish you out."

Her fear of the crossing was greatly diminished, thanks to Coldiron's seemingly easy crossing. She nudged the Appaloosa and entered the water boldly, no longer hounded by thoughts of drowning. It went as smoothly as she anticipated, until she reached the point where the bottom dropped off.

Startled, when it felt the bottom suddenly gone, the usually gentle Appaloosa lunged forward in an effort to find footing again. Caught by surprise, Myra came out of the saddle and into the water. The thought immediately flashed through her mind that the river had claimed her, just as she had feared. Screaming and flailing frantically, she was swept back to collide with her packhorse, which was now swimming after the Appaloosa. Myra's thrashing arms caught a strap of the packsaddle and she was pulled safely up onto the island.

An astonished Nate Coldiron gaped at the thoroughly soaked woman. "I never knowed you was one of them fancy trick riders," he dead-panned. "Rode into the river ridin' the Appaloosa, and come out ridin' the packhorse."

Having observed her antics from behind, Bret came out of the water after her and could not resist a comment as well. "Now you know that these aren't just packhorses. They're also lifeboats for river crossings."

Still sputtering from her impromptu dunking, Myra was not in a mood to appreciate the humor at her expense. Dripping wet, she still had a small channel of the river to cross before she could be done with the Missouri. "I reckon you can go awhile now before you have to take another bath," Coldiron remarked, remembering that she had felt such a strong need for one when they were back on the Musselshell.

"Now that I've given you two jackasses something to entertain you," she retorted, "can we get on across this damn river?"

"Yes, ma'am," Coldiron replied grandly, with a sly smile aside to Bret, who could not help beaming as well. "Would you like to lead, in case you decide to change horses again?"

She refused to dignify his question with a reply. Instead, climbing onto her horse again and giving it a kick, she plunged into the narrow channel of water, leading her packhorse behind her. She had already embarrassed herself by screaming frantically when she was dumped, and she was determined not to show her fear again. Much to her relief, the water did not rise above the stirrups. When she climbed up on dry land, she looked back and admonished them. "Well, come on. We're wasting time lollygagging around this crossing."

"I expect it'd be a good idea to stop for a little while to see if we can dry out the lady's clothes a little," Bret said when he joined his two companions on the bank. He and Coldiron were only wet from the thigh down, and would have simply let the sun dry them eventually. But Myra was soaked, and he knew she was uncomfortable, even though she was making a brave show of wanting to continue.

Now that she was on the north bank, she began to cool down a bit, both from the river water and a feeling of sheepishness over having lost her temper. "We don't have to lose any more time, if we just stop long enough for me to change," she said. "My dress is in one of the packs on top, and it doesn't look like they got wet."

"If you're sure you're all right," Bret said. "I mean, if you don't feel like you need to rest for a spell."

"I just got wet," she came back. "I haven't been doing anything to get tired."

"If it was me," Coldiron allowed, "I'd just let 'em dry on me. As wet as those clothes are, they'll shrink like hell. If you keep 'em on, they'll fit a lot better when they do dry."

"As much as I respect your advice, Mr. Coldiron," she replied sarcastically, "I think I'd rather ride into Fort Benton in dry clothes." Her tone was enough to inform the two men that there was no need for further discussion on the matter.

Bret couldn't suppress a smile. Then he realized that the river crossing had provided the first light moment in their journey. It only lasted for the time it took for Myra to get out of her wet clothes and put on her tattered dress. And then the grim purpose of their trip returned as they rode on into Fort Benton.

Chapter 8

Lucy Gentry sat at the back of the tipi, her legs drawn up to her chin, her arms wrapped around them, trying to get in as small a shell as possible. The voices of the people in the village carried to her as she cowered there, seemingly unconcerned that she was being held captive by one of their young warriors. She hoped with all her heart that Bloody Hand was feasting on the fresh antelope that the day's hunt had provided. Maybe if he filled his belly with meat and some of the whiskey that his cruel friend, Lame Dog, had brought back from the Blood village, he might be too sleepy to pay any attention to her.

Her life had effectively ended the day her husband was struck down and she was snatched off her feet by a screaming Blackfoot warrior. She had no idea how many days had passed since she was cast into a terrifying nightmare of scowling, leering Indians, who poked, prodded, cursed, and spat upon her, their faces filled with the contempt they felt for her. She had done them no harm, yet they seemed intent upon punishing her for something. It was too much for her mind to maintain its balance.

At first, she had Myra Buckley to help her hold on to her sanity, but now Myra was gone, maybe dead. She had not seen or heard of her since they were separated at a village on some river. Who was the more fortunate, Myra or her? She would never know, but she knew that Myra's fate could not have been worse than hers. Purchased from her captors by a Piegan warrior, who had an insane desire for her, she was certain that there was no greater hell than the one she had fallen into.

She had screamed and almost fainted when he came for her. One of the most feared warriors in the Piegan village, he was a vile-looking man with only one ear. On the left side of his head there was only a hole where his ear had been before being sliced off by a Lakota warrior's hatchet. On his left shoulder, there remained an ugly scar where the hatchet had struck him after it severed the ear. Bloody Hand had earned the respect of his fellow warriors when he opened the Lakota warrior's belly with his knife. The severed ear, dried and shriveled, was still worn on a rawhide cord around Bloody Hand's neck. The thought of it was enough to cause her to shiver.

After one night in the Piegan village, Lucy had

abandoned all hope of rescue. How could anyone find her? The village would be moving in a few days. Convinced that she could not endure the abuse from Bloody Hand, as well as that from his mother, Dark Moon, she decided that she would take her own life. That resolution was more difficult to accomplish, owing to the lack of means to effectively kill herself quickly. She was never allowed to use any object that might inflict damage on her or anyone else. Bloody Hand lived in his mother's tipi whenever he was in the village, and Dark Moon willingly took on the responsibility for keeping a constant eye on his captive. Lucy had considered the possibility of overpowering the vigilant Piegan woman, but feared it would only result in failure. Dark Moon was a strong old woman, and would undoubtedly win any contest between them. Lucy had attempted to starve herself to death, since that was the only option available to her. But Dark Moon, wise to what the white woman was trying to do, forcefully fed her, standing over her with a stick to make sure she swallowed every mouthful. Firmly believing there was no hope for her, Lucy could only pray that God would see fit to take her from this hell she found herself in.

"I am home, old woman," Bloody Hand slurred drunkenly as he pushed the tipi flap aside and entered. "You can go to your bed now."

"You've been drinking the white man's fire-water," Dark Moon scolded. "It is bad for you. It will make you crazy. Lame Dog should not bring it to our village. If he was a true warrior like you, he would not want the crazy water, but he has white blood in his body. He is not a good friend."

"You worry too much, old woman," Bloody Hand replied. "Lame Dog is a good friend. Now go to your bed." Grumbling under her breath, she did as he ordered. "Wait," he said. "Did you take her to make water?"

"She didn't have to," Dark Moon replied.

"You should have made her," he chided, knowing that as soon as he approached her, she would start making her frantic motions and crying over and over one of the few Piegan words Dark Moon had taught her: *Pee, pee, pee*! He was well aware that the only reason she did it was to try to kill his desire for her. It did her little good, for it only caused him to be especially brutal in his mating with her.

"Do you want me to take her now?" Dark Moon asked, making no effort to hide the disgust she felt for her son's infatuation with the white woman. It had been a dark day for the old woman when Bloody Hand brought the white woman back to the village, intent upon making her his wife. Dark Moon was reviled by the thought of mixing Bloody Hand's pure Piegan blood with that of the inferior white blood. She feared the union might result in another half-breed like his friend Lame Dog. *What a fitting name he chose for himself,* she thought, for she had no respect for the man.

"No, go to bed. I'll take her," Bloody Hand said in answer to her question. He turned to Lucy then. "Come!" When she did not respond as quickly as he preferred, he reached down, grabbed her arm, and pulled her roughly out of her balled-up protective position, causing her to emit a feeble yelp of pain. He then picked up a coil of rope with a noose tied on one end and looped it over her head to draw it tight around her neck. Much the same as leading a dog, he took her to the willows beside the river to let her perform her toilet.

The noose was now a standard practice, because the first time he took her, there was none. She had motioned for him to turn around, because she was shy. He decided to placate her, but when he turned around, she had tried to run away. She earned a severe beating for that little trick, plus the noose she now wore. When he took her to the willows on this night, she no longer had any modesty left in her. She didn't even bother to motion for him to turn around, knowing that he would refuse to.

Bloody Hand stood there, stoically watching his captive wife perform the most basic of bodily functions, his brooding face a reflection of his innermost thoughts. Although respected by the men of his village as a fearless and mighty warrior, he was never looked upon favorably by any of the women. He was aware that this was because of his hideous face, and his missing ear. When the opportunity came to buy himself a beautiful white woman, he did not hesitate to part with six good ponies to ensure that he would no longer be without a wife. He took solace in telling himself that she no longer fought him when he came to her because she was beginning to care for him.

"I'm not finished," she protested when he pulled on the rope, knowing he did not understand her words, but thinking he might understand her tone.

He, however, knew that she was merely stalling for time, so he jerked on the rope and commanded, "Come!" She blotted her bottom with the skirt of the long doeskin dress she now wore, her own dress and undergarments long ago destroyed. He led her back to Dark Moon's tipi and the living hell that was now her life.

Bret counted the money he had left in his saddlebags. There was still a substantial sum remaining from what he had withdrawn from the bank in Bozeman. He counted out twenty dollars and handed it to Myra, who seemed genuinely surprised. "What's this for?" she asked.

"I expect you might need a few new undergarments, and maybe some other personal things," he said. "Looks like this place might have something you can use." He nodded toward a store that claimed to have general merchandise.

"God bless you, Bret Hollister. You are the most thoughtful man I've ever met," Myra told him, beaming with the pleasant anticipation of shopping for underwear.

"Spend it wisely," Bret said, "because it'll be running out soon." He turned to face a grinning Coldiron.

"Most thoughtful man I've ever met," Coldiron echoed. "I reckon that just counts for women."

Bret smiled at his oversized friend. "I reckon I might go for a couple of shots of whiskey to cut some of that dust we've been breathing for the past couple of days."

Coldiron's grin extended almost to his ears. "I knew your heart was in the right place. Myra's right, you're a damn thoughtful man."

"Yeah, well, I said a *couple* of drinks. We've still got some riding to do today."

"Yes, sir, Lieutenant," Coldiron japed.

From where they stood in front of the Missouri Saloon, they could see the fourteen-foot adobe walls of the fort, and the blockhouses on the corners. The buildings looked in need of repair, from what they could see through the open gate. Bret could not help feeling a sense of injustice upon finding himself in close proximity to an army post, the first such occurrence since leaving Fort Ellis in disgrace. It reawakened the anger he held for the treatment he had received at the hands of his former commanding officers and peers, but only for a few moments before Coldiron broke into his thoughts.

"Somebody in the saloon oughta know where that Piegan camp is," he said, not willing to delay his drink of whiskey any longer.

"Right," Bret replied, and followed the big man into the saloon. As usual, the first appearance of the huge scout anywhere he went drew everyone's attention in the saloon. Coldiron went straight to the bar, where a sleepy-eyed bartender with a drooping mustache stood polishing a tray of shot glasses. Like everyone else in the saloon, Hank Lewis paused to gawk at the two strangers.

"Howdy, gents," he greeted them. "What'll it be?"

"You got some decent whiskey, somethin' that ain't kin to kerosene?" Coldiron asked.

Hank chuckled in response. "I reckon so. All my stock comes straight up the river from Bismark, and they get it from Omaha." He placed two of the recently polished glasses on the bar and poured. "Ain't seen you two fellers in here before," he remarked.

"Last time I was in Fort Benton this saloon weren't here," Coldiron said as he held the glass of whiskey up to let the light from the window shine through the amber liquid. "Clear as a mountain stream," he acclaimed, savoring the anticipation.

Then he tossed the shot back and paused to enjoy the burn, smacked his lips to express his approval, and set the glass back on the counter for a refill. Hank obliged.

Bret, as amused by Coldiron's sampling of the whiskey as the bartender, downed his shot of whiskey without the theatrics performed by his friend, and set his empty glass beside Coldiron's.

"I didn't know you were such an expert on whiskey," he said. "To tell you the truth, I figured you'd drink anything that wasn't used to remove paint."

"And you'd be right," Coldiron confessed. "But I ain't had a drink for quite a while, and I wanted to enjoy it. As quick as you knocked yours back, it was gone before you had a chance to let your belly know it was comin'. And since we're only gettin' two shots, you need to make 'em last longer'n just a quick fire in your gut." Practicing what he preached, he let his second drink sit there on the bar for a minute while he anticipated it.

Amused by the big man's show, Hank asked, "You fellers just passin' through town, or are you lookin' to sign on with the army as scouts?"

"Just passing through," Bret answered. "Maybe you can help us. We're looking for a village of Piegan Blackfeet that's supposed to be somewhere on the Marias River."

"The only one I know about was located about forty miles up the river, according to what a couple of trappers told me," Hank said. "That's about as close as they get to the army post here, and that's about as close as I want 'em."

"Much obliged," Bret said, satisfied to hear confirmation that they were camped on the Marias as they had been told by Jake Smart. "I guess we'll be on our way as soon as you get around to finishing that drink," he said to Coldiron.

"What's your hurry?" The question came from a trio of soldiers at the end of the long bar. "As long as you're buyin' drinks for that old buffalo, you might wanna buy a round for us soldiers, who are protectin' your ass from them Piegans." The one who spoke was a husky man, wearing corporal's stripes.

"Probably not," Bret answered simply, and turned his attention back to Coldiron. "How about it, are you gonna drink that drink? I expect Myra might be already waiting for us." The corporal had the look of a bully about him. Bret hoped he was wrong, but thought it best to avoid the possibility of further delay, just in case.

"Let's let it set for a minute," Coldiron replied softly. "And this old buffalo will drink it when he's good and ready."

"Well, whaddaya think of that, boys?" the corporal asked in a loud voice. "Soldiers ain't good enough for sorry drifters like that to have a drink with. Besides, Myra's waitin'. She must be their mama."

No such luck, Bret thought. The corporal was obviously intent upon causing a fight. He looked like a troublemaker, the type who enjoys a good barroom brawl. It would do little good to warn him that it would be a grave mistake to underestimate the huge scout by his gray whiskers and his long gray ponytail. He understood the corporal's motivation, however. He had been the biggest man in the saloon until Coldiron walked in, and being an obvious brawler, he felt moved to prove his worth. And there was not much chance that Coldiron would even consider backing down to the sneering corporal. Bret figured it worth a try, so he turned to face the corporal. "Why don't you just back off, soldier? We just came in here for a drink before we're on our way. We aren't looking for any trouble."

"Well, you've already stepped in it, sonny," the corporal shot back. "And the only way you're gonna get out of it is to get on your knees and crawl out that door."

Uh-oh, Coldiron thought as a grin spread under his heavy whiskers. *Bret don't like to be called sonny.*

"What the hell are you grinnin' at, old man?" the corporal asked as he moved down the bar to face them, his two companions walking close behind.

"You'll see," Coldiron said, still grinning.

Bret, fully irritated now, glanced at the bartender

and asked, "How much for that full bottle of whiskey?"

"Twelve dollars," Hank replied quickly, having seen the roll of bills earlier when Bret paid for the drinks.

"I'll take it," Bret said, and grabbed the bottle by the neck. If the last-minute transaction puzzled the corporal, he didn't show it, for he took a square stance confronting the two strangers. Bret took one deliberate step forward, bringing the full bottle of whiskey sharply up against the side of the corporal's head to land with a sickening thud. The surprised soldier's knees buckled under him and he dropped to the floor.

With no intention of missing out on the fun, Coldiron grabbed the soldier closest behind the fallen corporal, and lifting him in one powerful move, like a sack of grain, he threw him over the bar to land crashing against the wall. Seeing what had happened to his friends, the third soldier turned to run, once again a misjudgment of the big man's quickness. The chuckling monster caught him within three strides, grabbed him by his collar and the seat of his pants, and used his momentum to hurl him out the door, landing him in the street next to the horse trough. He wasted no time scrambling to his feet and heading toward the fort, passing an astonished Myra, who was standing by the horses.

"I guess we can go now," Bret said when

Coldiron came back to have his drink. He was still holding the bottle, which had not broken when it thudded against the side of the corporal's face. He held it up to make sure it was not cracked. "A damn expensive bottle of whiskey," he commented as he stepped aside to allow the soldier who scrambled out from behind the bar to run past him to the door.

"You can have it for six," Hank Lewis said, having enjoyed the altercation, even though some of his shelves behind the bar had been knocked down by the flying body.

"What about him?" Coldiron asked, nodding toward the body still not moving on the floor in front of the bar. "Want me to drag him outta here?"

"Murdock?" Hank replied. "No, just leave him there. He'll wake up directly and drag his ass back to the post. This'll give him a chance to see how the shoe fits on the other foot. It's usually him that leaves some poor feller on the floor. Maybe this'll take some of the orneriness out of him."

They said "so long" to Hank, promising to stop in again if they came back this way. "What in the world was going on in there?" Myra asked when the men returned to the horses. She looked from one of them to the other, questioning, as Coldiron tucked the bottle of whiskey inside one of the packs.

"Nothin' much," Coldiron answered her. "We

was just havin' a little drink with some soldiers. We even brought along a bottle, so you can have a little drink tonight with your supper."

"Well, you wasted your money if you bought it for me," she retorted. "I wouldn't drink the evil stuff."

"I know what you mean," Coldiron said, stepping up into the saddle. "It's nasty-tastin' stuff. I wish I had a barrel of it."

Bret gave her a boost up onto her horse. "Did you find anything you could use in that store?" he asked.

"I did. Thank you very much."

In the saddle again, they rode past the fort and the collection of buildings around it, to follow the river once more and look for its confluence with the Marias.

They reached the Marias early in the afternoon and stopped to rest the horses there before starting what they anticipated to be at least a forty-mile trip following that river. Since it was already too late to cover the entire distance that day, they only drove their horses for another few hours along the winding river before making camp for the night.

The spot they picked was at a sharp bend where the river almost doubled back on itself. It afforded them plenty of wood for a fire and grass for the horses. All three seemed to be tired that night, so when Myra produced flour for pan bread that she had bought with some of the money Bret had given her, it raised the spirits of them all.

Soon there was a good hot fire and pan bread baking in the skillet. Bret had to wonder at this point if all souls were still enthusiastic about the search for Lucy Gentry. It had been many days now, with no realistic reason to expect success in their search. Even if they finally found her, would it be too late to salvage the poor girl's sanity? These were troublesome thoughts, yet both Myra and Coldiron claimed there was no lessening of their determination to find the captured woman. As for Bret, he felt they had invested too much time and money in the search to turn back now that they were supposedly approaching the Piegan camp.

They were on their way again after a restful night of pan bread and smoked venison for supper, and a couple more drinks from the bottle Bret had used to get Corporal Murdock's attention. Spirits were high because they were closing in on the village where Lucy might be held. At the same time, their nerves were more than a little edgy because of the danger of being discovered. For the latter reason, Myra had put her foot down during the evening when the bottle was produced.

"I'm putting a limit on you two," she had informed them. "Two drinks each, and that's all for the night. I'll be damned if I'm gonna be left to defend myself from savage Indians while you two are lying around here drunk."

"The lady is surely talking sense," Bret had said, "so fine by me."

He had no intention of drinking more in the first place. The only reason he would participate at all was to make sure Coldiron didn't consume the whole bottle. As a result, all three set out on this morning with clear heads and alert brains.

The farther up the river they rode, the more signs they saw of tracks left by hunting parties, crossing trails made by people coming to and from the village. Finally they decided they were getting too close to continue riding in the open.

"Maybe we'd best find us a place to get outta sight till it gets a little closer to dark. That village can't be much farther. I'm gonna ride up that ridge over yonder, and take a look around."

"We'll ride around that point where the trees come down close to the river and pick a spot to rest the horses," Bret told him.

Coldiron untied the lead rope from his saddle and handed it to Bret, so he could take his pack-horse with him and Myra. Then he wheeled the buckskin and headed for the ridge at a lope. Bret and Myra continued on along the bank to the point where the snakelike river took another turn.

"That looks like a good spot," Bret said, pointing to an opening in the trees that came down close to the water. "We can build our fire there, and nobody could see it unless they were on the other side of the river, and that's pretty rough-looking rock on that bank."

By the time Coldiron returned from his scouting, Bret had unburdened the packhorses and unsaddled his and Myra's horses, while she was in the process of starting the fire.

"There's tracks all over that valley between here and the ridge," Coldiron reported. "I didn't see no sign of anybody, but I'm willin' to bet that their village is right ahead of us. From the top of that ridge, I could see a ring of hills, makin' a half circle next to the river. There's more'n likely open range inside the hills—perfect place to make a camp."

"Then I expect we'd better go have a look after it gets a little darker," Bret said. "That's gonna be a while yet, so we might as well fix something to eat while we've got the chance."

"If we see Lucy, how are we going to get her?" Myra asked. "Like you did me? I was tied outside a tipi. She might not be somewhere that'll be easy to get to her from."

"I don't know," Bret answered her. "We'll just have to wait and see what we find."

He didn't voice it, but he had his own doubts about the likelihood of successfully stealing the woman back. He felt the urgency of rescuing Lucy Gentry, but also the responsibility to ensure the safety of all of them. He could not forget that he had Myra to concern himself with. He had come to admire her willing spirit to persevere, no matter what the circumstances or conditions. But he would never forgive himself if he caused anything to happen to her.

When the sun dropped below the chalky cliffs on the other side of the river, they put out their fire and packed up the camp. In the silvery twilight, they set out once again, moving at a casual pace, so as to give the evening a chance to settle in. They approached the southern end of the ring of hills as darkness began to soften the edges of the rocks and ridges. Coldiron was a little puzzled as they guided their horses to climb up the slope of the hill.

"It's plenty dark enough now. We oughta see a little campfire glow in the sky from a village that size. Maybe I ain't so smart as I thought."

At the top of the hill, they stopped to look down in the valley below them. There was no village, nothing but a darkened prairie floor. Coldiron prodded the buckskin and started down the slope to the grassy meadow at the foot of the hills. His vindication came at the bottom when they reached the huge clearing and discovered rings where tipis had once stood and the remains of many campfires.

"Well, you were right," Bret said. "They were camped here, and quite a while from the looks of it."

"They ain't been gone long," Coldiron said, now on one knee brushing his hand back and forth over the grass. "This grass has been grazed down—ain't started to grow again."

He then went over to the ashes of a large fire in the middle of the circle of tipi impressions in the grass. Digging his hands in the ashes, he said, "Down a few inches, these ashes are still warm. They ain't been gone from here more'n a day or two. If we move fast, we oughta be able to catch up with 'em, as slow as a village moves."

"You need daylight to be able to see their tracks," Bret said.

"That'd help, right enough," Coldiron replied. "But a whole village leaves a helluva big track, even across grass, so we oughta be able to see enough to make sure which direction they're headin', and start after 'em right now. Common sense oughta tell us that they're most likely gonna follow the river. They ain't gonna be lookin' to set up their village away from the water. I just need to see which direction they headed."

Bret didn't comment for a moment, during which he exchanged questioning glances with Myra. "Well, common sense also oughta tell us that they headed north," he said. "If they had headed south, we would have run smack into them."

Coldiron hesitated, taking a long pause while he thought about it, then responded, "Well, yeah, there's that, too, come to think of it. That was what I was gonna point out next."

"So I guess we'd best get started north," Bret said, his grin unnoticed in the dark. "Are you up to it, Myra?"

"Hell yes," she replied at once, feeling a new sense of excitement, when it seemed they were drawing closer to Lucy. She pointed to a quarter moon climbing over the ridge behind them. "That'll help."

Back in the saddle, they started toward the hills in the northern end of the valley. As Myra suggested, the light from the moon was enough to allow them safe footing for their horses. They continued along the Marias until they had to stop to rest the horses, at which point they decided to camp until morning.

A little before noon on the next day, they spotted the camp stragglers in the distance ahead of them. Their first reaction was to hold up and hang back to keep the Indians from discovering them.

"Well, looks like we caught 'em," Coldiron said. "Ain't much we can do now but follow along behind 'em till they stop somewhere to rest."

"I'd like to get around in front of them," Bret said. "That way, we can find a place to watch them when they get on the move again, and we'd have a better chance of spotting Lucy Gentry as they're passing by us."

"I like that idea," Myra said.

Coldiron agreed. "This line of ridges beside the river will give us plenty of cover to get around 'em. Probably best to wait till they stop to rest and eat. Then we'd have plenty of time to ride up in front of 'em, find us a good spot, and rest our horses while we wait for them to get on the move again. If we're lucky, maybe they ain't already stopped this mornin'."

So they continued to trail along behind the Piegan camp for another hour before they realized the stragglers were catching up with the rest of the village. "I think they're stopping," Bret said.

"I think you're right," Coldiron agreed and immediately turned his horse toward a narrow ravine that split the ridge to the east of them.

Once through the ravine, they turned back to ride a parallel course to that of the Indian camp, with the ridge between them and the Blackfeet. Pushing their horses into a comfortable lope, they continued at that pace for half an hour before stopping to check their progress. Bret and Coldiron rode partway up the hill, then dismounted and crept carefully up to the top. Lying on their bellies, they looked down on the river valley to discover the forward part of the village directly below them. "We didn't ride quite far enough, did we?" Coldiron whispered. "We're damn lucky they don't see no use to have scouts ridin' out to the side and in front."

"I don't reckon they think they've got any reason to worry about anybody bothering them," Bret replied. "They're stopping, all right," he said when some of the boys circled around to turn the herd of several hundred ponies back to the river. "Maybe they're going to settle here for a while."

"I don't think so," Coldiron said. "There ain't enough grass here to feed a herd that size for more'n a week. They'll be on the move again after they rest a bit. We'll find us a place up ahead where we can watch 'em good when they go by." They remained where they were for another half hour while the Piegans built cook fires and prepared food. Both men strained hard to see every woman they could, but they could see no sign of a captive white woman. It was discouraging, but they had to give up and make sure they found a good place to watch the Piegan procession when the camp got started again. "We'll have a better chance of spottin' that woman when they're all walking by us," Coldiron said.

They pushed back from the top of the hill and returned to their horses. "Did you see her?" Myra asked when they rode down to rejoin her.

"No," Bret answered, "but it was pretty hard to tell from that ridge. We'll see if we can't get a better look when they get on the move again."

The path the village would take was fairly easy to determine, since there was obviously only one good choice. So they rode along the ridge for about half a mile before selecting a likely spot. The ridge was barren of trees of any kind, so the place they picked was a ravine with large rocks on each side. Making sure the back of the ravine was open, in case they had to make a hasty exit, they tied the horses to some scrubby bushes that had defied nature by growing up between the rocks. Once the horses were safely secured, they climbed up to the top of the ravine and picked their spots to wait for the Piegans. They waited more than an hour before the advance guard came into sight.

"Here they come," Coldiron announced as a column of warriors, two abreast, walked their horses along the river valley.

It was a better position from which to watch, than the hilltop Bret and Coldiron had scouted them from before, but it was still difficult to determine whether or not Lucy Gentry was among them. Myra strained to scan back and forth along the long line of women and children following behind the warriors, searching for the blue cotton dress Lucy wore when they were captured. But there was no sign of it. *She's not here,* she thought in despair. And then she saw one of the women, a slight, younger woman, trip and almost stumble. An older woman walking beside her immediately gave her a couple of swipes with a switch she was carrying. Myra stared harder at the young woman. *It's Lucy!* She had to catch herself to keep from blurting it aloud.

"I see her," she whispered. "She's wearing an Indian dress."

"Where?" Bret whispered back.

He was intent upon getting a good look at her, as was Coldiron. Even though she was white, she might be hard to identify in the dark of night, when their best chance of rescue was likely to be. He studied her features as best he could at that distance.

They remained where they were until the herd of horses was brought up behind the village. "Well, we're back to followin' 'em till they make camp," Coldiron said. "Then we're gonna have to see where they put her for the night."

The village traveled late that night, later than the nights before, until they reached a point where the Marias changed its course and turned sharply to the west through a wide expanse of grassy prairie. When the three searchers were able to move up close enough after dark to see into the camp, it appeared that the Indians were preparing to stay longer than overnight. After watching for a few minutes, Coldiron said, "They're fixin' to stay here. This must be the place they were movin' to." He took another look at the camp. "Yes, sir, that's what they're doin'. They got plenty of grass and water for their horses, and wood for their fires in the trees at the foot of the hill."

"And we're sitting here with two hundred yards of open grass between us and their camp," Bret pointed out. He took another few moments to consider the situation. "We need to be on the other side of the river."

"That's what I was thinkin'," Coldiron said.

The other bank was thick with willow trees and berry bushes. If there was any hope of working their way in close enough to be able to see what was going on, it would have to be under the cover of those willows.

Chapter 9

Bloody Hand sat by the fire, absentmindedly eating a piece of pemmican while gazing at the white woman sitting on the other side, her chin dropped almost to her breast. It was a position she always assumed whenever he was near her, and one that frustrated him sorely. A few feet from her, Dark Moon sat, a perpetual frown upon her face that had been there ever since her son brought the white woman home.

"Eat!" she demanded, and poked the young woman with a stick she used for a walking staff.

"Leave her alone, old woman," Bloody Hand said. Then speaking directly to Lucy, he said, "You should be proud to be the woman of Bloody Hand. No other warrior is respected more than I.

You must forget the white people. You are now a Piegan, and you are now my wife."

His words only served to increase his frustration, because he knew that she did not understand them. Sometimes he became so angry with her reluctance to be with him that he thought about killing her, but the hunger he felt for her would not let him take her life. Still she sat there, her head down, refusing to look up at him, until he spat out in anger, "Where is Lame Dog?" His verbal eruption caused the girl to jump, but she quickly resumed her position of silent protest.

"He's eating with Two Baskets and Iron Pony," Dark Moon answered him, making no attempt to hide her disgust for her son's weakness for the white woman. "He does not waste his time eating with white women." She knew why her son was asking for Lame Dog. The half-breed could talk white man talk, so he could tell the woman in her tongue what Bloody Hand wanted to say to her.

"Did you call my name?" Lame Dog walked up to Dark Moon's fire, having heard Bloody Hand's outburst.

"Come make the white man talk with this coyote bitch," Bloody Hand said.

"What do you want me to tell her?"

"Tell her I own her," Bloody Hand replied, his frustration creeping into his tone again. "Tell her I gave eight fine ponies for her, so I expect her to be a good wife. Tell her it is an honor to be the wife of Bloody Hand."

Lame Dog smirked, delighted to talk to the woman, and amused to see the frustration in one he wanted to call friend. Bloody Hand was a mighty warrior and, as he claimed, demanded much respect in the Piegan village. Lame Dog was accepted in the Piegan camp, but he had no status since he was not of pure blood.

"I will tell her," he said, but he couldn't resist correcting him. "You might have forgotten, but you only gave six ponies for the woman. Do you want me to tell her six or eight?"

"Tell her what I told you to say," Bloody Hand shot back with a flash of anger.

"All right," Lame Dog said, and turned to Lucy. "You make big mistake if you don't please Bloody Hand. You his wife now. He bought you, so he owns you. You don't act better pretty damn quick, you'll be dead."

Without lifting her head to look at him, she said, "I'm not his wife. I'm a married woman. I'm married to Carlton Gentry, so I can't be married to him."

"I'll tell him, but he ain't gonna like it. Your white husband's dead carcass is lyin' on the bank of the Yellowstone, rotting in the sun with no scalp. If you don't be good, Bloody Hand will take your scalp, too. You'd be better off if you just spread them pretty white legs and enjoy the ride."

He grinned wickedly when she recoiled with revulsion. He told Bloody Hand what she had said then, enjoyed the reactions of both parties. Adding to his entertainment, he glanced over to see the look of contempt on Dark Moon's face.

"Tell her I will kill her," Bloody Hand said. "Then maybe she can go join her white husband."

Lame Dog nodded and turned back to Lucy. "Bloody Hand says he'll kill you."

"So be it," Lucy replied. "I might as well be dead as live with that monster."

Lame Dog leered at her for a few moments while he decided whether or not to tell her what he had learned at his father's trading post. He decided it would drive her deeper into despair, so out he came with it.

"You know that other white woman who got captured with you? She got away. Some white men got her back. They came to the mouth of the Smith River, at the tradin' post, lookin' for you, but they don't know a Piegan's got you now. So they don't know where to look for you." He was at once gratified by her reaction, as she recoiled with the discouraging news. "You're never goin' back to your white folks. You're Bloody Hand's wife now." Turning back to Bloody Hand, he said, "I told her. I think she's thinking about killing herself."

Concerned at first that she might do as she claimed, Bloody Hand looked intently at the frail young woman for a few moments, then decided that she would not have the determination do it. He turned to his mother and told her to watch the white woman closely whenever she was not tied securely, however. "It would be better for you if she did kill herself," Dark Moon told him. "She is making you crazy. I will kill her for you and then you will soon forget this craziness for her."

His scarred face grew hot with anger. "Do not harm her, or I will beat you. I will take her to my bed tonight, so take her to the river and wash her. She stinks of sweat."

Many of the Piegan women went to the river to wash away the dust and sweat of a long day's travel. They went about fifty yards upstream where a thick stand of willows offered a screen from the eyes of the village. Several of the young girls were bathing together. One of them whispered to the others when she saw Dark Moon leading the white girl by a rope tied around her neck.

"Here comes Dark Moon with Bloody Hand's new wife." Her comment brought forth a titter of giggles from her friends.

"Bloody Hand has to go raid the white farms to find a wife," one of the girls remarked. "I hope she is strong enough to mate with a horse," another said.

"Shhh," the first who spoke warned, "or Dark Moon will hear you."

They feared the old woman as much as Bloody Hand. It was common knowledge among the people of Bloody Hand's village that the fearsome warrior's hideous facial features prevented his being considered a candidate for marriage, especially the ominous hole on one side of his head where his ear once resided.

Dark Moon was getting on in years, but her hearing was still sharp enough to hear the rude remarks from the young girls. She chose not to lash out at them with her stick, choosing instead to move farther upstream away from them. She pulled the doeskin dress over Lucy's head, then replaced the rope noose around her neck. She led her into the river and forcefully threw her down in the dark shallow water close to the bank.

"Wash!" she ordered when the startled girl came up sputtering for breath. "Wash!" Dark Moon demanded impatiently when it was obvious that Lucy did not understand what the old woman was screaming at her. "Maybe if I hold you under till you can't breathe, then you'll understand." As much as the thought appealed to her, she knew she had to control her urges. As patiently as she could, she made motions of washing herself, then pointed to Lucy. "You do!"

Lucy understood, and began rubbing her arms and torso with water. "There's no soap," she said, which resulted in a sharp tug on the rope, almost pulling her down. She had started to resume the motions when she was startled by a dark shadow on the bank behind the old woman. It rose out of the thick bushes until it loomed huge and ominous. Lucy froze, thinking it to be a demon rising out of the earth. Dark Moon was puzzled by the young woman's apparent refusal to do as she was told and started to scold her.

But in the next instant, she was snatched up with one massive arm locking her arms to her sides and a giant hand clamped over her mouth, throttling her impulse to scream. While Lucy stood staring in shock, the helpless Piegan woman was lifted out of the water and the huge dark form carried her helpless body back into the willows. Terrified, Lucy was unable to move.

"Lucy Gentry?" She heard the whispered question.

Bret waded out and extended his hand to help her out of the water. He quickly grabbed her with both hands when her knees suddenly failed her and she started to collapse.

"We've come to save you," Bret whispered. "You're all right now. Myra is with us. She's waiting to take care of you." Still finding it hard to believe, she managed to regain her composure a little, even while unsure she was not dreaming. "We need to move quickly," Bret encouraged as he helped her to the riverbank. Then he picked up the doeskin dress that Dark Moon had dropped on the ground. "Here, put this on. Let me take that

rope off your neck. I need it for something else."
Then he held the dress up while she inserted her
arms and let it fall over her shoulders. "Are you all
right now?" he asked when she appeared to be
stable.

She nodded rapidly, only then beginning to
realize that it was no dream.

"Can you walk?"

"Yes," she answered, and followed him into the
willow trees, where they found Coldiron waiting,
holding the squirming bundle that was Dark
Moon.

"Like tryin' to hold on to a coyote," Coldiron
said. "Pull that piece of cloth out of her belt and
tie it around her mouth so I can use this hand."

He paused then just long enough to say,
"Howdy, Mrs. Gentry." Then turning his attention
back to the wildcat he was struggling to restrain,
he waited while Bret firmly gagged her; then he
asked, "You get the rope?" Bret said that he did.
Holding her arms pinned to her side, Coldiron put
her facedown on the ground so Bret could pull her
hands behind her and tie them together.

When she was securely bound and gagged,
Coldiron said, "Come on, darlin'," picked her up,
and backed her up against a willow tree. "Use all
that rope you got left to tie her to the tree, and
make sure you don't leave the knot where she can
get to it."

When he was sure that the irate Indian woman

could not free herself from the tree, Bret stood back and said, "Take a look. Does that satisfy you?"

"Yep," Coldiron replied. "I reckon she'll stay here a while."

They paused to listen for any sound of alarm from the Piegan camp. There was nothing but the occasional lilt of the young maidens bathing a short distance downstream. He turned and started back the way they had come through the willows.

Standing dazed and dreamlike during the short time it took to truss Dark Moon to the willow tree, Lucy feared that Bloody Hand would somehow realize what was taking place, and would come down upon them before she was safely away. And she wasn't sure she could survive if recaptured. She jumped, startled, when she felt a hand on her shoulder, but relaxed when she heard Bret's gentle voice.

"Follow him, miss. I'll be right behind you, and we'll be away from here in just a few minutes."

Myra rushed past Coldiron to embrace Lucy when they returned to the small clearing where she waited with the horses. Bret allowed only a few moments for the reunion of the two women, but it was long enough for both women to sob in relief.

"I don't reckon I have to tell you that we've got to get the hell out of here," he said. "You can have your time to talk after we put some distance between us and those Indians. Can you ride?" he asked Lucy.

Myra answered before Lucy had a chance to. "She can ride. Put her on that horse and let's get going."

Coldiron was ready to do her bidding. He lifted Lucy and placed her on the black Indian pony, and in a matter of seconds they were galloping off into the darkness.

Fully aware that their six horses were not going to be hard to track if they continued to follow the river, they reined them back after about three-quarters of a mile, knowing they would wear them out if they maintained that pace for very long. There was also the fear of breaking a leg in the dark over such rough ground.

Continuing at a fast walk, Coldiron led and watched for a likely place to cross the river. He was more interested in the other side of the river than the side they now rode on. The spot he settled on was a wide place where the water flowed around an island in the middle. He held up and waited for everyone to catch up to him.

"We're gonna cross over right here. I want ever'body to follow me in single file, all right?" He waited until all three agreed, then looked at Myra, remembering her last river crossing. "The water ain't deep enough to reach your knees this time of year. So ever'body follow me, right behind me, 'specially when we cross over that little island." Assured that everyone understood, he guided his buckskin into the water. Bret held back to let Myra and Lucy go ahead of him, then followed.

Angling across to the island, Coldiron continued on the same course when he reached it, cutting across the little island at an angle also, generally leading in the same direction as when they were following the river. He looked back once to make sure everyone was on his line of travel. When Bret's packhorse was in the water, having just left the island, Coldiron reined his horse back again, remaining in the water.

"Here's where I hope we can slow 'em down a little," he explained. "We'll keep the horses in the water and head back downstream a ways before we come out onto the bank."

Bret understood why his big friend was so particular about following him exactly. By crossing the island at an angle, he hoped to give the impression that they were still running in the same direction as they were before entering the water. With everyone now in the water, they reversed their course and went back downstream for almost a quarter of a mile before reaching the place that Coldiron had spotted before. It was an expanse of chalky rock and gravel that the river swirled around. He nudged his horse and the big buckskin climbed out onto the rock. Then he waited while the rest of the party left the water.

"It might take 'em a while to find where we went into the water," he said. "I'm hopin' they waste some time lookin' north to find where we came out, before they give up and figure we doubled back on 'em." He pointed to the south. "We're headin' thataway, and there's grass once we get offa this rock, so spread out, 'cause ridin' single file will leave too heavy a track through that grass."

After Myra checked to make sure Lucy was all right, they left the banks of the Marias and set out for Fort Benton, which Coldiron estimated to be no more that thirty-five or forty miles. He didn't figure that a Piegan war party would risk following them there. They rode what he figured to be about half that distance when it became obvious that the horses were getting too tired to go much farther without rest and water.

"We're not gonna stand much of a chance if they figure out which way we went and we're trying to ride dead horses," Bret said. "So like it or not, we've got to rest these horses."

"I can't argue with that," Coldiron said. "Let's push 'em a little bit farther to see if there ain't some kind of water ahead. How you women holdin' up?"

"We're all right," Myra said after checking with Lucy. "Let's see if we can't find some water."

"All right," Bret said. "We'll push 'em a couple

more miles, but after that, we'd better dismount and walk ourselves." He wasn't sure if they were being trailed or not. Maybe they weren't good enough trackers to pick up their trail at night. But if they were, he didn't want to risk having horses too tired to run. So they pushed on for a mile or two farther before coming to a stream, barely more than a trickle, but enough to let the horses drink. They made their camp there.

Having waited for what he considered much too long for Lucy to have a bath, a thoroughly irritated Bloody Hand left his campfire and went in search of the two women. At the edge of the river, he met a group of younger women and girls on their way back to the camp. As usual, when he approached, they ceased their lighthearted chattering and became stony silent.

"Have you seen Dark Moon?" he asked.

"She went upstream, beyond where we were bathing," one of the girls answered.

"We did not see her again," another said.

Angry now, Bloody Hand walked past the girls without another word, intent upon scolding his mother when he found her. She knew he awaited his captive bride, and it made him furious when she tried to keep him away from her.

It was too dark along the river now to see very far ahead of him, but he kept walking, nearing a thick growth of willows. *She must have gone back to the camp a different way,* he thought, and that brought even more anger. He had turned around to go back when he heard a muffled sound he could not identify. It seemed to be coming from the willows. *An owl? Some other night bird?* He could not say, but his curiosity was piqued enough to try to find out.

When he reached the edge of the willow thicket, he discovered many broken branches as if a large animal had pushed through. Without consciously thinking about it, he dropped his hand down on the handle of his knife, and he became more alert. Making his way cautiously through the trees, he followed the trail of broken branches. Suddenly he heard the muffled sounds he had heard before, this time right in front of him. He took a cautious step back while he stared at the struggling figure only a few feet before him. In another few seconds, his eyes adjusted to the heavier darkness in the thicket, and he was astounded to discover Dark Moon tied to a tree.

As fast as he could, he untied the cloth in his mother's mouth to release her screeching protests upon his ears. She was almost insane with anger, screaming that she was attacked and no one would come to her aid.

"Where is the woman?" he demanded, ignoring her protests.

"Gone!" she screamed as she flung the ends of the rope from her as he untied them.

Impatient with her hysteria, he grabbed her by the shoulders and shook her violently. "What do you mean, gone?" he demanded. "Gone where? How did she tie you up like this?"

Calmed enough to answer his questions now, she railed at him. "They took her! They tied me up and took that bitch!"

"Who?" he asked in anger, and shook her again.

"Two white men," she finally told him, "one as big as a grizzly. They crept in while I was washing her and grabbed me from behind. There was nothing I could do to stop them."

Bloody Hand was stunned for a few moments, unable to believe what he was hearing. Then he was overcome with anger.

"Two white men walked right into our camp and stole her?" Suspicious then, for he knew his mother would go to any lengths to get rid of the white woman she hated. "That is not possible," he charged. "Someone would have seen them."

"I saw them," Dark Moon exclaimed. "I told you."

"Maybe you let her run away."

"Can you not see?" she screamed at him. "They tied me to a tree!"

Still harboring suspicion, he countered, "Maybe you let her go and told her to tie you to the tree."

Now it was she who could not believe her ears.

"Your desire for that white bitch has made you crazy. Two white men took her," she stated emphatically.

"Which way?" he asked, reminding himself that he was wasting time. He must go after her at once. She pointed upstream. Not bothering to wait for his mother, he ran back to the camp and called out to everyone sitting around their campfires. "Hear me! Our camp has been attacked!" He had everyone's attention immediately, and every warrior grabbed his weapons and prepared to defend the village.

"Who is attacking us?" White Hawk asked, since there were no shots or arrows flying.

Bloody Hand explained, "Two white men came into our camp, tied Dark Moon to a tree, and stole the white woman I have taken for my wife. We must go after them and bring her back." He was not totally convinced that Dark Moon's version of the kidnapping was true, but he decided to act upon it as if it were.

The warriors were gathered around their chief, White Hawk, now, but instead of the immediate outcry to take to their ponies and give chase, there was a rumbling of indecisive reactions. Seeing that, White Hawk spoke.

"I think it will be hard to track these two white men in the dark. Maybe we will have to wait until morning, when we can see."

Another man, the highly respected warrior Walks

Silently, spoke. "It seems to me that we have not been attacked by these white men. It appears that they came only to take the white woman back. And I would say to Bloody Hand that he and the village are well rid of her, for she clearly had no desire to remain here. I say let the woman go back to the people she belongs with."

His statement was representative of the feeling that most of the village held for Bloody Hand and the white woman. As far as they could see, she was a constant hazard to them if army or militia patrols came searching for her. Several more warriors spoke, encouraged by Walks Silently's statement. They were all in favor of letting the white woman go.

"By morning, when we can see to track them," White Hawk asked, "what if we still don't see their trail? We cannot look for them if we don't know who they are."

"I know who they are," Lame Dog said. "It is the army scout Coldiron and another man. I saw them at the trading post where my mother, Red Bonnet, lives. She told me that they have come here to find the white woman."

"Coldiron!" Bloody Hand exclaimed in disgust. "See! The hated fighter of my people has dared to come into a Piegan camp and steal a woman. I will find this man and kill him, and take back what is mine! Who will ride with me?"

"I will!" Lame Dog cried out at once. "I will

ride with Bloody Hand." He stepped forward and stood beside him.

No one else stepped forward. After a few tense moments of silence with Bloody Hand's grotesque features twisted in an angry grimace, White Hawk spoke again. "It is the feeling of your brothers that this is not a wise thing for you to do. Why not let the woman go back to her people? We are not at war with the soldiers now. It would not be a good thing for us to give them cause to fight us."

Bloody Hand was furious, feeling betrayed by his own people. "I, Bloody Hand, do not fear the white soldiers. You can sit around your campfires, stuffing your bellies. I will find these white men who stole from me, and I will kill them." He turned and stalked angrily to his horse.

"I go with Bloody Hand," Lame Dog stated, and followed the irate Piegan.

Although disgusted with her son's infatuation with the white woman, Dark Moon would not shirk her responsibility as the woman in his lodge. She prepared a sack of venison jerky and pemmican cakes for his sustenance, even including enough for Lame Dog, since the half-breed had no woman of his own. She tried to persuade him to wait until morning to set out after the woman, but he refused to remain in the camp with those who had betrayed him.

When their arms and provisions were ready,

Bloody Hand and Lame Dog went to the stand of willows by the river, hoping to pick up a trail in the darkness. It was easy to follow the rescuers through the willow thicket, because of the broken branches. Once they left the willows, however, it became a more challenging task. Finding only an occasional track here and there, they could guess that the white men had followed the river north. They continued until they could not find a single track, and were forced to conclude that their prey had crossed the river at some point, and they had missed it. With great reluctance, Bloody Hand finally succumbed to the dark, and decided he had no choice other than to wait for daylight. They made their camp right where they were.

"At first light, we will find their tracks," Bloody Hand vowed. "I will not stop until I have both of their scalps, and the woman is mine again."

Lame Dog, seeing this as a golden opportunity to curry favor with the fierce warrior, and possibly win his friendship as well, was quick to encourage him.

"These two white dogs have six horses. I saw them in Jake Smart's corral—and guns, they have guns that shoot many times, like my rifle. When we get your woman back, we will also get their guns and horses."

"That is a good thing," Bloody Hand agreed, thinking of his triumphant return to his village with the white woman and the spoils, including the scalps. Although he had never seen him, he had heard of Coldiron, and the warrior who took his scalp would be highly respected.

Chapter 10

Roughly twenty miles from the spot where Bloody Hand and Lame Dog had made their camp, the four people they were chasing sat around a small campfire. Alert to the night sounds, Bret and Coldiron remained in a state of cautious readiness while Myra and Lucy talked of the young woman's drawn-out ordeal at the hands of her captors.

"Who are these two men who risked their lives to save us?" Lucy asked. Myra told her about the unlikely happenings that caused Bret and Coldiron to decide to rescue them on their own, when the army apparently didn't care enough to pursue the issue.

"Who are they?" Myra echoed. "They're two by-God angels. That's who they are."

"What are we going to do?" Lucy asked. It was something she was wondering about, now that there was a chance there was a future in store for her, and her life might not end in an Indian camp. "Where are they taking us? I don't know what to do without Carlton." Thinking of her late husband, she started to cry softly.

Myra put her arm around her and pulled her close. "I think they'll take us wherever we want to go."

Lucy struggled to keep from sobbing. "I don't know where I want to go. I don't have a place to go. The only family I have left are my aunt and some cousins back in Missouri, and Carlton's folks. I can't go back there after what's happened to me."

Myra understood her young friend's despair. Lucy had not spoken of it, and Myra would not ask her, but she could imagine the abuse and violation that Lucy had suffered at the hands of the savage Bloody Hand. Lucy's mind might never heal, but if it did, it would surely take a long, long time. There were healing scars on her face and arms that spoke of the abuse she had endured. They would heal rapidly. It was the serious scarring, deep inside the girl's mind and body, that would take its toll.

"Honey," Myra told her, "you've got your ol' aunt Myra. You're not alone. Hell, I don't have any family to go back to, either. We'll just start over, you and me."

"What would we do to support ourselves?" Lucy asked. "Carlton was a farmer. I don't know much about raising crops. I don't own a thing to my name, but this ol' animal skin dress—not even a brush or comb."

"I don't know," Myra said. "We'll get somewhere

safe and then think about it. We'll find something. You just rest now. You look like you need to build up your strength, so I'm taking it as my responsibility to fatten you up a little. Why, when we get back to civilization, there ain't nothing that can stop two determined women like you and me."

She was not a great deal more confident about her abilities than her younger friend, but she would never admit it. Her greatest attribute was the belief that, like a cat, she would always land on her feet, no matter how far she was thrown. And this time, she was determined to put Lucy back on her feet as well.

And so it came to be that four souls set out the following morning, after a night that brought no attack by Piegan warriors, with no clear destination beyond Fort Benton, and no notion what they would do once they arrived. Still, they rode with a confident air, for they were within short miles of Fort Benton and the military stationed there. The abduction of the two women, which was the flashpoint that had started this ill-conceived adventure, had been successfully crushed, and the women rescued. This was as far into the future as Bret had planned. His years of education and military training had all gone for naught with his dismissal from the army. As he rode his paint Indian pony toward the Missouri River once again, he tried to turn his options over in his mind.

The only occupation that continued to come up as the most likely was to re-enlist in the army as a private, and he was determined not to do that.

Perhaps the only member of the rescue party with a firm idea of where he was heading was the big scout, Nate Coldiron, for he had seen the writing on the wall. He had always been a free and independent man. His skills in the wild were such that he needed no one to rely on for food or clothing. Things beyond those basics, like guns and ammunition, he could always trade animal hides for. Frequent agreements to scout for the army brought him the money he needed for his amusement.

But now Coldiron saw the end of his existence as a free soul getting closer every day. He had accumulated too many years. His life path was supposed to have ended a decade ago, before his eyesight began to deteriorate, and his hearing began to fade—and the onset of the trembling of his finger on the trigger.

Well, I might have one foot in the grave, he thought, *but it's gonna take a hell of a lot more to pull the other one in.*

Morning brought the light that Bloody Hand needed to follow the trail left by the six horses, and he was on it as soon as the predawn light found its way into the Marias River Valley. Retracing their steps of the night before, they confirmed their findings of that search in the dark. After careful study of the tracks, they found the spot where the white men had crossed the river, still heading north according to the tracks across the small island in the middle of the river.

"Yi!" Bloody Hand yelped in anger when there were no tracks leading out of the water on the other side. "They stayed in the water, hoping to lose us. A trick a child might use. Come!"

He kicked his horse firmly and the spotted gray war pony charged up out of the water to the bank.

"They had to come out somewhere."

Lame Dog followed him and they studied the riverbank carefully as they continued in a northerly direction.

After riding over half a mile, Lame Dog complained, "They must not have stayed in the water this long. I think they tried to trick us. I think they crossed back over the river again."

This seemed a possibility to Bloody Hand, so they crossed back to the other side, but they found no tracks on that side, either.

Almost at the same time, both men realized how easily they had been fooled. They crossed over for a third time and raced back to the spot where the little island showed the last tracks. From that point on, they traced the riverbank in the opposite direction until coming to the rocky outcropping, a likely place to leave the river if trying to conceal their tracks. Careful examination of the chalky rock revealed faint scarring by the iron shoes of the two packhorses. The trail through the grass beyond the rock was faint, but it was there, so they knew now that their prey was heading for Fort Benton. And it was likely that, with the head start the party had, the two hunters would not catch them before reaching that settlement. That fact seemed to be no deterrent to Bloody Hand. His obsession pushed him on in spite of the small chance of overtaking them before they reached the fort.

"I think maybe they are too far ahead of us," Lame Dog suggested to his fearsome companion.

"They will never be too far," Bloody Hand replied heatedly. "I will follow these two white men until I have them under my knife. Then I will kill the woman, too, for she is no longer worthy to be the wife of Bloody Hand. And as long as she lives, she brings shame to my tipi."

As the vengeance-crazed savage held doggedly to the trail across a rolling prairie, broken by ragged ridges and barren mesas, the four people he stalked were even then no more than a mile or two from Fort Benton. Making their way through a line of rocky hills, they had come down to the Teton River, which paralleled the mighty Missouri just north of the fort.

With no sense of alarm now, they paused to water the horses. They were grateful to find a few trees along the banks, after having traveled through a long stretch that had none. Since nothing had been discussed about what their plans were when they reached Fort Benton, Myra suggested that this might be a good time to do so.

"I don't know about the rest of you," she said, "but I could use a little coffee while we're spelling the horses."

Coldiron couldn't resist japing her, now that they were out of danger of being overtaken by a war party. "You mean, right now, before we cross this river?"

Accustomed by now to his tendency to tease when the situation was not dire, she responded in kind. "I can walk across this one and help an old man like you while I'm about it."

The river was shallow with gravel along the banks and apparently no deep holes in the moderately running current. There was nothing to concern her.

"I'm gonna build a fire and make some coffee, so if you want some of it, you'd best watch your mouth." Her sassy comment brought a chuckle from the big scout. She turned then to Bret. "If you don't mind, I think Lucy and I would like to talk over just what's gonna happen to us, now that we've reached Fort Benton and we're no longer in danger."

"Maybe you're right," Bret replied. "I guess it is time to make some plans for you and Lucy—hell, for all of us. And I suspect you're right about the Indians. You think so, Nate?"

"I reckon," Coldiron answered. "We had a good head start on 'em, and they'd be crazy to come in this close to Fort Benton."

Myra built her fire, and coffee was soon on to boil. However, the making of plans was not a simple matter, for in truth, no one knew what to do. There had really been no time to talk about it during their escape from the Piegan village.

"I reckon I could try to see you two ladies through to wherever you wanna go," Bret finally offered. "From the start of this thing, I guess I figured I'd be taking you back to Fort Ellis, or Benson's Landing on the Yellowstone, since that was where they captured you. I have to confess that part of the reason I was gonna take you back to Fort Ellis was to prove they were wrong to court-martial me. But the more I think about it, the more I don't care whether they know or not. Somehow I've kinda lost my interest in being reinstated in the army. And you've both been saying there's nothing and nobody to go back there to, so it wouldn't be right to drop you off at Benson's Landing and leave you without anything. I guess you're gonna have to decide what you're gonna do and where you want to go."

"What about you?" Coldiron asked him. "If you ain't wantin' to go back to bein' an officer in the army, what are you gonna do?"

Bret shook his head helplessly. "Damned if I know. After we take care of the ladies, I don't know where I'm heading." He could readily see the signs of despair in Lucy's face, so he said, "I plan to take the little bit of money I've got with me and spend it on some clothes for you women. You can't go anywhere dressed like that." Lucy looked relieved immediately, even though new clothes wouldn't solve her bigger dilemma.

Myra gave him a great big smile and said, "Damn, I'm gonna miss you."

Coldiron sipped his coffee and studied the remarks of his fellow travelers. When there was a lull in the discussion, he asked a question. "Why don't we just stick together? We're almost like a family, the four of us. Why don't we set up on our own?"

"And do what?" Bret asked.

"I've always had a hankerin' to find me some good pasture land and raise cattle and horses," Coldiron replied. "I never did anythin' about it, 'cause there weren't nobody but me, and I weren't sure I could cut it alone."

"You know anything about cattle?" Bret asked.

"A little bit," Coldiron answered.

The idea struck Bret as interesting, worthy of consideration. "Ranching, huh? I could help you with the horses, but I've never had much to do with cattle, except eating them. I reckon I'm not too old to learn. Of course, it's not as simple as that. You need some land to build your ranch on, and pasture land to raise livestock."

"Funny you should mention that," Coldiron said. "I've had the country picked out for a long time. We rode through it when we were trailing those Blackfeet, prettiest land there is anywhere. Above Big Timber, west of the Crazy Mountains, that's the place to raise stock—water, grass, everythin' you need—and most of it's free range."

"I believe you have been thinking about it," Bret said, really surprised. "I thought you wanted to be alone, preferred not to have anyone else around to bother you, holed up in that cabin of yours on the Gallatin River. Now you're telling me you want to be a family?"

Coldiron shrugged. "When you're young, maybe a man don't need nobody else. But when you get a little older, you get to feelin' that it wouldn't be bad to have somebody around."

Myra found the discussion very interesting. While there was a temporary lull, she looked at Lucy, questioning. Getting a shrug of noncommittal from her young friend, she chose to interpret it as indifferent, so she made a suggestion.

"Why don't we vote on it? I say we oughta try it as a family, and stick together. Lucy and I are already used to hard work on a farm, so we'll do our part. What about the rest of you?"

"I vote we make a family," Coldiron spoke up, a wide grin straining to shine through the whiskers.

Still insecure in her place among them, because of what she feared as a stigma as a result of the abuse she had suffered in the Piegan camp, Lucy nevertheless voted to join Myra, leaving Bret to make it unanimous.

"I guess we're gonna be a family," he said.

Myra cheered and Lucy's face lost its worried frown for the first time since she had been rescued. Coldiron grinned, knowing that he had formed a partnership with a strong, young, dependable man, and his recent worries about advancing age seemed no longer of importance.

Bret was not sure it was what he wanted to do with his life, but he believed that this was the best option at the moment. The thought of being part of a family was a strange one to him, for he had never really experienced it. He was the son of a career military man who was a widower. His young life was spent moving from post to post, with no roots sunk in any one place. And it had always been the natural progression for him to follow his father's profession. Maybe having a family, even one of unrelated members, would be a good thing for him. The idea caused him to smile to himself when he thought of the unlikely combination of characters.

Each of the four had reached a critical juncture in his or her life with no clear future in sight. *A family of misfits,* he thought, but one that might possibly have a stronger bond than a blood family.

So he made up his mind he would honor this commitment, knowing that of the four, he would contribute the most. The balance of money he had left in the bank at Bozeman was the only money available to finance their endeavor. He wondered if his late father would approve of his use of his inheritance.

They sat by the Teton River until the coffee was finished, then climbed into the saddle again to complete their trip to Fort Benton. High-spirited, they looked forward to a future. Even though it was not set in stone, it was a step in that direction. They rode into town at half past four o'clock in the afternoon. With a pretty strong notion that Lucy would like to throw away her doeskin dress, Bret led them directly to the dry goods store where Myra had purchased her clothes. He gave Myra some money to buy Lucy a complete set of clothes with a little extra in case Myra desired some clothes of a more feminine nature. Since they were across the street from the Missouri Saloon, he anticipated Coldiron's question and offered to buy a drink before he asked it.

"Just to make our new agreement official," Coldiron said with a twinkle in his eye. "Otherwise, I never touch the stuff."

Hank Lewis recognized the two men when they walked in the door. "Well, howdy, boys," he greeted them cheerfully. "Did you find that Injun camp you was lookin' for?"

"Yep, we sure did," Coldiron answered. "And we thought we'd give you a little business on our way back through town. Have you still got some of that good stuff you gave us last time?"

"I do, indeed," Hank said with a grin. Looking directly at Bret, he japed, "Want me to send somebody over to the fort to see if your ol' friend Corporal Murdock can come over and have a drink with you?"

"I'd just as soon you didn't," Bret replied. "We're kinda hoping to have a quiet drink and be on our way. We've got two ladies waiting for us outside."

"Oh," Hank said. "Well, you don't have to hurry off. Tell 'em to come on in and have a drink."

"I said two ladies," Bret repeated, emphasizing the word *ladies*.

"Beg your pardon," Hank was quick to reply. "No offense." He filled two shot glasses and stood ready to refill them if so directed.

Coldiron lifted his glass and held it out before him, proposing a toast. "Here's to our new partnership."

Bret brought his glass up to meet Coldiron's. "Luck to us," he said. "We're most likely gonna need it." They tossed the whiskey back. "One more and we'll go meet the ladies."

Hank obliged. "Where you fellers headin', now that you've found that lady?"

"Headin' south," Coldiron said, "down across

the Musselshell to that big valley of grass above Big Timber." He looked at Bret and grinned. "And we can't get there too soon, right, partner?"

"South, huh?" Hank asked. "I might can give you a little piece of advice. A couple of soldiers were in here the other night. And they was talkin' about goin' out on patrol down that way, because of some trouble some Blackfeet was causin' east of the Little Belt Mountains. I don't know if that's the way you was thinkin' about goin', but if it is, you might wanna ride to the west of them mountains."

"Much obliged," Bret said. "We were going that way. Maybe we oughta take your advice and go west of the mountains. Whaddaya think, Nate?"

"Maybe you're right," Coldiron said. "It'll put us outta our way a little, but what the hell have we gotta be in a hurry for, anyway?"

The women were still inside the dry goods store when Bret and Coldiron walked back across the dusty street.

"Might as well go in and look around," Bret suggested, "see what they've got to sell in there."

Seeing Myra at the counter with an accumulation of items stacked up before her, including some basic supplies like flour, salt, lard, leavening, and sugar, Bret stepped up to give her a hand.

"I figured you'd use all the money I gave you on things to wear," he said.

She smiled and replied, "I thought you might rather have some biscuits. I'm satisfied to wear the clothes I've got right now."

"Where's Lucy?"

"She's in the storeroom in back, changing clothes," Myra told him. "She couldn't wait to get outta them Injun clothes."

"I reckon," Coldiron said, then walked over to the other side of the store to look at a rack of firearms.

"I'll carry this stuff out and load it on the packhorses," Bret volunteered. "You all paid up?" Myra said that she was, and the store clerk thanked them for the business.

"Whoa," Private Bowden said. "Look who's comin' outta the dry goods store with his hands full of stuff, Murdock. Ain't that the feller that bounced a whiskey bottle offa your head?"

Corporal Murdock stopped to glare at the tall man wearing buckskins, his arms loaded with parcels as he walked to a packhorse.

"It's him, all right," Murdock growled. "The son of a bitch almost cracked my skull."

"I don't see that ol' big'n he had with him last time," Bowden said, the memory of flying over the counter still fresh in his mind.

It was a coincidence that the two soldiers happened to be in town that day, and a lucky one in Murdock's mind, for he longed to seek revenge for the tender bump on his head. He didn't hesitate, and hurried up the street, pulling his army model Colt as he ran, intending to catch Bret while his hands were still occupied and his back was turned.

"Well, look who's back in town," he taunted when he tapped the barrel of the .44 against the back of Bret's head. "Turn around, you long-legged bastard. You made a helluva mistake showin' your ass back in this town."

Bret turned slowly to face his aggressor. "Well, Corporal," he said calmly, "I see that little rap on the head didn't do any permanent damage." He took a quick look at Private Bowden, who was standing beside Murdock, his hand resting on the handle of his pistol, but the weapon still holstered. Shifting his eyes back on the corporal, he said, "I hope you aren't getting ready to make another mistake."

"Ha!" Murdock blurted. "Mistake! I'm fixin' to spill your guts all over this street. The only mistake is you showin' up here again. Now, suppose you just drop down on your knees, and mind you don't drop any of them parcels when you do." Bret was far too calm to suit Murdock. "Damn you!" he cursed. "Down on your knees!"

"I don't reckon that'll be necessary," Bret told him with no hint of panic in his tone for the two soldiers facing him, for he could see Myra coming out the door behind them. His expression never changed as he watched her pick up a long-handled shovel on display beside the door, testing its weight.

"Necessary?" Murdock roared in disbelief. "I'll show you what's—"

That was as far as he got before his words were replaced by the sound of the shovel as it rang loudly against the side of his head. Stunned, he went to his knees, dropping the pistol as he did. Bret, his hands still occupied with Myra's purchases, raised one foot and kicked him over on the ground. Stunned almost as completely as the corporal, Private Bowden turned to see Coldiron charging out of the store. With no desire to engage the monstrous man a second time, he took off at a dead run, back the way he had come. Coldiron chased after him for a dozen yards or so before conceding the race to the more motivated competitor.

Across the street, having heard an altercation taking place in the street, Hank Lewis stood in the saloon door. "Murdock," he commented to no one, "he don't never learn."

In the street, Coldiron returned to the scene of the short skirmish. "You all right?" he asked Myra, who was still standing poised over the body, lest Murdock show signs of needing another swing of the shovel.

"Yes, I'm all right," she replied, "but this buzzard better think again before he threatens a member of this family."

Coldiron threw his head back and laughed. "Damn right," he said, then placed his foot in the middle of Murdock's back and flattened him on the ground again when the dazed and confused corporal started to stir. He laughed when Bret, still standing with his arms full, asked if anyone was going to help him load the parcels on the packhorse.

"Why, shore," he replied. "It's a good thing you held on to what you got. Myra mighta tried out that shovel on you if you'da dropped that bag of flour and let it bust." He picked up Murdock's pistol and handed it to her. "Here, this'll be easier to handle. I'll put the man's shovel back, unless you're thinkin' about buyin' it now that you've tried it out." He propped it up against the side of the door just as Lucy came out, dressed in a riding skirt and jacket, keeping only the moccasins she had been given to wear while a captive.

"Well, lookee here," Coldiron remarked. "Ain't you pretty as a picture?"

Unaware of what had gone on while she was changing clothes, she gazed, astonished, at her new family and the prone soldier in the street. By this time, Murdock was clearing some of the cobwebs from his brain, but he wisely chose to remain where he was and count himself lucky to have suffered no worse.

"Let's mount up," Bret said. "We're ready to travel."

Chapter 11

It was approaching twilight when the two warriors came to the banks of the Teton River. The tracks of the six horses they had followed were plain to see, telling them that the four people they followed had no longer felt it necessary to try to hide their trail. It struck Bloody Hand as an insult. He slid down from his lathered horse and let the exhausted animal go down to the water's edge to drink with Lame Dog's horse.

Lame Dog knew better than to make any comment at this point, aware of the fury burning inside his violent companion. They had ridden their ponies to the point of collapse in Bloody Hand's determination to overtake the fleeing white raiders. Now they had no choice but to wait for their horses to recover from the grueling pace they had been held to all day.

Bloody Hand stood at the edge of the river, staring at the tracks left by the six horses while absentmindedly fondling the dried ear on the rawhide cord around his neck. He remained in that trancelike pose for a long time before suddenly turning to walk over to the ashes of a fire higher up the bank. He knelt down and stirred the ashes with his fingers. They told him that it had been only a few hours since the woman and her rescuers sat beside the fire, eating and drinking coffee. The thought of it was enough to make him pick up a sizable stub of half-burned wood and fling it in anger into the water, causing the horses to jump, startled. Drowning in the frustration of knowing he was so close to overtaking the hated white raiders, but could not dare to follow them into Fort Benton, he stood up and kicked at the ashes.

After a few moments, when Bloody Hand appeared calm enough to question, Lame Dog spoke. "We cannot kill the white dogs in the town full of soldiers. What are we going to do now? I fear the woman has gotten away. Maybe it is just as well. Maybe it is best for you to forget this white coyote bitch. She is not worth the trouble to search for her any longer."

Bloody Hand cocked his head around sharply to glare at Lame Dog. His expression plainly told the half-breed that his advice had not been solicited and was not welcome.

"I will not stop until I have the unworthy woman under my knife, and I have the scalps of the two men who took her. I did not ask you to come with me. You came because you wanted to. Now, if you no longer want to ride with me to avenge this wrong, you may turn back. I will go on alone. I am Bloody Hand. I need no one."

Afraid that he was about to lose the somewhat shaky status he thought he was gaining by volunteering to accompany the incensed warrior, Lame Dog was quick to make amends. "I will ride with you until vengeance is done," he pleaded. "I can be of great help to you. I have many friends in Chief Black Bear's village near here. I camp with them when I go to visit my mother. They are Bloods, but are friendly with the soldiers at the fort. I can go into the town. I have done so many times before. Maybe I can find them, and maybe find out where they are heading."

The suggestion gave Bloody Hand new hope. It made sense that the soldiers and the white merchants did not know one Indian from another. Black Bear's people were on friendly terms with the town, so they could not know that he and Lame Dog were from the hostile Piegan band. The risk they ran was being seen by the woman. She could identify both him and Lame Dog, so they must find her and her rescuers without being spotted.

It was an uncomfortable subject to comment upon, but Lame Dog felt that he must suggest that he should go into town alone. "Your fierce appearance would be very noticeable to anyone who saw you, and they might talk to other people about seeing you," he said, hoping that Bloody Hand would accept it without going into another rage. Surely he would agree that a warrior with such a grotesquely scarred face, and missing an ear, would have an impact on everyone who saw him. And if it generated enough talk, the word was bound to get around to the white woman. "I can go into town and the soldiers would pay me no mind."

Lame Dog was relieved to find that Bloody Hand considered what he suggested without a flare-up of fury.

"What you say is true," the fearsome warrior said, after thinking about it for a few moments. "We will do as you say."

Having decided what they were going to do, the people that Bloody Hand was so desperate to overtake were making camp just west of Fort Benton on the banks of the Missouri. Their plan was to start out in the morning and retrace their previous journey back to Jake Smart's trading post. They figured it to be a ride of a day and a half to reach the confluence of Hound Creek and the Smith River.

While there was no particular need to stop at Jake Smart's store since they had ample supplies, Bret figured it a good place for an overnight camp—even though there had been trouble with a horse thief when they camped there before. As Jake had said, it had been a rare occurrence and the thief was most likely a rogue Indian from one of the bands up on the Judith.

Bret was concerned about pushing Lucy too hard. She was still in a fragile state both physically and mentally, even though she insisted she was not. Maybe half a day of rest would help. Coldiron and Myra were in agreement, knowing the treatment the young woman had suffered while in the Piegan camp. Also, Coldiron and Bret agreed that it would be a good opportunity to use that half day to hunt for fresh game.

"Get that fire good and hot," Myra commanded, " 'cause I'm gonna bake some biscuits. It's time we ate like civilized people for a change. I'd cook some beans, too, if I'da had a chance to soak 'em long enough. I might boil up some of 'em anyway, if you don't mind a little crunch in your beans."

"Suits me whatever you do with 'em," Coldiron said. "It's the biscuits I want." He winked at Bret. "It'll be a good chance to see if she can bake biscuits."

Equally as sassy, Myra responded, "They'll be the best biscuits cooked in a skillet that you ever ate. You'll get a chance to eat a real baked biscuit when we get settled on our cattle ranch and get me a good iron stove. We'll show 'em some real cookin', won't we, Lucy?"

Lucy responded with a shy smile, but said nothing. It was going to be some time yet before she felt completely at ease. While she was extremely grateful to have been rescued, she could not yet fully believe their acceptance of her as genuine. She feared that deep down they judged her as damaged goods, somehow blaming her for the misfortune that had befallen her.

Myra seemed so at ease with the two men who had come to her salvation, but Lucy had not had the time to really come to know them. The one, Coldiron, was such an ominous-looking giant of a man, who appeared to be capable of unrestrained violence, yet joked with Myra like a jolly old uncle. The other was harder to define. A much younger man than the grizzly he partnered with, probably close to the age of Carlton, her late husband, he spoke like an educated man. Tall and confident. Myra said he had been an officer in the army, and had been cashiered unfairly, because of a lying witness. But that was his version of his departure. What if there was another version? Greatly troubled by these thoughts and still-fresh memories of her captivity, she had no choice other than to wait to see what happened as time passed. Her thoughts were suddenly interrupted by a request from Myra.

"Come help me with these biscuits. I wish I had a board to roll this dough out on. They're gonna be funny-looking biscuits."

"Long as they eat good," Coldiron said, having overheard her comment as he walked up with an armload of limbs to feed the fire. A loner for most all of his life, the big man was wallowing in the glow of being a member of a family.

Well, I guess it's a typical family scene, Bret

thought as he paused to watch Coldiron. His oversized friend seemed almost joyful with their situation, but Bret still wondered if he truly was. Maybe he wasn't ready to be responsible for a family, especially one not of his own making.

"Hell," he muttered to himself. "It is what it is. I said I was for it, so I'll live up to what I said."

Besides, he thought, *fresh biscuits come with the deal.* He went back to work on the Indian saddle he was trying to adjust to fit Lucy's slender legs.

Harold Carter, owner of Carter's Dry Goods, walked back inside his store carrying the shovel and pitchfork he had displayed out front. He was met just inside by his wife, Flora. "What were you talking to that Indian about?" she asked. "Another one begging for something?"

"No," Harold replied. "He wasn't begging. I've seen that one around here a time or two. He was looking for those two fellows who are escorting the two white women that were in here buying clothes."

"What in the world did he want with those folks?" Flora asked.

"He said they hired him as a guide, but he can't find them anywhere, wondered if I had seen them."

"He's not much of a guide if he can't even find the people who hired him," Flora commented. "What did you tell him?"

Harold shrugged. "I told him those folks were already gone. He wanted to know which way they went, but I told him I didn't know. When they left here, they rode out the west road, but I didn't know where they were heading."

"I expect those folks are better off without him," Flora remarked. "He was a surly-looking fellow."

Lame Dog whipped his horse when it settled into a slower lope, demanding it keep up the pace on his way back to the Teton River. There was really no need for his haste, since it was already getting dark, and there was little chance Bloody Hand would insist upon starting after them before daylight. Still, he was anxious to report his findings to the savage Piegan.

Upon reaching the Teton, he turned his pony's head to follow the river westward for half a mile, walking his horse more carefully now as it made its way along the bank.

"Hy-yi!" he called out as he approached the camp.

Bloody Hand stepped out from behind a tree, where he had taken cover when he heard a horse approaching, and released the hammer on his rifle. Anxious to hear Lame Dog's report, he exclaimed, "You saw them?"

"No," Lame Dog replied as he slid off his pony. "They have already gone from there."

Bloody Hand's frightening features immediately twisted into a storm warning of coming rage.

"Gone?" he roared, for he had assumed that Fort Benton was their destination, at least for a time. "Where? Did you find out where they went?"

"The storekeeper told me he didn't know where they were heading, but he said they left Fort Benton on the road west. Maybe they are going back the way they came, and I know that trail."

"Did you only ask one person?" Bloody Hand asked. "Maybe they talked to someone else."

"I asked several people," Lame Dog lied, afraid to tell Bloody Hand that he had not. "None of them knew as much as the storekeeper. And they will not allow Indians in the saloon, so I couldn't ask anyone there." Seeing Bloody Hand's angry grimace, Lame Dog was quick to say, "I know the road that leads out of town. If they leave the road and cross the river, then I am sure they are going to the trading post where my mother lives. It will be easy to catch them there, and they will be away from the soldier fort. There would be no one to help them."

"We will go there as soon as the sun is up tomorrow," Bloody Hand decided.

"They cannot outrun us forever," Lame Dog encouraged. He could have taken Bloody Hand to the road leading out of town that night, but he was glad the irate Piegan did not insist upon it. He wanted to eat and rest.

• • •

It was still not midmorning by the time they circled around the fort and struck the west road out of town. There were many tracks on the wagon road, some from shod horses, some from unshod, most of them old, but many that were relatively new. It was impossible, however, to isolate the tracks of the six horses they had followed from their camp on the Marias. With no other option available to them, they continued along the road. Lame Dog's sharp eyesight was responsible for the first lucky break in their search. No more than two or three miles from town, he spotted a place beside the road where a party of horses had turned off and gone down beside the river.

After dismounting and taking a close look, the two trackers could not be sure there were six horses that had left the tracks, but at least two of the horses were shod. They had to be the same tracks they had followed from the Marias. It could not be a coincidence. Eager now, they jumped onto their ponies and followed the tracks down to the water's edge, where they discovered the remains of a camp. It was recent, so recent that there was no doubt that it was the party they trailed, and they had found their camp from the night before. It made sense that they would have camped there, for there were signs of older camps evident in the shady clearing.

Bloody Hand stood erect, his hands clenched into fists so tight that his fingernails brought blood to his palms. He felt the nearness of his prey and his nostrils flared with the scent of the woman he thought he could smell on the wind. She was only hours away! Quickly returning from the trancelike daze that had taken over his brain, he was now impatient to finish his quest.

"Hurry!" he implored.

"Here!" Lame Dog exclaimed. "This is where the horses were tied. The tracks lead back toward the road."

Kneeling, he bent close to the ground, examining each clear hoofprint closely, hoping to find some identifying mark that would set it apart from the many other prints on the wagon road. Realizing then what Lame Dog was looking for, Bloody Hand reined in his impatience and dropped to his knee to join in the search. It had not been necessary to look so closely while following the six horses to Fort Benton, for they had been the only set of tracks to follow. Now they would be mixed in again with the traffic on the river road.

"There!" Lame Dog exclaimed triumphantly. Bloody Hand bent close to see. Pointing to the print of one of the shod horses, Lame Dog touched the forward arch of the shoe with his finger where it showed a small nick.

Bloody Hand was pleased. "You have sharp

eyes," he said. "I am glad that you came with me. Now we must ride!"

Finally feeling Bloody Hand's acceptance, Lame Dog sprang to his feet, glowing with confidence. They rode up from the riverbank to once again follow the wagon track along the Missouri. Riding side by side, both men looked for signs of tracks leading away from the road again. They found only one set before reaching a common crossing to the other side of the river. It took a few minutes to examine the tracks before they decided they were not the ones they sought. When they reached the crossing, they found that almost every traveler had left the road to cross over to the other side. Just to be sure, they looked closely until they found the hoofprint that told them what they needed to know.

Once they had crossed the river, another search of the tracks was performed to make sure their party had not doubled back. When that was confirmed, Lame Dog felt sure he knew where the four white people were going.

"They're heading back the same way they came," he said. "Maybe they will stop at the trading post at Hound Creek, like they did before."

"If this is so," Bloody Hand replied excitedly, "we can move much faster. How far is it to the trading post?"

"Maybe one long day," Lame Dog said. "With

two women, they will probably take a day and a half."

"I think you are right. We will catch them when they make camp tonight."

"Is that saddle a little better for you?" Bret asked as he reined his horse back to let Lucy come up beside him.

"Yes, I think it is," Lucy answered. "Thank you for fixing it."

"No trouble at all," he said. "Might as well be as comfortable as you can."

The young woman was still extremely guarded in her relationship with him, maybe even more so than she was with Coldiron. He hoped that more casual conversation would set her mind more at rest as the days passed. Knowing the treatment she must have endured during her captivity, he felt true compassion for her, and he hoped she would allow herself to forget those painful memories.

She concentrated her gaze on his back as he nudged the paint horse ahead again, wondering what role he had in mind for her, if this talk they had about being a family really was in earnest. On this ranch they talked about building, could she be little more than a servant girl, working in the kitchen, helping Myra? She was not fooling herself. She had no skills to offer. She could cook and clean, work in the fields, if called upon to do so. Beyond that, she had no real worth to them.

"What are you thinking about?" Myra asked, interrupting Lucy's reverie. She had been studying her young friend's face after Bret rode back up in front of her. She saw the same signs of worried distress that had often played across Lucy's face since her rescue.

"Nothing, really," Lucy answered, and formed a halfhearted smile.

It was not enough to convince Myra.

"Lucy, honey, what's in the past is just that—past, and it ain't here no more unless you just hang on to it in your mind. This is a new day, and we're lucky that we got away with our lives. Not only that, we were rescued by two decent men who will take care of us. So I want you to start looking at the bright side of things. I'll always be here for you if things don't work out for us with Bret and Nate. We'll just find something else to do if that happens. All right?"

"All right," Lucy said, with the same attempt to smile as before, but she was still just as uncertain about her future.

Along toward the middle of the day, they crossed a healthy stream on its way to join the mighty Missouri. It seemed to offer a good place to make camp, but they decided that they wanted to continue on, since Jake Smart's place was still over half a day's ride.

So they stopped only long enough to rest the horses and let them drink. They passed several other streams before finally selecting a spot by a healthy creek where they could ride off the trail a couple of hundred feet into a grove of pines. The men unloaded the horses while the women gathered wood and built a fire. The supper that night was to be leftover pan biscuits and smoked venison, washed down with coffee. But Myra promised better fare when they got to the trading post.

"I'll take some time to cook something," she promised.

"And me and Bret'll take time to do a little huntin'," Coldiron said. "We ought not be ridin' for more'n half a day tomorrow—give you ladies a little time to rest."

"Maybe we can spend a little time gossiping with Jake's wife," Myra said, then laughed at her facetious remark.

Coldiron laughed with her, thinking about the grim-looking Blackfoot woman. "I expect you might. She's a real chatterbox."

The mood was cheerful as the evening approached, and all the fears and uncertainty seemed far behind them.

There was just barely enough light to examine the hoofprint closely, but both agreed that it was the print with the nicked shoe they had identified before. Bloody Hand peered through the growing gloom of evening toward a grove of pine trees.

"I think they may be camped in those trees," he said. "We will wait a little while longer until they have settled down for the night."

He wanted to be sure there would be no time for the two men to react when they struck.

"We need to be careful," Lame Dog warned. "I have heard many stories about the scout Coldiron. I have heard that he is as big as a bear and has many kills. The other man, I don't know, but I know that they both have the rifles that shoot many times."

He didn't tell Bloody Hand that he knew this because they had sent him scurrying with a heavy barrage of gunfire when he attempted to steal their horses.

Patient, now that he knew his prey was treed, Bloody Hand said, "It is best to wait until they are asleep. Then we will kill the men in their beds before they have time to protect the women."

Soon it was dark enough to see occasional sparks flying up into the night air, so the two warriors left their horses and crept up closer to the camp. The glow of the campfire could now be seen through the veil of trees and bushes. They waited a while longer, and then Bloody Hand decided to move almost to the edge of the trees to see if he could determine where the men were sleeping.

After a few minutes, he was back. "They are already in their beds close to the fire, their weapons lying beside them. I could not see the women, but I think they are behind them, close to the horses."

He checked his rifle once more to make sure it was ready to fire, then told Lame Dog to aim at the man to the left of the fire, and he would take the one on the right.

"Watch for the women. They might have guns also, but be careful you don't shoot the young one. I must take her alive." He got to his feet. "I will have the woman again, and the six horses I paid for the bitch," he boasted.

"Some of them," Lame Dog corrected. "We will share the horses. You can have the woman."

He got up and together they stole silently through the underbrush and onto the clean floor beneath the pines. When both were in position, Bloody Hand nodded and they charged into the clearing, screaming a terrifying Piegan war cry and firing at the still forms by the fire.

Shocked from a sound sleep by a howling nightmare descending upon him, the man scrambled from his blanket and reached for his rifle just as the first .44 slug caught him squarely in the chest. Still, he managed to cock his weapon, loading a cartridge before a second slug ripped into his stomach, and he dropped back on his blanket. Lying helpless, he heard the rifle on the other side of the fire and knew that his partner had gotten off a shot. But there were no more as his partner went down. Seconds later, the final slug ended it.

"Head the women off!" Bloody Hand shouted. "Don't let them get across the creek!"

Reacting to Bloody Hand's commands, Lame Dog sprinted through the trees to splash across the creek, effectively cutting off any alley of escape from the camp. But there was no sign of the women. Baffled, for they could not have gotten across before he did, Lame Dog closed in on the camp, looking for their hiding place. He heard Bloody Hand yelling for him.

"I'm here," he answered, "at the creek!"

In a few seconds, Bloody Hand ran to meet him, eager for the reunion he had suffered to have.

"Where is she?" he demanded. "Where is the bitch?"

"There's no one here," Lame Dog told him. "They're gone."

"How can that be? They must be here some-where!" Bloody Hand was close to a blind rage. He looked all around him frantically, looking for any possible hiding place. "The horses," he said. "They're hiding among the horses."

Both warriors ran then to see, but there was no one hiding there. Choking with rage and confusion, Bloody Hand stopped short when it struck him that there were only four horses. They must have escaped! But how could they have escaped without being seem by them? No one had ridden out of the camp.

"They are not here," he stated emphatically. "Let's look at the two men we killed."

He turned and walked back to the fire, where the two bodies lay sprawled near their blankets. Pulling a half-burned limb from the fire, he poked it around in the glowing coals until it burst again into flames. Then using it as a light, he held it close to the faces of both corpses. He stood back then and stared at the two insignificant bodies of two old trappers while thinking of the description of the bear of a man named Coldiron. In a deadly calm voice, he asked, "Are these the men you saw at the trading post?"

Unable to explain the mistake, Lame Dog fumbled for words. "We both saw the hoofprints, the marked horseshoe . . ."

In a sudden search for redemption, he went to the four horses tied by the creek and began inspecting hooves of the two that were shod. When he found a rough place on the right front hoof of one of them, he exclaimed, "See, here is the horse that left the print." He seemed to imply that it justified their mistake in following the wrong party.

Once more awash in frustration, Bloody Hand stood staring at the two bodies, idly rubbing the shriveled ear on the cord around his neck between his thumb and forefinger. Lame Dog stood by, hesitant to say more, his head hanging, much like the animal whose name he had chosen. After a long stretch of angry silence, Bloody Hand finally took control of his overtaxed emotions.

"This changes nothing. Let us see if these two white dogs have anything of value."

Lame Dog enthusiastically joined his savage partner in the stripping of the bodies, ripping pockets to get to their contents, slashing them with their knives if they were too coarse to tear with their hands. All told, their massacre of two unsuspecting trappers netted them four dollars in silver, four horses of average quality, two Colt revolvers, and two single-shot Springfield army rifles.

They loaded their spoils on the horses and rode away, satisfied that they had at least rid the world of two white men who had no business in Blackfeet country. Now half a day behind again, they rode for only a short distance before making camp for the rest of that night. Tomorrow, they would ride to Lame Dog's father's trading post to see if the four white people they trailed had stopped there.

Chapter 12

"Well, I'll be . . . ," Jake Smart started, then called back toward the store, "Ruby, they're back! And they've got the other woman with 'em." He replaced the rail to close the corral where his horses and the cow were eating hay he had brought from the barn. "I swear, I wouldn'ta been surprised if we never saw them again."

Ruby Red Bonnet came from the store to see for herself. Sure enough, there was the big gray-haired scout and his tall dark-haired young friend, turning off and coming down the path to the store. Behind them were the two white women. Like her husband, Ruby had not expected them to successfully steal the young woman out of the Piegan camp. But unlike Jake, she was not happy to see them.

How many of my people died because of this? she wondered.

"Hey-yo, Nate," Jake called out. "I see you got what you went after."

"Yep," Coldiron answered. "Me and Bret most of the time get what we go after," he boasted. "Ain't that right, partner?"

"If you say so," Bret replied, content to let Coldiron be the one to do the bragging. "This is Lucy Gentry," he said as Lucy reined her horse to a stop beside his.

"Pleased to meet you, ma'am," Jake said. "Welcome to my little business here. I'm real sorry you had to go through all your troubles with the Injuns, but I'm mighty glad they was able to find you."

"We thought we'd stay over for a day or two," Coldiron interrupted, thinking Lucy would prefer not to talk about her ordeal right away. "We'll camp down by the creek where we did last time, if it's all right with you. Me and Bret plan on doin' a little huntin' to see if we can't add some fresh meat to our supplies. Might share a little with you and Ruby, if we have any luck."

"You oughta do just fine," Jake said. "Mule deer and antelope, too, have been runnin' all along Hound Creek of late. I saw three young does right up at the edge of the yard yesterday."

"That's even better," Coldiron joked. "Maybe we won't have to hunt 'em up. Me and Bret'll just lay back on your front porch and shoot 'em when they come a-callin'."

Jake chuckled. "Maybe so, but I ain't givin' no guarantees." He changed the subject abruptly then. "Did you run into much trouble rescuing the lady?"

Not finished joking yet, Coldiron answered, "Why, not a bit. That fine, upstandin' gentleman that grabbed her said he was happy to see she got back with her people again. They wanted us to hang around for a while, but we told 'em we had to get back home."

"Is that a fact?" Jake replied, going along with Coldiron's nonsense. "Well, them Piegans are known for their hospitality." He noticed then that the young lady in question did not appear to appreciate the humor in her capture by the Piegan Blackfeet. So he apologized for his own lack of hospitality. "I reckon you ladies are most likely weary. Why don't you step down and come inside? Ruby can make you a pot of coffee, and maybe set you out a little somethin' to eat."

"That's mighty kind of you, Mr. Smart," Myra was quick to reply. "But we don't want to put your wife to all that trouble. We'll just wait till we set up camp. We've got some deer meat that's fixing to spoil if we don't eat it pretty soon."

She realized that it might be idle suspicion on her part, but she didn't want to eat anything the sullen Blackfoot woman prepared for them. She might pepper it with gunpowder or some strange Indian herb designed to make a white person sick. Catching the look of disappointment on Coldiron's face, she gave in a little.

"A good cup of coffee would be welcome, though. That would be plenty."

"That'd be no trouble a'tall," Jake spoke for his wife, who was still hanging back at the door of the store. "Ruby, how 'bout buildin' a pot of coffee for these travelers?"

Without a word to the visitors, she turned and disappeared inside the store.

"I swear, she's something, ain't she?" Myra commented later while setting up their camp. She was referring to Jake's wife and her obvious distrust of white people. "That's one Indian who ain't signed any peace treaty with the government."

She handed the pot she had purchased in Fort Benton to Lucy. "If you want, you can fill this with some water, and we'll let some of those beans soak till it's time to fix supper."

Lucy paused a moment to reply before going to the creek. "She looked at me the same way those Piegan women looked at me. She doesn't seem very friendly."

"Ha," Myra responded. "She ain't. You might think I'm being silly, but I didn't take a sip of that coffee till I saw her pour her husband and herself some of it. I don't trust her no farther than I can throw her. I reckon Jake means well, but I don't really believe he knows what a mountain lion he's married to."

"Do you think we're in any danger here?" Lucy asked, concerned now.

"Oh no, I don't think so," Myra was quick to reassure her. "That's the reason we stopped here— 'cause it's close to the trading post, and the Indians in Black Bear's village don't bother it. The only thing we need to do is keep an eye on that wife of Jake's."

They had set up their camp in the same spot they had used the time before, upstream from Jake's outhouse perched on the bank above the creek—a location Myra had insisted upon when the proximity of the structure seemed to be of no importance to either of the men. It was little more than a cabinet of vile odors, at any rate, and Myra advised Lucy to avoid it, recommending the willows downstream instead.

"Think that'll do?" Bret asked, after dropping another armload of wood for the fire.

"That oughta hold me for a while," Myra replied.

"Nate and I are gonna ride on up the creek this evening to see if we can come up on some deer—see if there're as many around here as Jake claims. I'm hoping we can kill a couple so we can smoke a good supply to take us down to that valley Nate's so set on." He paused then to take a look at Lucy, kneeling at the creek. "How's she doing?"

Myra turned to look at her as well. "She's doing just fine. She's just having a hard time letting go of the awful things that happened to her. But she's getting a little better. I can't see how anybody else would handle it any differently."

Bret smiled and asked, "How about you? Are you doing all right?"

"Me?" Myra responded, surprised. "Hell, I'm gonna always do all right. Ain't you figured that out by now? If you're worrying about having a couple of weepy women on your hands, you can stop now." Her response caused them both to chuckle. "One thing, though," she said, turning serious for a moment. "I need some ammunition for my pistol. The only cartridges I've got are the ones it's loaded with, and if you and Coidiron are going riding off into the woods somewhere,

I'd feel better with a gun and plenty of bullets."

"Oh," Bret said, surprised by the request. He had forgotten that she still had the revolver that Corporal Murdock had carried. "I've got plenty of forty-fours. I'll leave you some."

A little before the sun dropped behind the hills west of the river, Myra and Lucy served up plates of beans and deer jerky, with some more of Myra's fresh-baked biscuits, causing Coldiron to comment, "If I keep fillin' up on your biscuits, I ain't gonna be able to climb on my horse. I believe I could get used to this."

"I expect you'd better," Myra told him, " 'cause I aim to be doing a lot more of it, me and Lucy. Ain't that right, Lucy?" Lucy nodded with a faint smile.

In a little while, Jake walked down from the store and helped them finish up the coffee. "I thought I'd give you a little tip on how to get your deer right quick," he volunteered. "If you ride back up the creek about a mile, you'll see a little meadow that runs down to the water. The deer like to cross there, comin' outta the woods on the other side to get to that meadow. You'll know it when you see it. There's an old cottonwood tree layin' on its side—got hit by lightnin'. I have sat on that tree and shot a deer comin' across the creek."

"Is that a fact?" Coldiron replied. "Well, we'll go see if the deer will do that for us."

Jake stayed and talked until Bret said it was time to go. Twilight was setting in and he figured that the deer would be coming out of the thick forests to feed. With a promise to bring Jake and Ruby some of the fresh meat, Coldiron and Bret rode off, following the creek upstream. When Jake said good night to the women and returned to the store, Lucy asked Myra, "How long do you think they'll be gone?"

Myra saw right away that her young friend was nervous without the men around. She attempted to set her mind at ease.

"They won't be gone long. Didn't you hear what Jake said? He said that place was only about a mile away. Us ladies could use a little time without the men around, anyway." Lucy appeared to find no comfort in Myra's words, so she added, "Anyways, I've got my Colt pistol handy in case we need it, but I don't think we will this close to the trading post."

She couldn't help wondering just how severely damaged Lucy was, and whether or not she was ever going to rid herself of the fears that held her mind captive.

It was already growing dark by the time Jake walked back by the corral and stopped for a few minutes to take a look at his horses and the cow. He didn't have any reason for concern; it was just from habit. There was a time when he would have put his livestock inside the barn and padlocked the door, but that was long ago. His friendly terms with Black Bear over the last decade ensured his peaceful relations with the Blackfeet tribes that hunted and lived in the Missouri River Valley.

Satisfied that his livestock was all right, he stepped inside the door of the trading post and pulled up short, startled to find Lame Dog talking to his mother.

"John!" Jake blurted. "When did you get here? I didn't see your horse in the corral. Hell, I didn't figure you'd be back here for at least a month."

"Why do you still call me John, old man? I am Lame Dog," he growled. "I go and come when it pleases me. My horse is where I left it—in the trees."

"Well, what the hell did you leave it there for?" Jake asked.

Lame Dog ignored the question. "Those two white men, they're camping here tonight, right?" Jake said that was true. Lame Dog scowled when he asked, "They have two white women with them?"

"That's right," Jake said. "But they're peaceful folk set on stayin' over for a day or two to do some huntin'. Then they'll be on their way. Ain't nobody you've got any reason to be interested in."

Lame Dog continued to question. "Did they camp in the same spot they did last time they were here?"

Jake was beginning to dislike the way the questioning was going. "What have you got workin' in that ornery mind of yours? You come sneakin' in here at night, leaving your horse in the woods—didn't you learn your lesson last time when you tried to steal their horses? And don't try to tell me that wasn't you they ran off that night."

Lame Dog rankled with the accusation. "If I had wanted their horses, I would have taken them. I had no interest in their horses."

"Is that a fact?" Jake replied sarcastically, recognizing a lie when he heard one. "Well, let me give you a piece of advice. If you've got any crazy notions about those people, you'd best forget about it, 'cause you'd be goin' up against more'n you can handle." His advice was met with a sullen smile from his renegade son.

"You should just worry yourself about your store here," Lame Dog said. "And don't worry about what I'm doing."

Faced with the usual exasperation in trying to communicate with his son, Jake gave up on the attempt. "How long you stayin' this time?"

"I'm leaving right now," Lame Dog replied smugly.

He picked up a sack of dried meat and coffee beans his mother had given him, and turned to give her a smile before going out the door. There was nothing more he needed at the moment. His mother had told him that the two white men planned to go hunting that evening, so he was anxious to tell Bloody Hand that the women would probably stay behind in their camp. And with Coldiron and the other man gone, it would be a simple matter to snatch the women.

Lucy wanted to release her fears, but the memory of the horror she had endured was still too fresh in her mind. The image of Bloody Hand's horrible face came to her in her dreams, to the point where she sometimes feared that he was more an evil spirit and not a mortal man at all. His savage friend, Lame Dog, treated him as such. She shuddered when she thought of the pleasure the vile half-breed enjoyed in translating Bloody Hand's threats.

Realizing that she was letting herself be pulled into one of her frequent panic spells again, she shook her head in an effort to rid her brain of these fearful thoughts. The night must come, where every shadow might be the one-eared monster coming for her. She could not live in eternal sunshine, so she resolved to overcome her fears. The men had gone to hunt. They would return, and all her worrying would have availed her nothing but a nervous stomach.

In spite of her resolve, she was reluctant to leave Myra and the fire to walk a little way into the willow trees to answer nature's call. She had held on as long as she thought she could, hoping that the men would return, but they had not, even though it was well after dark. Myra speculated that they must have had no luck in finding game, and so had to ride farther. If they had had luck as close as Jake predicted, the women would have heard gunshots. Finally Lucy's bladder won the standoff.

"I've got to pee," she announced.

Myra looked up, noticing the slight tremor in Lucy's voice. "You want me to go with you?"

"No, of course not," Lucy replied. "I'm just going over in the willows there."

She was ashamed to say that it would have made her more comfortable had Myra chosen to go with her. However, she had challenged her urge to go for so long that now the possibility of wetting her underwear became a bigger concern than who might be lurking in the willows.

Stepping as quickly as she could while straining to hold on until she could reach the cover of the trees, she barely made it in time to pull her underpants down and squat. She had held on for so long that she now wondered if she was ever going to finish. When at last she did, she relaxed for a moment to enjoy the relief. A moment later she was sprawled on the ground, having bolted sideways when she was startled by the touch of a hand on her shoulder.

Her worst fears seemed confirmed, as she stared up at the dark shadow standing above her. He had found her, and she was too paralyzed with terror to scream.

"You and the other woman must get away from here," the voice told her.

Still terrified, Lucy could only lie there on the ground, confused by the strange voice. It was not the harsh guttural tone so familiar to her when Bloody Hand had cursed her.

"You are not safe here." The warning was repeated. "You and the other one must get away from here as quick as you can."

Cowering in fear, Lucy realized that it had to be Jake Smart's wife.

"Bloody Hand comes for you," Ruby said. "You not have much time. Go into the woods and hide." When Lucy was slow in responding, she finally scolded, "Get up!" The harsh command was enough to shake Lucy out of her fearful paralysis.

Satisfied that the frightened girl was at last responding, Ruby said, "I must go now." With that, she turned and disappeared into the dark shadows of the willows.

Intent upon slipping back into the house before she was seen, Ruby made her way quickly through the trees. Lame Dog had told her that Bloody Hand was waiting for him with their horses. She had not told Jake what the two warriors were planning, and she wanted to get back before he knew she had gone.

Myra's opinion of Ruby Red Bonnet was nearly accurate. The Blackfoot woman had no use for whites in general, and she encouraged her son's adoption of the Blackfoot ways. But there was a modicum of conscience in the otherwise savage woman, and this obsession Bloody Hand had for this white woman was not a good thing. The conflict between white man and red man should be a war between warriors and soldiers, and not involve women. Consequently, she felt no sense of betrayal to her son and the Piegan brute he rode with. She had warned the woman. It was now up to Lucy to save herself.

Behind her, the frightened young woman, having scrambled to her feet, stumbled through the willow branches, oblivious of the thrashing her arms and legs suffered.

"Myra!" she screamed in a half whisper as she ran to the fire. "We've got to run!" she implored as Myra watched her approach, baffled by her bizarre behavior. While pulling a reluctant Myra away from the fire, Lucy told her what had just happened.

When Myra realized that Lucy wasn't having fearful hallucinations, she quickly responded. Snatching up her revolver, she put a handful of extra cartridges in her pocket and took command.

"Come on," Myra said, "across the creek, over by those big trees!"

The two women crossed over the shallow creek as quickly and as quietly as they could manage in their panic to find safety.

With Myra leading, they followed the creek upstream, moving as fast as they possibly could on the dark bank. It was imperative that they should warn Bret and Coldiron before they rode into an ambush. She only hoped the men would return on the same trail on which they had departed, and that she and Lucy would intercept them before they got too close to the camp.

On foot, leading his horse, Bret stopped dead still when he caught a slight movement in the bushes on the left side of the creek bank ahead. Thinking it likely caused by a deer, he signaled Coldiron behind him. Both men dropped their horses's reins and pulled their rifles out of their saddle slings and cocked them. Walking silently, they watched the bank, following the movement in the foliage as it tracked along a line that would bring it to a gap about five yards wide. It appeared that the gap was the only chance they had for an open shot, so they both knelt, aimed, and waited. The bushes parted.

"What the hell . . . ?" Bret exclaimed, and reacted quickly enough to shove Coldiron's rifle barrel sideways, causing his big friend to send a .44 slug ripping through the treetops. The rifle shot forced a scream of fright from both women.

"Myra!" Bret exclaimed. "What the hell are you doing, trying to get yourself killed?"

"Jesus' whiskers!" Coldiron gasped. "I damn near shot you!" He was visibly shaken by the close call, and extremely grateful for Bret's younger and sharper eyes.

"What are you doing here?" Bret repeated as Myra and Lucy scurried out of the berry bushes and ran to meet them.

"Bloody Hand," Myra exclaimed. "The son of a bitch followed us here!"

"You saw them?" Bret demanded, assuming it was a war party from the Piegan camp. "How many?"

"I don't know," Myra said. "We didn't see them. Ruby told Lucy to run, that Bloody Hand was coming to get her."

"Ruby?" Coldiron asked, finding it hard to believe the hostile Blackfoot woman would bother to warn them.

"Yes," Lucy exclaimed. "It was her. She sneaked up on me when I was in the bushes and told me I had to run and hide, because Bloody Hand had come to take me back."

"We didn't see any Indians," Myra repeated. "But I didn't see any sense in taking any chances that the woman was just up to some mischief—out to frighten two white women."

"You did the right thing," Bret said. "She doesn't strike me as the kind to do much joking, so I expect we'd best take her word for it and get ready to have some visitors. We've got to figure they heard that shot, so they'll be coming this way pretty quick." He turned to Coldiron. "What do you think, Nate? Better to pick us a spot to sit and wait awhile, instead of taking a chance on bumping into a war party in the dark. Whaddaya think?"

"I think you're right," Coldiron agreed. "It's best we sit tight till we find out what we've got to deal with." He had to pause to comment then. "I swear, though, I wouldn'ta believed they'd come after us, after we got to Fort Benton."

"It's Bloody Hand," Lucy cried. "He said I'd never get away from him, and now he's here, just like he said. I think he's the devil and he's determined to take me back to his hell."

"Well, it's gonna cost him more than he might wanna pay," Bret assured her. "Let's quit wasting time and find a place to make a stand."

Myra put her arm around the near-hysterical girl and tried to calm her. "There's three of us that son of a bitch has to go through to get to you."

Bloody Hand looked up when he heard the rifle shot echoing through the darkness. He dropped the strip of smoked venison he had found on a metal plate beside the fire. Lame Dog came from the creek, where he had been looking at the horses left to graze there.

"That was not far away," he said. They both paused, waiting to see if there were other shots fired. When there were none, Lame Dog said, "Maybe they shot a deer."

"Why would they take the women with them?" Bloody Hand wondered aloud. He could not understand why it happened that the women were not in the camp. When he and Lame Dog were scouting the campsite, it appeared that the party had left in a hurry, because of the plates by the fire and a coffeepot still sitting in the coals.

In a fit of anger, he kicked the coffeepot, sending it bouncing over the ground, splashing coffee. What he had expected to be a simple capture of the two women had resulted in adding to his wrath and frustration. Simple logic told him that the two white men had not taken the women hunting with them.

"Somehow they found out that we were coming, and they have run into the woods to hide." He cast an accusing gaze at Lame Dog. "The white trader, Smart, must have warned them."

His nostrils flared in anger at the thought.

"No," Lame Dog responded immediately. "I didn't tell Jake Smart that you were here to take your woman back." He was still reluctant to refer to his father in any context other than the third person. "He doesn't know you're with me."

"Your mother, then," Bloody Hand said.

Again Lame Dog was quick to refute. "No, my

mother is pure Blackfoot. She has no use for any white man except Jack Smart, and she doesn't tell him anything about me, or what I'm doing. He is only good for providing a house and food for my mother, and with his trade goods, he is useful to the Blackfeet. If that were not so, he would be dead already, by her knife or mine."

Bloody Hand was still not convinced. "If they ran to hide because they saw us approaching this camp, then they cannot be far away. They didn't have time to take their horses, so they must be hiding somewhere near the creek banks like frightened fawns." Convinced that was the case, he said, "Come, we'll search both sides of the creek and flush them from their hiding places."

"What about Coldiron and the other man?" Lame Dog asked. "They might show up here, if they killed a deer."

"Then we will kill them," Bloody Hand stated frankly. "I came to kill them. It will save me the trouble of having to find them."

He pulled a limb from the fire and, using it for a torch, crossed over the creek, searching for likely hiding places. Lame Dog set out combing the darkened bank on the near side.

While he searched, under every bush and vine, he thought about Bloody Hand's suspicions earlier, and he wondered if his mother *had* told his father. How else would he know to warn the women? If that was what really happened, then

Jake Smart had betrayed him in favor of the white men. That made Jake Smart his enemy, and he wished death to his enemies. He decided then to kill Jake and rid his conscience of his shameful ties to the white man. His mother would no longer need the miserable little man for her food and lodging. He, Lame Dog, would take her back to the Piegan village with him and she would be free to live as she was born to live, with her people.

"Here!" Bloody Hand called and held up a scrap of material that had been torn from Lucy's sleeve by a broken laurel limb. "They ran this way!" He pushed through the laurel, coming to a clear patch of sand near the water. He stopped there and held his torch close to the ground, and discovered a clear footprint. It was a woman's print.

"They're running to the sound of the gunshot," he said, "trying to find the hunters." He started up the creek at a trot, hoping to overtake them.

"What about our horses?" Lame Dog called after him. He didn't think it wise to become separated from their ponies.

Bloody Hand paused for only a second, too intent upon catching two frightened women running for their lives.

"Go back and get our horses, and then bring them along behind me."

He was off again, at a trot, confident he could run the women down before they reached safety.

On he went, stopping occasionally to search a

sandy spot for footprints, becoming more and more anxious as he found them, knowing that the feeble light from the burning limb was nearing exhaustion. A dozen yards farther found him nearing a sharp bend in the creek where it changed course to flow around a twelve-foot bluff. He paused to try to get a better look at the ground ahead a moment too late. For in the next instant, he felt the blow of a .44 slug, knocking the smoking limb from his hand. Too startled to keep from emitting a yelp of pain, he was quick enough to drop to the ground and roll over the edge of the creek bank.

"Damn it, I shoulda waited," Coldiron swore. "I think I hit him, though—don't know how bad he's hurt."

The target he had was just a tiny flicker of flame, but he was afraid he wouldn't get a much better one, so he took the shot. There were no answering shots, so they were not sure of what might be coming at them.

After several minutes had passed with still no return fire, Coldiron asked, "You think maybe I got him?"

"Maybe," Bret answered, his eyes scanning the dark creek bank below them, searching for movement of any kind, something that would tell him if there was a war party even now working around their position on the bluff. He looked behind him then where Myra and Lucy were huddled up against the steep face of a low hill with his and Coldiron's horses beside them. A few more minutes ticked slowly by with nothing to break the deep silence of the creek but an occasional ripple from a muskrat.

Finally Bret declared, "I don't think there's a war party down there. I think the man you shot at was alone, and the only way we're gonna find out if I'm right is for me to go down there to see."

"Well, that don't make a helluva lotta sense," Coldiron said. "That might be just what they're hopin' you'll do."

"Maybe," Bret said. "But I don't intend to sit up here all night, waiting for somebody to come after us. I'll go back and cross the creek upstream and see if I can work around behind them."

He didn't wait to get Coldiron's opinion, and was scrambling down from the bluffs in a matter of seconds. He knew it was risky, but he was tired of running from a vengeful Indian, who seemed to have set his mind on dogging Lucy until he caught her and dragged her back to his tipi. Of additional concern to him was the thought of the horses and packs with all their possessions back at the camp.

As he made his way in a wide circle around the section of the creek bank where they had seen the flame, he became more and more convinced that it had been only one man stalking the women. There was no sign of horses or a large party of warriors combing the creek banks.

When he came up behind the place where he thought Bloody Hand had been shot, there was no one there. He was sure it was the right spot, because he saw the smoking limb that had served as the Indian's torch lying on the edge of the bank. He turned to call Coldiron at once.

"He's not here, Nate! We've got to get back to the camp before we lose everything we own."

The same thought must have occurred to Coldiron, because within seconds, the big man came crashing down through the bushes leading the two horses with a frightened woman on the back of each.

"Might be the same son of a bitch that tried to steal our horses before," he said, panting for breath. "Keep a sharp eye," he warned needlessly, and they started back down the dark creek at a trot, leading their horses and fearing that they might be too late to stop the raider, or raiders, from absconding with all their possessions.

Bret was of a different opinion. If the Indian was only after the horses and their other possessions, he would have taken the four horses back at camp and gone with them and their possibles while he had a chance to escape with no damage done. Bret was convinced that it was the crazed Piegan warrior coming after Lucy, just as Ruby had warned.

Although it seemed far, they were actually no more than a quarter of a mile from the camp behind Jake Smart's store. Intent upon getting to their camp as soon as possible, they were forced to become cautious as they approached the clearing.

In the darkness they could not be certain where their enemy was, or how many, even though Bret's gut feeling was that there was no war party, and probably only the one Piegan obsessed with Lucy. But because he couldn't be sure of that, he and Coldiron were hampered by the necessity to keep the women with them, lest they be found in some hiding place without his protection.

Moving through the pine trees that surrounded the clearing on three sides, Bret told the women to stay with the horses while he and Coldiron crawled a few yards to the edge of the trees where they could get a better look into the clearing. The campfire had died to little more than a rosy glow that gave very little light beyond about a six-foot circle.

"Can't see a helluva lot, can you?" Coldiron expressed the obvious. "With those young eyes of yours, can you see the horses?"

"Just barely," Bret answered. "I can see them moving a little bit, at least enough to know they're still there." After a few moments more of straining to make out anything else on the edges of the clearing, he concluded, "The packs and saddles are right where we left them. It doesn't look like anybody bothered them. But there could be a regiment on the other side of that fire and you couldn't see them."

"Got any great ideas?" Coldiron asked. "I know I ain't got any big desire to walk into that camp."

"We gotta figure that you musta wounded that Indian back there by the bluffs, but not bad enough to keep him from running. He knows we've got to come back here to protect our horses and supplies, so the best thing for him to do is sit right here and wait for us to show up. That way, he can just pick us off when we come riding into that clearing. Is that about the way you see it?"

"I expect it's what I would do," Coldiron said. "Looks like that's what he's got in mind, else he'da stole the horses and anything else he could find and be gone." He shook his head, perplexed, having come to the same conclusion that Bret had already arrived at. "Nah, he's got killin' on his mind—and gettin' Lucy. I expect Jake's wife told Lucy the truth when she said that it was Bloody Hand come to fetch her."

"Looks to me like we've got a standoff until daylight," Bret said, "and that's a pretty long time yet."

"Looks like," Coldiron agreed. "And don't you get no ideas about sneakin' across the clearin' before daylight," he scolded, thinking of Bret's impatience back there on the bluffs. "We'll just sit tight, till we've got a better idea what we're up against. We can't see him, and if we ain't made too much noise, he can't see us."

With little choice in the matter, they withdrew

from the edge of the trees to do what they could to find protection for Myra and Lucy as well as the two horses. Once they were satisfied they had done all they could for them, they settled in for a long sleepless night.

Chapter 13

Bloody Hand unwound the bandanna from his hand to look at the mutilated stumps where two of his fingers once were. Without the makeshift bandage, the bleeding began anew, causing him to scowl with anger. He wrapped the bandanna around his hand again and let Lame Dog tie a rawhide thong around it to hold it in place.

"It's lucky it's my left hand," he said, and to test it, he quickly brought his rifle up as if to shoot. "They will have to come back here, and when they do, remember not to shoot the young woman. I will kill her in time, but I have use for her before then."

He thought of the slender girl, so vulnerable and helpless in his lust for her, powerless to deny him his way. Then an image of her obvious disgust for him whenever he had approached her came to him, causing his anger to overpower the pain throbbing in his wounded hand. Unable to prevent the surge of frustration that rose from deep inside his bowels, he emitted a low thin whine that startled Lame Dog, who knelt beside him beneath the bank of the creek.

"Your hand?" he asked. "Does it pain you?"

"This wound is nothing," Bloody Hand snapped in contempt for the question. "The pain I feel is an aching to kill the white men."

Out of habit, he clutched the shriveled ear in his right hand so hard that his fingernails brought blood to his palms. Finally pushed to the limit of his patience, he suddenly rose to his feet and sang out his war song, daring the white men to face him in battle. Shocked by the unexpected wail of the tortured warrior, Lame Dog quickly drew away from him, expecting a barrage of rifle shots to follow.

On the other side of the clearing from the warriors, the four white people were also jolted by the sudden release of Bloody Hand's frustration. Lucy moved closer to Myra when the eerie howl drifted to them across the open grass of the meadow.

"What the hell is that?" Coldiron blurted.

"You're the Indian expert," Bret replied. "You tell me."

The war chant continued for a couple of minutes. "I know a little Blackfoot talk," Coldiron said. "Sounds like he's singin' his war song, somethin' about how many enemies he's killed, and some other stuff I can't make out."

"Can you tell where it's coming from?" Bret

asked. "Sounds to me like it's over close to the creek bank, near those two tallest trees."

"Maybe," Coldiron replied, "hard to tell."

Bret thought about it for a couple of seconds before suggesting, "Maybe he's hoping he can tempt us to fire a few rounds in that direction so he can see our muzzle blasts and get a target."

"He might at that," Coldiron allowed. "I hadn't thoughta that. Wonder if it would work on him, and give us a target to shoot at? Hell, I can sing him a war song if that's what he wants."

"It might beat sitting here waiting for daylight," Bret said, not expecting Coldiron to actually attempt it.

A second later he was stunned by an outburst akin to a rusty pipe organ. The big man sang out lustily to the tune of an old Irish drinking ditty, but the words were of his own creation. Devoid of rhyme, he sang a confusion of insults to the Piegan warrior, labeling him a coward and next in kin to a groundhog. His offering was met almost immediately by a barrage of rifle fire, clipping the limbs above their heads and filling the air around them with stinging hot metal.

"Damn!" Coldiron blurted as he dived to the ground.

"Get flat on the ground, ladies!" Bret called back behind him. "To the right of that biggest tree!" he exclaimed to Coldiron, and pumped three quick shots at the spot where he had seen the muzzle flashes. Coldiron fired three of his own; then they both moved to the side several yards. "Everybody all right back there?" Bret called to Myra.

"We're all right," Myra called back. "But I hope to hell Nate ain't got any encore numbers. I don't think that Indian appreciates his singing."

Under less dire situations, Bret might have laughed at Myra's graveyard humor. As it was, he shook his head in amazement at the woman's calm. After the sudden eruption of gunfire, everything went quiet again. "That was a helluva lot of fire for one man," he said.

"Yeah," Coldiron agreed. "He's got help—two of 'em is what I think. At least it looked like two different muzzle flashes. Course it could mean there's a hundred of 'em over there, but only two of 'em shot at us."

It was a signal to both of them that they were going to have to be even more cautious, knowing for sure that it was not one man alone.

There were still several hours to wait before daylight, and the more thought Bret gave to their situation, the less inclined he was to sit there. With the coming of dawn, the clearing would be even more of a no-man's land, leading to the prospect of the two sides sniping away at each other, probably with no clear winner. The time to act was now, he decided, under the cover of the darkness that now held them helpless. His mind made up, he told Coldiron to stay close to the women and to keep a sharp eye on the clearing. "What the hell are you gonna do?" Coldiron demanded.

"I'm gonna fall back and take a wide circle around behind their position," Bret said. "If I can get in behind them, I might be able to end this standoff. If we wait for sunlight, we're not gonna be in any better position than we are right now."

"There you go again," Coldiron scolded. "What if you work your way around them and find out you walked right into a whole bunch of Blackfoot warriors just lyin' low and waitin' for us to make some dumb-fool move like that?"

"Then I'd be the one to wear the dunce hat, wouldn't I? But there ain't any Blackfoot war party over there. That's for sure. So look after our women. If you need help, Myra's got her forty-four."

His last comment was an attempt to joke, but he felt confident that the plucky woman would step up if she was needed. Then, while Coldiron was formulating his objections, he was off before the big scout could put them into words.

The ring of pines that framed the creek was about thirty yards wide. Outside the ring was an almost treeless ridge with a common wagon road running along it. It was the road that he, Coldiron, and Myra had followed to the trading post on their trip down the Smith River. Reasonably satisfied that he could not be seen on the road, he ran along it at a trot, planning to leave it at a point some seventy-five yards short of the path that led down to Jake Smart's store, and work his way back into the trees behind the two warriors. There was no sign from the trading post of any possibility that Jake might be investigating the shooting that he had surely heard. But what Bret should have considered, maybe even expected, was the possibility that his adversaries might have had similar thoughts.

In fact, Lame Dog had already suggested the same tactic to Bloody Hand. The tormented Piegan eagerly accepted the plan and insisted that he should be the one to carry it out. The mangled mess that Coldiron's bullet had made of Bloody Hand's fingers, however, refused to stop bleeding to the point where the soaked bandanna was no longer effective. The pain from the wound caused his arm to throb all the way to his shoulder, which served to increase his frustration.

Lame Dog, seeing an opportunity to gain the respect of his fearsome friend, sought to convince Bloody Hand that he could drive the white men out of the trees and into the clearing, where he could kill them. Finally admitting that his left arm was becoming more and more stiff and useless, Bloody Hand gave in to Lame Dog's plan. Since fate has its own agenda, it would seem more than coincidence that Lame Dog decided to circle around the clearing by way of the wagon road.

With rifle in hand, Bret trotted along the wagon track, slumped slightly in a subconscious attempt to make as small a target as possible. When he reached the spot he had picked to leave the road to make his way down through the trees, he paused a moment to look back the way he had come, and listen for any sounds that might alert him. There was nothing. The road behind him stood out in the eerie light like a bright ribbon in the faint light of a nearly eclipsed moon. With one last look toward the trading post, and seeing no activity from that quarter, he left the narrow road and started toward the ring of trees, to suddenly find himself face-to-face with the lean, dark figure of a Blackfoot warrior.

Equally startled, both men stood frozen for a long moment, unprepared to encounter a combative adversary. In the next instant, both men recovered and sprang into action, each one trying to level his rifle and fire, and each one grabbing the barrel of the other's rifle to prevent the rifle from being aimed at him. A desperate battle of strength ensued as each man strained to overpower his opponent in what proved to be a fairly equal contest. Back and forth they struggled, knowing that to weaken would result in the ultimate penalty, one that neither man was willing to accept.

Finally Lame Dog managed to swing his foot to catch on Bret's ankle, causing him to trip and fall. Refusing to release his grip on Lame Dog's rifle,

Bret pulled the half-breed toward him as he fell, causing him to flip over him to land on his back. The collision with the hard ground was enough to make them both lose their grip on their rifles, resulting in a frantic scramble to recover their weapons.

Lame Dog was quick, reaching his rifle first, but not quick enough to keep Bret from diving on him to prevent him from bringing it to bear on him. With one hand under Bret's chin, Lame Dog strained furiously to push him away, but to no avail, as Bret fought to gain control of Lame Dog's rifle. Thinking of the long skinning knife he wore on his belt, and feeling the drain on his strength, Lame Dog suddenly released his hold on his rifle and reached for the knife. It was a mistake. Bret, acting instantly, grabbed the rifle with both hands and rolled away from the half-breed. With his knife raised to strike, Lame Dog launched his body to land the killing thrust. Praying that there was a cartridge already chambered, Bret only had time to pull the trigger. The bullet caught Lame Dog in the chest, killing him instantly. His lifeless body landed across Bret's legs.

Bret kicked the body off him, not sure if the half-breed was dead or not. When there was no response from the corpse, he quickly crawled over to retrieve his Winchester, looking around him cautiously, in case the dead man had friends close by. But he saw no one.

It's a damn good thing there isn't anyone, because I damn sure had my hands full with this one. I wonder if he was Bloody Hand, he thought, lacking the presence of mind to remember Lucy's description of the Indian. It would have been fairly easy to identify a man with only one ear.

He sat there for a minute, exhausted, before moving forward again, this time with a rifle in each hand. He had other immediate worries now, and he needed the cover of the thick band of trees that circled the clearing. Everyone had to have heard the shot, and he couldn't be sure who might be on their way to investigate.

Once in the trees, he stopped again to listen. There were no sounds that would signal an attack by other members of a war party, so he felt reasonably certain that he and Coldiron had been right in concluding that they were dealing with two Indians only. So now the question was, where was the other one?

Keeping the spot across the clearing where he had seen the muzzle flashes in mind, he started making his way through the thick band of pines with the intention of circling all the way around and coming up behind it. As he moved through the dark forest, he remained mindful of the fact that the other Indian had heard the shot, and Bret could not know if he had remained where he was. Suspecting that Coldiron had wounded the man, Bret thought there was still a good possibility that he might confront him unexpectedly in the trees.

The question was answered in the next few minutes when he was nearing the edge of the creek. A movement across the creek caught his eye and he turned in time to glimpse a horse moving up toward the clearing through a stand of willows. It disappeared from sight almost as soon as it had appeared. Bret went after it, almost certain the horse was being led up through the willows. By the time he reached the spot where he first saw it, the horse was gone, but there was another horse tied there. It further convinced him that there were two warriors only. Because of the broken willow switches, it was not hard to follow a man leading a horse. He didn't have to follow him very far before he realized that the warrior was on a path to circle around behind Coldiron and the women.

Damn! he cursed to himself, and tried to hurry after the Indian. Then, thinking he should alert Coldiron, he fired his rifle three times in the air. He hoped that that would at least keep his big friend on his toes.

Pushing hurriedly on then, he suddenly dropped to his knee when he emerged from the willows to find a warrior standing some forty yards before him, his rifle aimed at him. The slug whistled only inches over his head, his reflex action of dropping to his knee having saved him. He brought the Winchester up and got off one round before diving flat on the ground. He had no time to take careful aim, but he saw the Indian stagger when his shot turned him halfway around. Bret scrambled to his feet as fast as he could, but it was not in time to get off a clear shot as his target used his horse to shield himself.

Not anxious to run into an ambush, even though he was sure the Indian was wounded, Bret followed the man cautiously, hoping to get the clear shot he needed to end it. It was not to be, however, for when he came again to the creek, he got just one glimpse of the wounded warrior galloping over the top of a small ridge. Seconds later, he was gone.

Damn! Bret thought. *I should have shot the damn horse when he was using it for cover.* "Well, I can't do anything about it now," he muttered, and turned to call out to Coldiron, "Nate! It's all over! There were two of them, all right. One of 'em's dead. The other one got away, but he's wounded. I think he's got two bullets in him."

"All right," Coldiron called back. "We're comin' out if you think it's clear."

"Come on, then," Bret confirmed, confident that it was all right for the time being, but thinking that it would be wise to pack up and leave as soon as it was daylight. "I'm going to take a look to make sure that Indian isn't waiting on the other side of that hill," he called out again. Then he started out in the direction Bloody Hand had fled, moving at a steady trot, still carrying two rifles. When he reached the top of the hill, there was no sign of the wounded man on the other side of it, and none on the rolling expanse of treeless prairie beyond. It seemed likely that the man was intent only upon escaping.

By the time he returned to the clearing, Coldiron and the women were already in the process of packing up. "Somebody put a dent in your new coffeepot," Myra said when he walked up to join them. "I found it halfway across the clearing."

"You all right?" Coldiron asked. When Bret said that he was, the big bearlike man went on. "I wasn't much help," he said. "I shoulda been down here helpin' you."

Bret realized that his oversized friend was feeling genuine remorse for not having taken part in the fight. "You were protecting Lucy and Myra so I didn't have to worry about them."

"Yeah, well, you gotta start tellin' me what you're thinkin' about doin' next time before you go ahead and do it. Now, where's the one you killed?"

"He's up by the road," Bret said.

"Let's go take a look at him," Coldiron said.

"I'm going with you," Lucy spoke up then.

Myra quickly responded, "You don't need to see a dead Indian. It might not be a pretty sight."

"I want to see if it's him," Lucy insisted. "I have to know he's dead."

"You're having enough nightmares as it is," Myra told her. "There's no sense in adding another one. Bret can tell you if it's Bloody Hand. From the way you described him, it shouldn't be too hard." She turned to Bret then. "Can't you, Bret?"

He realized that he was not absolutely certain, because of the desperate struggle in the dark, but he didn't recall noticing that an ear was missing. He remembered wondering afterward if the man he killed was Bloody Hand, but that was after he had already left the body.

"I suppose," he hedged. "It was so dark, and I was pretty busy at the time, but I'll take a closer look for you."

"Looks like you picked up an extra rifle," Myra commented as the two men started to walk up to the road.

"What?" Bret replied absentmindedly. "Oh . . . yeah, a Winchester."

"Well, unless you think you need both of them, then I could use one," she suggested.

"I hadn't thought about it," Bret said. "Sure, you're welcome to it. You know how to use it?"

"Just like the one I shot that deer with, I suppose."

He chuckled at that. He had forgotten about it. "Right, just like that one." He handed her Lame Dog's rifle.

"And that means I get the pistol you've been carrying," Lucy was quick to advise Myra.

"Damn," Coldiron chuckled. "Everybody totin' a weapon. We best be careful we don't go to shootin' each other."

With the coming of daylight, Jake Smart ventured out of his store to see what all the shooting had been about. Bleary-eyed from spending the night moving from window to window, he had sought to protect his store in the event the shooting got closer. Also unable to sleep, Ruby suffered more concern than her husband. She was well aware of the cause of the shooting, for she knew what Lame Dog and Bloody Hand had planned. Soon after first light, and all was quiet in the valley, she implored Jake to investigate. And this was how he came upon Bret and Coldiron standing over the body of his son. When still not close enough to identify the deceased, he called out to the two men, "Sounds like you fellers had another busy night. Somebody tryin' to steal your horses again?"

"Not this time," Coldiron replied. "They had somethin' more in mind. It was that crazy son of a bitch after Lucy again. That's why we're packin' up. This place ain't brought us nothin' but bad luck."

"Well, looks like that one won't be botherin' you no more," Jake said. "So he was after—"

That was as far as he got when he came close enough to see the body. Stunned, he stared in disbelief, unable to speak.

"Damn, Jake," Coldiron said. "You look white as a sheet. You know this feller?"

"He's my son," Jake answered softly, his voice barely above a whisper.

His simple statement cast all three men into a stony silence. Bret and Coldiron exchanged shocked glances, left speechless, for what words were appropriate for such an occasion? After what seemed an eternity, it was Jake who broke the silence.

"I knew he was runnin' with a mean bunch, but I didn't know he was plannin' nothin' like this against you boys." He stood there, continuing to stare at the corpse.

Bret knew he should say something to justify the killing, so he offered his condolences and tried to explain how it happened.

"I didn't have any choice, Jake. He was trying to kill me, and I was just the lucky one who came out on top. It was him or me."

Bret's attempt to explain loosened Coldiron's tongue, and he wanted to make sure that Jake understood the facts of the matter.

"Don't go blamin' Bret for what happened here. We didn't have no idea your boy was one of them two out to kill us and steal the girl again. God's honest truth, neither one of us woulda knowed your son from any other Blackfoot warrior. Bret did what he had to do. Your son was the one did the choosin'. And that's the truth of it."

Jake considered what Coldiron said for only a moment before replying, "I know what you say is most likely the way of it, but what can I tell his mama?" There was no answer coming forth from either Coldiron or Bret. "Maybe you can help me carry him to the barn, and then I expect it'd be best if you fellers get on your horses and get on outta here." He didn't have to explain why.

"We can surely do that," Coldiron said, "and we'll be outta here by the time you go to the house to tell Ruby. I'm real sorry your son had to come to an end like this, but like I said, he didn't give Bret no choice." He turned to Bret then and said, "I can tote him to the barn. You go back and get the women on their horses and meet me here at the road."

"Right," Bret replied. "We'll be ready to ride."

He turned at once and hurried back down through the trees to the clearing, feeling as if he had somehow committed a crime. He wasn't sure how he should feel, however, sorry for Jake and Ruby maybe, but also knowing that their son was an evil son of a bitch that deserved killing. He was going to have to tell Lucy that the man he killed was not the one-eared monster as she hoped. But when he recalled how Bloody Hand was lying low on his horse's neck, he felt confident that he was critically wounded. If he didn't die, he would be a long time recovering, and by that time, they would be long gone from this territory.

When he got back to their camp, he found the women packed up and ready to leave, so he told them to climb on their horses, and in a matter of minutes, they were heading up through the trees toward the wagon track. Lucy wanted confirmation of Bloody Hand's death before she got on her horse.

"Bloody Hand's gone," he told her. "You don't have to worry about him anymore. Right now we've got to ride. I'll tell you all about it when we stop to rest the horses and maybe eat some breakfast."

She was perplexed by his reluctance to simply tell her that the Piegan monster was dead, but it was obvious that he was not going to take time to discuss it then. So she didn't resist when he hurriedly cupped his hands to give her a boost up on her horse.

When they reached the road up above the creek, Myra asked, "Where's Nate? Ain't he going with us?"

The big man was nowhere in sight, but within a few minutes' time, he suddenly appeared, shuffling along at a rapid walk.

"We're all set to go," he said as he took his reins from Bret and climbed aboard the big buckskin.

Finally it was too much for Myra to hold her tongue.

"Will somebody tell me why we're running

away from here like we robbed the place? Are there some more Indians coming after us?"

"No," Bret told her. "But we need to make tracks. We'll tell you why after we put some distance between us and this place."

With that said, he asked the paint gelding for a fast lope, and they headed south along the river. He had a notion that when Ruby found out about her son's death, she would come looking for vengeance equally dangerous to that of a war party.

Approximately twenty miles north of the trading post, Bloody Hand lay where he had fallen from his pony. Weak from blood loss, and in severe pain, he gazed at his bloody hand but was in too much pain to appreciate the irony in the appropriateness of his name. His shirttail was soaked with blood from the bullet wound in his back, and he was not sure he had the strength to get back on his horse. When the afternoon sun began to settle closer to the hills, he began to chant his death song.

The angry explosion back at the trading post that Bret and Coldiron predicted came about as anticipated. Ruby Red Bonnet screamed in agony when Jake told her that they had to bury her son. Brought to her knees by the news that Lame Dog had been killed by Bret Hollister, she cried out her pain and began ripping her arms and face with her fingernails. Jake tried to comfort her, but she pushed him away. "Where is he?" she demanded.

"I carried him into the barn," Jake said.

"Into the barn!" she exploded again. "You treat him like a horse or cow?"

"I just took him there so I could tell you about it before I just came carryin' him in the house," he tried to explain quickly.

She wasted no more words on him but got up from the floor and rushed out the front door. She found him lying on a bed of hay in the back stall and collapsed by his side, her grief overpowering. Jake could only stand by, helplessly watching her, as she sobbed and moaned with her pain.

After a long period, her grieving tears suddenly turned to anger. Without a word to Jake, she got to her feet and ran to the store. Jake wanted to give her comfort, but he didn't know how he could, so he followed her to the store, only to be met by her on her way back, carrying his shotgun.

"Whoa, hon," Jake attempted to reason with her. "Where you goin' with that shotgun? Them folks has already pulled outta here. They're gone."

It was too much for her angry frustration. Using the shotgun as a club, she swung it at him, barely missing his head. He jumped back a couple of steps in fright.

"Why you didn't kill them?" she asked. "He was your son!"

"Why, hon, I thought about it," he whined defensively. "But I couldn't hardly see how I could blame them folks for defendin' theirselves. Could you?"

"He was your son," she repeated, thinking that was reason enough.

"You shoulda told me John was fixin' to ride into that camp to kill them folks and take that young woman back. He ought'nta done that."

"Why you call him John? His name is Lame Dog, Blackfoot warrior," she said.

"Yes'm," Jake replied respectfully. "But I expect we'd best get him in the ground."

They buried Lame Dog on the hill behind the barn, and Ruby stayed there by the grave, mourning long after Jake returned to the store. Later in the afternoon, she came back and got the shotgun again, then disappeared into the trees between the trading post and the clearing where Bret and the others had camped. Jake figured she went to their camp to mourn, but he began to worry when she didn't return by nightfall. Deciding it was too dark to try to find her, he decided he had no choice but to wait until morning.

The next day, he looked for her, but she was nowhere around the clearing, and he feared she might be trying to track Coldiron and his friends, seeking revenge. He shook his head in frustration, knowing she had little chance of catching up with them on foot.

Two days passed before she returned to the trading post, looking half-starved and bleeding from the many self-inflicted wounds that testified to the intensity of her mourning. He greeted her at the door.

"Damn, hon, I'm glad to see you. You look like you could use a cup of coffee and a biscuit or two, although them biscuits ain't as good as the ones you make."

He hoped she'd gotten over Lame Dog's death. He knew that he had. A man couldn't begin to explain the why or the wherefore for the way things happened. It didn't do any good to worry about it, one way or the other, and he wouldn't have to worry about hiding the forty-four cartridges anymore.

"I reckon the best thing for us to do is to put all that meanness behind us now and go back to livin' with what we got," he counseled.

"What do you know about living, white man?" she responded curtly.

Chapter 14

Three full days of hard riding found Bret and his "family of misfits" in camp by a healthy creek at the foot of the Crazy Mountains. They had planned to stop there for the night only, but after finding deer sign all around the creek, they decided to stay over for a day or two more. The tragic happenings on their last night at their camp at the confluence of Hound Creek and the Smith River were well behind them now. There had been no sign that anyone was following them, and even Lucy seemed to be less tense and nervous. It was a good opportunity to release the tensions that had captured everyone since Lucy's rescue from the Piegan village.

After a successful day's hunting, while butchering two fine young deer, Coldiron spoke the words that were on everybody's minds.

"I could sure get used to this little valley between the Crazies and the Big Belts. This is all a free man could ask for right here—the mountains behind you with plenty of game to hunt—a sea of grass in front of you to graze on between the mountains."

"I was thinking the same thing," Myra said, having overheard Coldiron's comment. "I brought you some more coffee." She filled the cups for both men. "Plenty of lumber in the foothills behind us to build a house and a barn." She turned to look at Lucy beside the fire. "What do you think, Lucy?"

"Whatever you say, Myra," the young lady replied.

The concept began to take hold on all four minds, even to the extent of creating interest on Bret's part. This even though he suspected the three of them of ganging up on him to sell the idea.

"Who owns all this grazing land between these mountain ranges?" he asked.

"Nobody," Coldiron said. "It's free range. At least, last I heard."

"Then I say why don't we homestead it?" Myra suggested. "It sounds like the place we talked about before when we decided to stick together like a family."

Bret shrugged. "I don't know. How far is it to Bozeman?" He was thinking about supplies and tools.

"'Bout fifty miles," Coldiron answered, a big smile struggling to be seen beneath the heavy gray beard.

"Hell, I don't know," Bret confessed. "We said we were gonna set up a place somewhere. Whatever the rest of you think, I reckon I'll go along."

Myra and Coldiron looked at each other, both grinning, so Myra spoke for both of them. "Then I guess we're home."

They all laughed at that, and began exchanging handshakes, oblivious of the deer blood passed from Bret's and Coldiron's hands.

The following days were busy ones for everyone, the first order of business being to establish a permanent camp. Coldiron and Bret were able to cut enough small trees with the hatchets they carried in the packs to build a sizable lean-to that would keep the four bedrolls dry in anything less than a driving rainstorm.

Since they were in the dry season on the plains, they hoped to get a cabin built before having to face winter storms. But there were tools and other things needed to build a good cabin, including a two-man saw to cut the larger logs for the cabin walls.

"There are some other things we're gonna need if we're gonna raise cattle and horses," Bret said. "It's a little difficult to raise horses when you don't even own a mare. Same thing goes for cattle."

"Hell," Coldiron said, "that ain't no problem. We'll use that money of yours you've been keepin' in the bank. We can buy some breedin' stock from one of those big ranches up at Deer Lodge. We'll have us a herd started in no time."

Bret had to laugh. "Well, I'm happy that you're gonna let me have a hand in your big stock enterprise."

The work that followed in the next couple of weeks seemed to have been a cathartic for everyone, especially Lucy, who was gradually healing inside. Her downcast manner was soon replaced by one without the constant shame she had come to them with.

Much progress was made, but the summer days were waning, and winter was not far away. It was time to make the trip into Bozeman to buy a wagon, and the tools and supplies they would need to build a proper cabin. Bret, of course, had to go, for he had to withdraw the money from the bank. They could not all go, they decided, because they were not comfortable leaving the temporary camp they had built and running the risk that it might be found by some other wanderers looking for a place to settle. There was no one Bret could think of who was a better protector of their homestead than the huge bear of a man he now partnered with, so Coldiron stayed at home.

"I guess either me or Lucy oughta go with you," Myra suggested.

"Why?" Bret asked. "I don't need anyone to go with me." He grinned and added, "Besides, somebody's got to be here to feed Coldiron."

"Because you might decide to just keep on going," she said, joking. She turned serious then. "You need to go tell those officers at Fort Ellis that you brought a witness for the defense," she said. "You told us what they did to end your military career."

Her words were sobering. He had not thought about it for a long time.

"We talked about this before," he said. "I told you when we made our agreement to work together that I didn't care to return to the army. And I meant it."

"The three of us appreciate that," Myra said. "But it might be the right thing to do to clear your name. And I'd be proud to tell the bastards that you and Nate rescued us."

He couldn't help considering the possibility. "I don't know, Myra. It might be a waste of time to tell them. The charge against me that cost me my commission was that Nate and I ran when the Blackfeet attacked. The fact is that we went on to rescue you and Lucy after we came back the first time without you. So you see, that doesn't disprove what those two soldiers testified—that we ran from the fight."

"Yes, but it seems to me that you would want the truth to be known," she persisted.

"Tell you the truth, I don't give a damn what the army thinks anymore," Bret told her emphatically. Then he shrugged and said, "If you just want to ride into Bozeman with me, that's fine, if Lucy and Nate can get along without you for a few days."

"I think they can," Myra said, then looked at Lucy for confirmation. "Can't you, honey?"

"We'll be all right," Lucy said. Her response was encouraging to Myra, for she knew the injured girl had come a long way back from her fears. In the beginning, Lucy had feared the intimidating Coldiron almost as much as she had her Indian captors. But in the time since, she had come to realize that he was her protector, and was genuinely concerned for her well-being. Thinking of that progress, Myra smiled to herself. They really were becoming a family.

"All right, then," Bret said. "No use delaying any longer. We'll head out in the morning."

After discussing it with Coldiron, he decided to ride the two packhorses to Bozeman, because both his paint and Myra's Appaloosa were Indian ponies and might not adapt very well to pulling a wagon. Myra started to protest but thought better of it. Plans all settled then, Bret and Myra left early the next morning.

Coldiron cautioned Bret to keep a sharp eye out for any roving bands of Indians.

"There's still some Sioux and Cheyenne renegades that ain't took to the reservation yet." Bret was well aware of that, and promised to be careful. "I'm glad you're takin' Myra along for protection," Coldiron joked. "Me and Lucy won't worry about you as much."

The trip into town was uneventful. They made it in one long day, causing Bret to think the distance was shorter than the fifty miles Coldiron had estimated. They arrived in Bozeman just at dusk and rode into the stable to find the owner, Ned Oliver, preparing to leave for supper.

"Evenin'," Ned greeted them, and tipped his hat to Myra. "You lookin' to board those horses?"

He studied the young man dressed in buckskins intently, thinking that he had seen him before, but unable to recall when.

"That's right," Bret answered. "And in the morning, I might do a little business with you on some other things I need." This perked Ned's interest up a bit more. Bret went on. "I'm gonna need to find a wagon and harness to hitch these two horses to it. Can you help me with that?"

"I sure can," Ned replied. "I've done business with you before, I'm thinkin. I just can't remember when."

"I bought one of these horses from you, the sorrel," Bret said, "and another one, a paint Indian pony."

It struck Ned then, and his face seemed to light up. "I remember now. You got two good horses, and a saddle and pack outfit to boot." He grinned at them both. "I got it now. You were wearin' an army suit. Them buckskins is what threw me off. Yes, sir, I can help you. I can even help you with a wagon. I just bought one from a homesteader who decided he'd had enough hard winters and dry summers and headed back East."

"Good," Bret said. "We'll see you in the morning, then."

"Yes, sir, I can sure fix you up," Ned muttered to himself as he watched them walk up the street toward the hotel.

It's a good thing I'm going to the bank in the morning, Bret thought when he paid for two rooms in the hotel. Thinking then of the many places his money would have to go to set up their ranch, he wondered how many cattle he would be able to buy with whatever amount was left. *Might not be but one cow,* he thought. *I hope to hell she's carrying a calf.* He smiled at the mental picture.

"What are you grinning about?" Myra asked, already looking forward to sleeping in a bed.

"Nothing," Bret replied. "We'll go on upstairs and take a look at the rooms. Then if you're ready, we'll go on down to the dining room for some supper."

"I won't have to take much of a look," Myra said, anticipating the luxury of having someone cook for her. "I hope Lucy and Nate are enjoying their deer jerky tonight while we're dining like rich folks."

Colonel John Grice, acting commander of nearby Fort Ellis, sat at a table near the back corner of the room with Mrs. Grice and her sister and her sister's husband, a prominent lawyer from Omaha.

Since his wife's sister was only going to be in town for the night, Colonel and Martha Grice met them for supper in the hotel dining room.

Looking up to signal their waitress for more wine, Grice suddenly paused, astonished, when he saw the tall young man wearing animal skins walk into the dining room with a woman dressed in men's clothes. Grice forgot the waitress then, his gaze following the couple to a table on the other side of the room. There was no doubt in his mind, it was Bret Hollister.

Knowing what he had to do, Grice told his guests to excuse him for a moment and he would be right back. He got up from his chair then and walked across the room.

Bret, seated with his back to the center of the room, was not aware of the visitor until Myra looked up and nodded. Bret turned then to see what she was staring at so intently.

"Bret?" Colonel Grice spoke.

"Colonel Grice," Bret acknowledged calmly, even though he was as startled as the colonel had been. He was surprised that Grice would approach him.

"Ma'am," Grice greeted Myra politely before saying his piece. "Now, before you tell me to go to hell, Bret, hear me out. All right?"

"I thought all our talking was over," Bret replied. "I know I've got nothing to say to you."

"I know you're angry," Grice went on. "And I

don't blame you one bit, but I'm trying to make amends here."

"Well, you're wasting your time. You and the army have done all the damage to my life that you're capable of doing. So go on back to your table and let us eat in peace."

Myra quickly put two and two together and came up with who the colonel was.

"Let me introduce myself," she interrupted. "My name's Myra Buckley. I was kidnapped by Blackfoot Indians along with Lucy Gentry. After your army gave up on us, Mr. Hollister and his friend Mr. Coldiron refused to quit until they rescued both Lucy and me. And I wouldn't be here today if he had abandoned his search for us."

Grice listened, impatient to continue what he had to say. "I believe you, ma'am, but please listen to me for a minute, and then I'll leave you in peace. I want to tell you about a fight between two men in the Second Cavalry last week. These men were supposed to be friends. I think you will recall Private McCoy and Private Weaver." Bret blanched at the mention of their names. Seeing then that he had Bret's attention, Grice continued. "I don't know what started the fight, but it got ugly, with Weaver cutting McCoy nearly in half with a bayonet. The sergeant of the guard got there in time to stop the fight before Weaver killed McCoy. He threw Weaver in the guardhouse and McCoy in the hospital."

Not really interested, Bret interrupted. "All very entertaining, Colonel, but I don't give a damn if those two liars kill each other."

"Well, maybe you'll be interested in this," Grice insisted. "That little fight turned McCoy into a parrot that wouldn't stop talking. He told the doctor that Weaver was the cause of that massacre of your detail that night on the Yellowstone. Weaver was on guard, but he went to sleep, and when he saw the fighting going on, he ran to save his own hide. He said the two of them cooked up that story to make heroes of themselves and shift the blame on you. He also said that it was you and Coldiron that drove the Indians off, saving his life."

Finished then, Grice stood back to judge Bret's reaction.

It was profound. Bret did not speak for a long moment, sitting there as if just having his life pass before his eyes. There was really nothing he felt appropriate to say. He wondered if the colonel thought he should be dancing a jig to celebrate. If he did, he was to be disappointed, for Bret still felt the injustice of his sentence. Only Myra seemed openly pleased.

Finally Bret spoke. "Well, I'm glad that you and that panel that tried me know the truth now. I appreciate your taking the time to tell me."

"I tried to find you to give you the news," Grice said. "I don't think you understand what this means. I'm pretty sure I can get you reinstated, and your rank and commission back."

Bret took another pause to think about what the colonel had just told him. Then he glanced over at Myra, whose expression of joy had now turned to one of serious concern. He gave her a brief smile, then turned his attention fully on Grice.

"I know what you're telling me, Colonel, but I've got other plans."

Grice seemed shocked. "Do you fully understand what I just said? You can regain your status as a second lieutenant, and that court-martial will be cleared from your record."

"Maybe you should think about that, Bret," Myra felt compelled to say, even though she feared that he might.

"It's a rare occasion when a man gets a chance to see what's best for him. When I left the academy, I was fully primed with the sense of integrity and honor that comes with being an officer. Reality struck me when I found that that integrity could be questioned on the word of two newly enlisted privates, while the word of an officer was rejected. If it happened once, it could happen again, and I do not choose to serve under those conditions. I count myself fortunate to have the opportunity to start my life anew. Now here comes our supper, and I'm sure yours is probably getting cold, so good evening to you, Colonel. Thanks for telling me."

"Suit yourself," Grice snapped, feeling properly rebuffed. He turned on his heel and marched back to join his dinner party.

Myra cast a serious look at Bret. "Are you sure you're doing the right thing?" she asked. "You might be throwing away a great career."

"And miss an opportunity to be a cattle baron?" Bret replied with a grin. "I decided being a soldier just because my father was one is a mistake. Now let's eat this stew before it gets cold."

She fairly beamed. "If I was twenty years younger, I swear, I'd ask you to marry me."

Bret and Myra were waiting at the bank when it opened the next morning. Instead of drawing out all his money, as he had originally planned, he decided to withdraw only what he figured he would need for the time being. When the time came to buy stock, it might be better to do it with a bank draft.

"That way," he jokingly told Myra, "I won't have to find a hiding place to keep you and Lucy out of it."

From the bank, they went directly to see Ned Oliver at the stable. There was a fairly new-looking farm wagon parked conspicuously in front of the stable when they walked up. It occurred to Bret that Myra probably knew more about wagons than he did. She certainly had more experience farming than he, so he asked her to look it over and tell him what she thought. She did, and told him that it looked to be in good shape, so he bought it. She next helped him hitch the horses up to the wagon, making him wonder how he would have gotten along without her.

Next stop was the hardware store, where they loaded their new wagon up with the tools they thought they would need to build a cabin. From there, they went to the general store, which was really the other side of the hardware, where they loaded basic supplies they would need, like flour, sugar, molasses, lard, cornmeal, dried beans, and coffee. One last stop was at the saloon, where Bret picked up a bottle of whiskey and made Myra swear not to tell Coldiron about it until there was a proper occasion to open it.

Starting back, they had barely cleared the sawmill at the edge of town when the two horses decided they didn't like working as a team. Both sorrels, they began protesting and kicking at each other, resulting in a jerky, lurching ride for the passengers. When they refused to settle down after a quarter of a mile, Myra suggested switching them. The idea sounded as good as anything else they could try, so they pulled up and hitched Coldiron's horse on the right of the wagon tongue and Bret's on the left. It worked, for no logical reason, and the ride smoothed out from that point forward.

"Just goes to show you how crazy horses are," Myra said.

"I don't know," Bret joked. "Maybe Nate's horse is just like his master, he always wants to be on the right side of things."

The trip back to their homestead was a good deal slower because of the wagon, so they had to camp overnight. Late in the afternoon, they came upon the first water they had seen in the last six or seven miles, so they decided to stop there. The stream was little more than a trickle coming down a ravine from the hills at the south end of the Crazy Mountains, but it was enough to satisfy their needs. The ravine provided a place to pull the wagon out of sight of anyone out on the prairie, as well as a good place to build a fire where the smoke would not be easily seen.

After a hastily prepared supper of coffee and bacon, Myra promised to do some real cooking when they got back to their camp. When Bret returned to the fire after climbing up the ravine to the top of the hill to take a look around, he found Myra in a mood to talk about their future.

Although they had speculated about building a ranch of serious consequence, he had never really thought much beyond what he would do the next day. Myra was more interested in what he saw in the future, not just his, but all four of their futures. Her concern was what might happen to Lucy and herself. As young and virile as he was, he might simply decide one day to ride away and not come back. There was nothing really holding him to the casual promise to remain with them. True, he was investing all his money in the current project, but he didn't seem to be the kind of man who treasured his money so much that he couldn't ride away and leave it. And she was convinced that the three of them, Lucy, Coldiron, and herself, needed his strong hand to make it work.

"Have you ever thought about getting married one day?" she suddenly asked.

The question surprised him. "Why, no, I don't reckon I ever have," he answered honestly. Remembering her joking remark a few days before, he asked, "Are you fixing to propose?"

She laughed at the thought. "No, I don't think I'd wanna take on a man as young as you are at my age. It might be the death of me. I'll just be your aunt Myra, how about that?" She reconsidered then. "Maybe your older cousin would be better."

"All right, Cousin Myra," he said, laughing.

"No, I expect you'd do better with someone about Lucy's age," Myra said.

Alerted then that she was leading into some more of her devious ways to try to shape the future of the family, he quickly retreated. "I reckon the last thing I need right now is a wife. I doubt I'll ever marry, or ever want to." Then he laughed and said, "Unless I can find a nice Blackfoot woman like Jake Smart did."

"Huh," Myra grunted at the thought of the sinister woman. "Every man should have to be married to a bitch like that for a while. Then they'd all be better husbands the next time around."

She let the subject die for a brief moment before returning to it again.

After pouring him another cup of coffee, she commented anew, "I worry about Lucy. She's so young and full of promise. She didn't have a chance to even get her marriage started." When he made no reply to her comment, she continued. "After what she's been through, I don't guess most men would consider her for marriage." She quickly added, "And they'd be so wrong. Lucy would make the best wife a man could have."

Bret was not so naive that he couldn't recognize the web that the scheming Myra was hoping to weave. She was already thinking about expanding their little family, hoping to start a breeding program. And he was the only eligible candidate for stud service, so he decided to stop her before she ventured farther.

"I don't hold anything against Lucy for what she's been through. None of that's her fault. You're right, I suppose she'd make some lucky man a good wife. I hope for her sake one comes along. Like I told you, I doubt I'll ever get married. I just don't see it in the cards right now."

"Oh, I wasn't talking about you," Myra quickly

responded. It was a lie, and she knew that he knew it by the doubting expression on his face. She would let it rest for now, but he and Lucy were both young. Myra would not abandon the project. She had a strong desire to build a real family, and she was convinced that the best way to do it was to have good breeding stock, like Lucy and Bret, to raise many children. There was a part of her that felt the insecurity of a partnership without marriage ties, something to hold a young man to his responsibilities. She had not yet learned that Bret never made casual promises, and when he promised to help her build a family unit, that's exactly what he would do—without marital ties.

They got an early start the next morning, hoping to make it back to their camp by supper-time. The horses had adjusted to their harnesses and no longer fought against the wagon tongue, so the day's pace went well, and the sun had not yet set when the hills behind the camp came into view.

"I hope Lucy's cooked plenty of food," Myra commented. "She'll be surprised to have company for supper, I expect."

"We'll find out in thirty or forty minutes," Bret said. "Maybe we can get there before Nate finishes it off."

Chapter 15

"Supper's ready!" Lucy called out to Coldiron. The big man was a couple of dozen yards down the creek where he had been marking off a site for the cabin they would build. Always ready when called to supper, he sank his hatchet in a small stump and came at once.

"Hmmm," he sighed when he approached the fire. "Those biscuits smell pretty good. If I'da known you was bakin' biscuits, I'da been here a lot sooner."

Lucy laughed. "I thought I'd give you a chance to test some of my biscuits. They might not be as good as Myra's, but nobody's ever thrown them back at me."

"Well, they smell just as good as Myra's," he said.

She dipped a heaping serving of beans from the pot sitting in the coals and deposited them on a metal plate, being careful to see that she got plenty of the salt pork with it. She handed him the plate, then poured his coffee before she served her plate. After she seated herself across the fire from him, she asked, "When do you suppose they'll be back?"

"Don't know," he said through a mouthful of biscuit. "Depends on whether or not he finds everything we need, I reckon. It might be hard to find a wagon without goin' to Helena. Course, if he finds one, they'll be a lot slower comin' back than they were goin'."

She got quiet again, but he was aware of the fact that she was beginning to talk more and more lately as she got farther away from her despair. He knew she did better when she had Myra close by, but there was no doubt that she was healing. He took a big gulp of coffee and looked around him at the valley they had settled in. He liked it. It already felt like home. He glanced at Lucy and gave her a wide grin. Nathaniel Coldiron wasn't going to grow old and alone in the mountains, and that was enough to grin about.

Unknown by the two homesteaders at the edge of the valley below, a lone observer knelt on a rocky ledge jutting from the ridge behind them. Watching the peaceful scene with great interest, he shifted his gaze from the two people by the fire to the four horses grazing on the lush grass across the creek, then back to the packs piled up near the fire. He was patient now, because he could tell by the camp they had built that they were going to be there for a while.

Feeling a phantom twitch of pain, he looked down at his mutilated hand and the ragged stumps where two fingers had once been, wondering how he could feel pain in fingers that were no longer there. It was part of the curse the white man had somehow put upon him. There was no other explanation for it, but he was satisfied that the curse would be destroyed when the white man was destroyed.

Still calm, he arched his back and stretched his neck back and forth. The bullet that was still in his back would be buried there forever, for the wound had healed around it. It still pained him, but not as much as his hand. The medicine man in Black Bear's village had told him that it would have been too dangerous to try to get the bullet out. He had ridden there for help after being shot, refusing to die until he had fulfilled the quest he had set for himself. They had told him there that Lame Dog had been killed. He felt no sorrow for the half-breed's death, only anger that Lame Dog had not gotten around behind the white men and driven them out into the clearing as he had planned.

Returning his concentration to the scene below him, he wondered if it was possible that the other white man and woman were not coming back to join these two. His passion for vengeance told him that to be fulfilled, he must kill all four of the white devils who had brought him grief. But the woman who had been stolen from him was there in the camp below with the big grizzly called Coldiron. His brain was still tormented by his obsession for her, and her death would be long and painful. He had watched her for two days, waiting for the missing two people to return. His desire for the woman was too much to delay any longer. He decided he would wait no more, and strike while there was still daylight. He fingered the shriveled blob of cartilage on the cord around his neck while he thought of the satisfaction he would enjoy with the killing of Coldiron.

Lucy covered the biscuits in the pan with a cloth, knowing Coldiron would probably finish them off before he turned in for the night. She picked up the plates and cups, dropped them in the iron pot with their spoons, and carried them down to the creek to wash them. She glanced at the gentle giant as he walked down to lead the horses back closer to the camp, and smiled when she thought of the compliments he gave her on her biscuits.

Looking down again to wash her dishes, she jumped, startled by the sound of a rifle shot somewhere behind her. She looked up again to see Coldiron fall, and her heart stopped for a moment before racing with terror.

It was all happening again! He had come back!

Terrified, she didn't know which way to run, but knowing in her heart that it was none other than Bloody Hand, she could not wait for him to come for her.

With her pulse pounding in her head, she ran for the nearest possible place to hide, a long ravine leading up to the ridge behind the camp. Stumbling in her panic, and hoping he could not see where she had fled, she prayed he could not find her. As she struggled to race up the ravine, she was aware of the absence of the heavy revolver bumping against her thigh. She had stopped carrying the pistol in her skirt pocket only a couple of days before. She thought of Coldiron, lying, maybe dead, in the long grass of the valley floor, her protector. There was no one to protect her now! The thought of it caused her to give in more to her panic, and soon she felt she couldn't breathe.

Gasping for breath, she made it to a pine thicket halfway up the ridge. Desperate to hide from the monster coming after her, she crawled between the crowded trunks of the pines and crouched in the carpet of needles like a mouse hiding from a great cat. Afraid to make a sound, she reached back to try to smooth over the needles she had scuffed up in her haste to hide. There was no sound in the forest, save that of her hurried breathing, all the ordinary sounds of the clicking and chirping of the vermin and insects had been stilled by the sound of one rifle shot. Then the silence was broken.

"Woman!"

It came from the bottom of the ravine, and the guttural gruffness of the Piegan warrior's voice chilled the blood in her veins, threatening to cause her to faint. So choked with fear she was now barely able to breathe, and she tried to wiggle back deeper into the thicket.

"I come to get you now, woman," Bloody Hand called out, confident that there was no longer anyone to stop him. "Did you think you could run and hide from me? You will beg for your death before I let you die."

He knew she did not understand what he was saying, but it gave him satisfaction to threaten her. Running at a trot, he followed her up the ravine, certain that it was where she had fled. Fearing to move now, lest he see her in the thicket, she balled up as small as she could in hopes he would not find her.

Searching the narrow ravine, right and left, as he climbed up toward the ridge, he taunted her continuously with his violent promises to make her pay for her rejection of him. Higher he climbed until reaching the heavy pine thicket, where he stopped upon noticing a slight disturbance of the pine needles at the edge. A lascivious grin spread across the grotesque face of the evil brute, for he was certain he had found her. Pushing into the thicket a few feet confirmed his discovery, for there among the slender pines lay his pitiful prey, trying with all her might to become part of the earth beneath her. Growling lustfully, he reached out and grabbed her foot from under her balled-up body and pulled her out of the thicket. In a desperate fight for her life, she tried to hold on to the tree trunks with her hands. It was to no avail, for his strength was too great, and he pulled her out into the middle of the ravine.

Like a rattlesnake about to strike, he gazed lustfully at his captured prey, his eyes reflecting the evil he was promising to cast upon her. With his mangled hand, he grabbed her chin and forced it up so she had to look at him. But she would not, and closed her eyes, hoping the nightmare would end. He slapped her hard.

"Look at me!" he demanded, and grabbed the collar of her blouse. With one powerful yank, he tore the blouse halfway off.

"Take your filthy hands off her, you God-damned dirty savage!"

The command was like the roar of an angry cougar as it reverberated off the sides of the rocky ravine. Bloody Hand released her at once and spun around to see the ominous avenger advancing toward him, poised to strike like the mountain cat he resembled.

Bloody Hand tried to bring his rifle to bear on the enraged avenger, but had no time to cock it before the human projectile launched his body into Bloody Hand's midsection, driving the hapless brute into the rocky ground behind him. Almost blind in his fury to destroy the evil predator, Bret did not think to use his rifle, driven instead to wrench the life out of him with his two hands.

Fighting for his very life, Bloody Hand realized his rifle was useless, so he dropped it and tried desperately to draw the knife from his belt, even as the breath was being crushed from his wind-pipe. Blindly grasping for the knife handle, he was forced to abandon the attempt when the last breath of life was wrenched from his lungs and his struggling ceased. Mauled like a prairie dog snared by a mountain lion, his body relaxed in death.

"Bret. . . . Bret." The sound of someone calling his name finally penetrated the shroud of fury that had enveloped him. Gradually he came back from the fog of rage that had consumed him. "Bret, he's dead. He's done for. It's over."

He recognized Myra's voice then, and rolled off Bloody Hand's body to sit exhausted beside it while he tried to regain his senses.

After a few minutes, he was able to bring his mind back to the moments before the attack, and he remembered the rifle shot that had set him into motion.

"Where's Nate?" he asked.

"I don't know," Myra answered, relieved to see he evidently had his wits about him again. She was holding Lucy close to her as the terrified girl was still trembling from the touch of the Piegan monster.

"He's down there with the horses," Lucy managed to say between uncontrollable sobs.

Bret was immediately alert again. Fearing the worst, he got to his feet and started back down the ravine. Behind him, Myra and Lucy followed, but not before Myra cocked her rifle and pumped two rounds into Bloody Hand's corpse.

"Just in case," she explained.

When he reached the bottom of the ravine, he saw Coldiron on his hands and knees, trying to crawl back to the creek. "Nate!" he yelled, and splashed across the creek as fast as he could run. "Stay there!" Bret yelled again. "We'll take care of you!" He slid down in the grass beside his wounded friend. "Just be still," he ordered, "and we'll see what we need to do. Where are you shot?"

"In the back," Coldiron said—his words labored with the pain he was suffering. "Where else would a back-shootin' son of a bitch shootcha?"

He lay down on his side then and Bret could see the bloody stain spreading on his back. His spunky remark was a good sign to Bret, however. The big grizzly still had his bite. Myra and Lucy arrived then after they, too, ran through the creek. Bret checked the front of Coldiron's shirt, but there was no exit wound.

"Well, we know what we've got to deal with," Myra said. "First thing is we've gotta get him back across the creek and close to the fire. It's gonna be dark pretty quick now, and I'd like to be able to see while I still can."

She apparently felt it her responsibility to take care of the doctoring, which Bret was thankful for, because he was afraid he might do more harm than good if he was called upon to do it. The alarm for the wounded man had also evidently pushed the hysteria aside for Lucy, because of her concern for Coldiron.

Getting the wounded man across the creek was no easy chore, even considering Bret's strength. They finally decided that the best way to accomplish the task was to get Coldiron to ride piggyback on him while Bret waded across through water about four feet deep in the middle. This was decided upon as a safer alternative than attempting to jump from rock to rock with a man the size of a small horse on his back.

Once Coldiron was safely across, they settled him close to the fire, and Myra, with Lucy's help, went to work on the bullet wound. In spite of there being no indication that Bloody Hand was not alone in the attack, Bret scouted a wide area around the camp just to be sure. When he was, he went back up the ravine to drag Bloody Hand's body away and dump it in a deep gully where Lucy was not likely to see it again.

Grotesque in life, the bloody monster's appearance was even more menacing in death. Bret took a long look at the face that had terrified Lucy, and had little wonder that the poor girl had nightmares. He puzzled for a moment over what appeared to be a piece of dried gristle on a cord around the Piegan's neck. It occurred to him then that it might have at one time been attached to his head beside the unprotected hole where an earlobe had been.

Finished with Bloody Hand for good and all, Bret returned to the campfire to see how Coldiron was doing.

"He's gonna make it," Myra told him as soon as he walked up. "That bullet's in too deep for me to try to get it out, but I don't see any signs that it's hit anything that would make him bleed out."

"How 'bout it, partner?" Bret asked the patient. "You think you're gonna make it?"

"You heard the boss," Coldiron answered, obviously trying to talk through considerable pain. "If she says I'll make it, then I reckon I ain't got no choice." He grimaced when he tried to shift his body and was rewarded with a stab of pain. "When I got hit, it knocked me to my knees, and I thought I was shot pretty bad, but I don't think it's as bad as I thought now."

"Well, it looks like you've got a couple of good nurses," Bret said. "Just don't get too used to lying around taking it easy. We've got a lot of work to do to build us a cabin." To Myra then, he said, "You might wanna make use of that bottle we brought back from town. When I bought it, I didn't know it was for medicinal purposes."

"You'd better get out of those wet trousers and

let them dry by the fire," Lucy said. "If you're shy about it, you can wrap a blanket around you."

Her comment caused all three of the others to stare at her in disbelief. "Are you all right, honey?" Myra was the first to speak, astonished by the young woman's apparent recovery of her fears and emotions.

"Yes, I think so," Lucy answered calmly. "We have a lot of work to do to build our home, so I think it's time I started taking a bigger part in it, especially with Nate in the condition he's in."

She couldn't explain to herself why she had suddenly let go of her fears and taken a good look at the possibilities the future held for her "family." She could not deny, however, the impact on her brain when Myra put two shots in the evil Bloody Hand's body. She was convinced at last that the demon was really dead.

I guess I have to believe in miracles, Myra thought. She was fairly beaming then with the prospects that the future she was planning for the four of them had a better than average chance for success.

Still thinking about the rage Bret had exhibited when he saw Bloody Hand threatening Lucy, a rage he had never exhibited before, she said, "Lucy, why don't you make us some coffee? I think we have something to celebrate."

It might take a little time, she thought. *But what the hell? They're young. They've got plenty of time.*

Center Point Large Print
600 Brooks Road / PO Box 1
Thorndike ME 04986-0001 USA

(207) 568-3717

US & Canada:
1 800 929-9108
www.centerpointlargeprint.com